Party Games

Fiona Cuthbertson

First Published in 2020 by Blossom Spring Publishing

Party Games Copyright © 2020 Fiona Cuthbertson

ISBN 978-1-8380188-0-1

E: admin@blossomspringpublishing.com

W: www.blossomspringpublishing.com

Chapter 1

The bell rang out. She knew that this was just the beginning. Her heels tapped on the intricately tiled corridor as she quickly made her way down towards Central Lobby, keen to make it to her appointment on time. She entered the massive octogen shaped hall and her heart pumped wildly in her chest. The grand stone crossroads of the Palace of Westminster: the spot where the House of Commons and House of Lords come together.

She stopped as Big Ben finished chiming. She looked up at the mosaics on the Venetian Glass windows, the sunlight exposing the floral emblems and heraldic badges high above where she was standing. All around her were the statues of past Kings and Queens of England and Scotland standing guard, adding their judgement onto those who stepped into this, the Mother of all Parliaments.

Taking a moment, she walked to the side of the lobby and fingered the intricate copper designs that masked one of the many secret passages in this old building. Politics had come so far since these metal grilles had been over the Ladies' Gallery above the Chamber to prevent MPs from getting distracted by their presence.

She sighed contentedly. She was part of the new generation with not only the opportunity to interpret the law, but to shape it. She walked back into the main space, took her new security pass in her hand and breathed in slowly. Examining the photo staring back up at her, she caressed its smooth, laminate front fondly and ran her finger over the title stated under her name. Assistant Parliamentary Counsel.

She pushed a stray wisp of her blonde hair behind her ear and looked round at the unassuming men and women. They were all part of the massive legislative machine that she had now become part of. She pulled the cuffs of her crisp shirt exposing shining new cufflinks and turned a full 360 degrees. Her eyes addressed each of the patron saints in turn. They were swathed in gold leaf, resplendent in their traditional poses and ever bathed in the light from the enormous chandelier.

The heels of her new Louboutin shoes hurt her calves and the balls of her feet. She winced slightly as she turned, slightly regretting such a high heel, but she knew that whilst appearances shouldn't be important, in this world they always mattered. She would be judged quickly and instantly.

Nervousness began to rise in her gut. She wasn't sure which direction her new boss was going to emerge from. The Permanent Secretary could have had meetings with anyone before he welcomed her on her first day. She worried if she would remember what he looked like but chastised herself.

A ridiculous concern. His face was plastered all over the department website, a face that was crumpled by age but was still in possession of the remnants of a handsome youth.

She smiled, remembering her interview. She remembered the anticipation of his staff when they received the message of his impending arrival at the Department, and the presence he exuded as he entered, his years of service adding up to a glittering career. Josephine suddenly felt a tap on her shoulder and heard a deep booming voice annunciate her name. "Josephine, welcome."

She looked around and saw Patrick smiling broadly. As his hand came towards hers in greeting, she noticed his tailored suit and manicured nails, alongside a crisp white open necked shirt picked out to exude casual perfection.

A light scent of cologne wafted through the air around him. His white hair was slicked back, no hair out of place. Lego hair, she thought, smiling slightly to herself. She looked him up and down and reassured herself that she knew what she was doing. He was tough, particular and a perfectionist, but she thrived under such working conditions.

She put out her hand which he took quickly exerting a firm handshake. "Patrick," she smiled,

"Then let's get on," he responded quickly. He maintained his hold on her hand as he slightly pulled her towards the panel of St. David and towards Members Lobby. A touch unbalanced by his gesture, her free hand instinctively went out to check that nothing was out of place. Reassured that her skirt had not risen, she quickly picked up an equivalent stride alongside him.

The corridor was long, and they walked towards Members Lobby in silence. Josephine noticed the policeman watch the assembled crowd in front of him whilst he made sure that no one without the proper accreditation was allowed down the corridor leading to the Commons Chamber. He stepped slightly towards them to ensure the validity of their presence and soon saw Patrick's distinctive pass around his neck. Stepping aside, they passed through unencumbered, as the policemen lowered his head slightly out of respect.

They passed by quickly and Patrick gave her little time to take in her surroundings before he stopped and turned towards her: "We have yet to get your desk organised at the Department, but that's not why I wanted to meet you over here. I want to impress on you the importance of the work you are about to undertake. We may not be well known outside the Estate but without us the Government machine can't work."

He drew her across the lobby quickly and rubbed the burnished foot of the bronze statue of Churchill that stood guarding the entrance to the Chamber. He told her: "It's good luck for MPs to rub Churchill's foot when they enter and exit the chamber, but I think we can try and get some of that luck for ourselves." Quickly, Josephine stretched out and grasped Churchill's statue, rubbing it whilst making a silent wish like so many had done so before. Empowered but nervous now, she didn't want to leave anything to chance.

The door of the Commons Chamber was open, and she looked inside, past the Doorkeepers on guard dressed smartly in their black uniform, with their brass shoe buckles that shone brightly and their immaculate white gloves. They guarded the sanctity of the Chamber to ensure that only MP's passed the threshold. This was where the magic happened, where Members of Parliament debated matters of state and passed the Laws that she was going to spend time drawing up.

As she watched, both sides of the House fell into silence. The Speaker rose from his chair to call an MP to contribute to the debate. "Robert Simmons," he bellowed then sitting down to allow the Honourable Member for Chatsworth to start speaking.

The new MP stood up: "I have listened carefully to what the Home Secretary said and whilst appreciate her sentiment, she must understand the other side of the argument." Braying from opposition benches meant he stumbled slightly over his words. He looked at the Speaker for help, who rose again to calm everyone down and make a joke to bring the House back to order.

Patrick took this moment to move towards

a different exit, signalling Josephine along with him, and they soon entered a dark wood corridor. Patrick noticed that Josephine was still looking behind them, a look of shock on her face and he cleared his throat to re-engage her attention. Meeting the gaze of his piercing grey eyes, she felt that he was looking into her soul: "You will soon get used to their ways," he said: "They are much politer than it might seem and there is a lot more cross party communication than one might think."

He took a moment to evaluate her. He often found that by taking physical control of those he met often unnerved his targets and helped him gain the upper hand so they wouldn't know what to expect. She was different though. Her slight tenseness was obvious as they moved through their tour, but even though through there was no doubt this was an assault on her senses, she wasn't letting it bother her, not really.

She obviously took time over her clothing and was well dressed in a suit that allowed her to keep up with his pace without sacrificing any style. Her green eyes were earnest and thoughtful, and her blonde hair was swept up into a chignon that showed off a slender neck and a sharp jawline.

Josephine returned his gaze in a welcoming, warm and confident manner that showed him she would be able to hide any nervousness well if the situation needed it and would remain in control of herself even if she had to deal with something unexpected. A good characteristic to have in a world where political intrigue, 24-hour media and opposing views were the order of the day.

Soon they were winding their way down through one of the many corridors - the green carpet stretched in front of them marking the territory of the House of Commons, a separate governing body from the House of Lords, an area even more ornate and festooned in red leather and gold leaf. They passed a number of arches and she looked quickly left and right to orientate herself. Putting his hand out as a signal to each one they passed, Patrick quickly explained, "Party offices, Opposition Whips Office, Members Tea Room, Library." He didn't give any more explanation, and quickly fell back into silence to see how she would tolerate the change of tempo.

Turning right at the end of the corridor, big heavy wooden doors ran beside them, and before Patrick could comment again, their silence was broken by the sound of the division bell. Its familiar ring soon had an effect on the surrounding area. Bodies emerged through the heavy doors around them, the heavy door handles creaking as they were turned whilst the numerous lifts opened quickly and regularly spilling out MP's that were restricted to the 8 minute deadline now that the division had been called.

Patrick suddenly stopped by a TV monitor behind the Speaker's Chair - the old beside the new. His eyes quickly scanned it, and he eyed Josephine again: "It may not seem like much. It's not as if the monitors give any more information beyond which clause within a Bill is being discussed, but you and I both know that just one of these innocuous sentences can alter a policy drastically and that politics impinges on everything."

Patrick nodded towards the back of the Speaker's Chair, acknowledging its authority as expected by the tradition of the house. A large green leather armchair raised from the ground, emblazoned with the royal coat of arms, no one could forget that the Speaker's authority ultimately came from the Crown.

Pausing for a second, they both listened to the division bell continue in its call for the Parliamentary representatives. He saw the crowds file the other way and slowly started to talk again, his voice taking on a serious tone: "Every decision validated from that chair is political. A division voted through or voted down, it all counts, and it is down to us to make sure that there is a firm basis on which to start the decision-making process. After all, Parliament doesn't work in a vacuum."

Watching for Josephine's reaction, he saw the serious look on her face and continued: "Influence on the Parliamentarians comes from many different sources – organisations, constituents, interest groups, unions – who all work in sync to create debate and push opinions forward. Some view this as interference but personally I feel it's better to embrace it. If we know the opinions of the external stakeholders it means we can truly understand the mood around a piece of legislation, and then we can make sure the legislation we write fits the bill, as it were." He smiled at his unintentional pun, and strode on, leaving her to absorb his words.

As quickly as the–hustle and bustle had started, it had stopped. MPs had all congregated to vote in the lobbies, leaving visitors to sit where they were left, unable to move unaccompanied around the building without the very real possibility of being stopped by one of the armed policemen that were scattered through the building.

Josephine and Patrick turned down a quiet corner, a corner that showed even more of a rabbit warren of corridors, lined with glass cabinets built all the way to the ceiling. They were full of old copies of Hansard, bound in green leather, and obviously organised with great care, and under lock and key.

They soon reached a set of intricately carved wooden doors, to the side of the cabinets. Deftly opening the door, Patrick stepped aside. Quickly Josephine caught up with him, peered in and stepped inside. All the walls were all carved in a similar style to the door, with high ceilings above made of brown wood, creating a relatively dark room.

It was no surprise that the newspapers regularly reported quite how much money it took to keep the building in prime condition. Just keeping the rooms clean was a job in itself, let alone protecting them from the heavy usage undertaken during each Parliamentary session.

Josephine looked round the enormous room. It had been furnished with fine leather chairs that had obviously been in service for many years. Patrick soon spotted a gentleman lounging in the depths of a sunken chair and lead the way towards him.

The man's legs were awkwardly crossed exposing brightly coloured socks under trousers that were too short. Though his nose was stuck in a file, he quickly spotted the new arrivals and leaned forward. His head protruding out like a scrawny bird and his black-rimmed spectacles perched on the end of a long pointed nose.

He stood up, and motioned Patrick and Josephine towards him, frightened that they would change their mind and head towards someone else. He looked around him, and a sudden impulse of manliness took over. He reached out to pull a chair closer towards his table. However, his skinny arms were no match for the old fashioned high-backed solid oak chair, and after five seconds of trying to pull it the foot across the room, he retreated, beaten, and contented himself with a continuation of his elaborate hand gestures to welcome them to the table he was occupying.

Falling back into the seat he had briefly exited, he exclaimed, "Patrick!" as they arrived at the table. Patrick nodded towards him and pulled up two chairs with ease. Sitting down, he looked at the man he had known for these many years.

"How are you, Bernard?" he asked. The man in question repositioned himself and crossed his legs again, the smug look on his face betraying his feelings of self-worth. He often banished his feelings of physical inadequacy from his mind by the fact that he was here, in this place. Bernard had been a member of the House of Lords since 1982, having been ennobled because of his services to business.

Bernard smiled at Patrick: "It has been a long time since we started on this road together. Is it 35 or 40 years since we went up to Cambridge?" Patrick smiled and put his hands together: "40 now, and still after all the twists and turns life can throw, we end up working in the same place."

"Indeed," nodded Bernard, "Of course how was I to know that the little kids soft play centres I opened would be such a big thing. After all, they didn't even exist when you and I were of an age. Now all parents seem to do is dump their kids in a Jungle Jim and have a coffee. Anyway," he sighed contentedly, "made me money."

He exhaled and turned to Josephine. He

stuck out a sweaty hand, taking in her physique. She sighed. She had been used to this all her working life. She worked hard to keep fit, getting up early to go to the gym, but in many men's eyes that just made her something to look at. Of course, she knew that if she took an attitude similar to those of many those very same men, she would be judged a slob and wondered how such double standards were allowed in this day and age.

She looked him up and down and quickly broke off the contact. She had heard that Lord Cole of Weston Abbey didn't feel he needed to make much of an effort on how he looked. His brown corduroy trousers had seen many better days and his jacket had patches on the elbows. She looked at his creased shirt and it hardened her resolve. He obviously didn't see the irony of his own behaviour towards her.

He swung his arm rapidly in the space between himself and Patrick in a gesture to create a link and establish an alignment of agendas. "Of course, it's important that we stick together, us old hands: progressive but not making changes for the sake of it." His tinny voice became all the more earnest. He found his footing and now looked straight in her direction, his eyes slightly watery with excitement as he continued: "There are so many interlopers now who just feel they can be fast-tracked because they are women or on some scheme."

He turned to Patrick: "You and I both know that it's an art, it's not something you can pick up." He nodded to Josephine: "You are a lucky girl to be given the role of Patrick's secretary. After all, there is plenty of time for a young thrusting character like yourself to make your mark once you have learned the trade."

Josephine raised an eyebrow, but before she could defend her position, Patrick stepped in: "No, I still have Sharon working in my office. It's important that the administrative side of the office remains constant. Josephine is joining the Counsel team, using her skills to provide those legislators with their Bills."

Bernard snorted, feeling slightly castigated by his colleague, and Patrick put a hand on his shoulder: "as you say, continuity is so important, and I wouldn't want to undermine the status quo or the delicate balance of my office. Plus, Josephine understands she has a lot to learn, and that whilst Sharon is more administrative, her way of dealing with organisation is second to none."

Bernard shifted slightly in his seat, his tongue slightly lolling at Patrick's inclusion of Sharon in the conversation and nodded: "Yes. No one wants to get on Sharon's wrong side. She'll stab you with a heel from her boot." His voice then hushed: "A favourite of many though. Works hard. Plays hard. But understands how important it is for a strong man to have a good woman to rely on."

13

He moved again, not quite able to get himself comfortable all of a sudden, his cheeks suddenly puce.

Josephine thought back to her interview. Sharon had been calm and collected, keen to check out the potential new recruit. She had the hint of an accent that had been diluted by effective elocution lessons, asking quick fire questions about Josephine's qualifications, background and ambitions. Keen to engage, Josephine responded to her questions, but soon enough their encounter was cut short when Patrick had entered the room allowing Sharon to pick up the phone, sift through her roller-deck with her polished nails and quiz those that she had picked out about various aspects of Parliamentary life.

Coming back to the present, Josephine looked from side to side, catching snippets of the conversation and suddenly wondering if she was in a Benny Hill sketch. She looked at Bernard, wondering how much she would have to deal with him. She hoped it would be minimal. He was stuck in the dark ages, prattling on about times long gone and people that had long left. Sensing a break in the boy's chat, and that the attention was back on her she smiled sweetly, lowering her head slightly before saying: "Well I am here to do a job and am looking forward to learning from all of you."

Bernard honked in approval and moved ever so slightly closer to her: "And I look forward to taking the opportunity to teach you what I know." She shifted slightly in her seat, an action subtle enough in itself, but strong enough to alert Patrick to the fact that she wanted to move on.

Chapter 2

Josephine and Patrick stepped out onto Parliament Square. They walked over the road and made their way towards Whitehall. Josephine was immediately struck by the noise on the street. She had entered Parliament before the rush of tourists had arrived with their cameras in hand, clicking away at everything and everyone. However, the number of people crowding around now meant that Patrick and Josephine had to zig zag across the pavement a few feet away from each other as they made their way towards the Department.

Josephine couldn't help but think about what a different world this was from that in which was brought up. On this road, everything was cramped and intense with a constant barrage of noise, police cars and buses. The village of Mayfield in Leicestershire where she had spent her formative years only had a population of a thousand people. Just one shop and a pub serviced the houses nestled together by the small stream that lead towards the hills and woods that went on for miles around providing her and her friends with fresh air, silence and space.

Eventually Josephine and Patrick managed to leave the tourists behind as they headed down a side entrance and came to the open black door of the Treasury. Opposite St James Park, with fabulous views of the lake, Josephine had just enough time to watch a flock of geese take off over Duck Island before she noticed that Patrick had stepped into the Treasury building.

Josephine stepped up the four stone steps and watched him step between the two heavy black doors that lead towards the main hall. He swiped his pass against the small scanner on the side of the three tubular entrances - a bullet proof security system that only allowed registered pass holders through and remained impenetrable without the proper documentation.

The security gates registered his pass with a click. The side of the tube closest to Patrick opened with a small buzz, and he stepped in. It quickly closed behind him, and his weight triggered off the second part of the tube that opened to allow him access the department. Having stepped out, he looked behind him to beckon Josephine through.

With a deep breath she pushed her security pass against the black scanner. She half expected to set off the alarm but instead, the tube obediently buzzed open and she could step inside. A palpable feeling of relief came over her as she found herself inside the Atrium, alongside a fountain that trickled obediently in the centre of the room and plants in order to give a sense of peace to this insular and busy world.

She looked up towards the glass lifts that were slowly moving people from floor to floor like ants in a glass sided ants nest, busying themselves with the paperwork and files they were carrying, files stamped red with the security stamps that made it obvious if someone tried to take them off site. There was no messing about here.

Patrick briefly held her arm and guided her along a corridor that was surrounded by modern wood bookcases, aware that he was taking her through corridors she would not have seen when she entered through the visitors' entrance. Josephine mused on how different the inside of this building was to the Palace. Though steeped in history it was no longer a remnant of the old world. Now it was all contemporary artwork and break out pods with brightly coloured sofas, on which numbers civil servants emitted a soft hum of chatter, occasionally wandering back to their desks to check something on their computers.

The staff looked up as they became aware of Patrick's signature cologne. He often used it to forewarn his arrival in the building, a sign that he could emerge from behind the bookcases at any time. He prided himself on not micromanaging his staff, but he expected them to be up to speed on their brief at a moment's notice. He had been around long enough to know that a week truly could be a long time in politics, and considering it was a rule he lived by himself, he expected all his staff to understand this mantra too.

Soon Patrick opened some frosted glass

doors to a set of offices along a side corridor. Josephine recognised the rectangular shaped space and breathed deeply. To the left and right of the entrance were two partially open doors that revealed two wider and more comfortable looking offices. One housed a single desk and sofa where Patrick quickly put his papers, whilst the other contained two wooden desks opposite each other. Apart from this, however, they were pretty much identical, and both decorated with the soft grey fabric suitable for the heavy usage of a civil service office.

"I don't care what she said," said a mop of blonde hair sitting at the computer in the ante room in the middle. The figure turned around from the desk, her phone attached to her ear, and she rolled her eyes at Patrick: "Rhiannon cannot authorise any comment from this office. Her boss may be on the Bill Committee but that doesn't give her the right to try and pre-empt anything. Seriously, that girl needs to learn where the boundaries are."

She stared Patrick straight in the eye. She listened to the caller on the other end of the line and then smiled: "Last night huh? Oh really. Well that surprises me not one iota. Yes, keep me informed – on all of it." Josephine recognised Sharon immediately, and watched her new colleague put the phone down with a crack.

Her long legs were crossed, and her skirt crawled up her thighs. She didn't wear tights, preferring to show off her tanned legs, freshly topped up from a recent trip home for the brief Baltic summer over the recess period. Her lipstick a scarlet red, and her perfume overpowering and ever so slightly masculine, she was well maintained for her 52 years and exuded poise and confidence.

Having dismissed the caller, she stood up. At 5'8 without her high heels, she towered over Josephine as she walked across the room. Sharon came closer and looked Josephine up and down remembering how accommodating she had been with her answers during the interview process. A definite sign of youth, she mused about how new staff had got younger and younger. She reached the water cooler and set the water to ice cold. "Can't believe it's already 2pm," she started, "when I worked for Charlie, we would have the drinks trolley out by now," before adding, "those were the days," with a wistful sigh.

The water slowly filled the first of the two glasses she was filling, she pictured a different office with her old boss sitting with his advisor, their feet on the table, smoking cigarettes whilst they plotted and schemed before he laughed that deep pub laugh that filled the room when a new idea popped into his head.

Hearing the click of the water when it stopped running, she placed the second in position and handed Patrick the one she had filled. She assessed this boss, here, now. Patrick was different, always straightforward. A safe pair of hands. He smiled and took it from her, but before he could even thank her, his phone began to ring.

He backed away slightly to protect the identity of those that called him, and quickly answered it. Telling the person on the other end of the phone to hold on, he quickly tasked Sharon with showing Josephine round the office and headed out the door.

Walking along the silent corridor and into an empty committee room, he spoke quickly into the phone. He could have taken the call in the office but he wanted to give Sharon the opportunity to start bonding with her new colleague, and he knew she would never do that if he was on the phone because she would be much more likely to spend her time busying herself round his office trying to listen in. She thought he didn't notice it, but he noticed everything.

"Hi Charlie, thanks for calling me back," he smiled. He closed the door to the room: "It's a just a courtesy call really to let you know we have a new member of staff, Josephine, and I have tasked her with ensuring we have the right people at the evidence session next week."

He sat down, brought out his note pad out and began writing as he continued speaking: "Yes, I agree, the Bill Committee are doing this at our request so it's even more important that those being questioned feel that they are part of the process.

That's why I want you there. You always seem to manage to make everyone feel warm and fuzzy. And of course, it will be a good test for Josephine."

He laughed at the response from the end of the phone. "Yes," he continued: "Young thing, though obviously very determined. Bit wet behind the ears mind so Bernard made an immediate beeline. For all her naivety though, she didn't seem massively impressed so I don't think we need to be concerned that she will be taken advantage of by the more predatory beasts."

Back in the office, Sharon knew it was Charlie on the other end of the phone. Patrick only reacted that way when he called. She sighed and turned to face Josephine: "It's got much more corporate around here now which just makes life a bit less fun." She drew back the half open door to their right, she guided Josephine in towards the two desks, continuing: "And this will be your office. You will share with Rebekah."

Behind the desk further away, sat her new colleague, and Josephine noted that she was more of her own age. Tall and slim, she had bright brown eyes that crinkled when she smiled. Fair skin and minimal makeup, she leapt out of her chair to welcome the guests and Josephine immediately felt a warmth, a flicker of potential friendship from the girl she had only just met.

"Hi there!" Rebekah trilled, "Welcome to the madhouse!" as her sing song tone immediately brightened the room. Josephine laughed: "It all looks pretty orderly to me."

"Appearances can be deceptive," Rebekah continued. She sat back down, and before Josephine could enquire what she meant, the phone rang.

Sharon moved towards the desk that Josephine was about to take to check the drawers were empty. Rebekah watched her, used to her slightly overbearing presence. She often found excuses to come in whilst she was in the phone or in a meeting and seemed to think no one realised what she was up to. Rebekah sighed and picked it up to answer its plea for attention. Listening carefully but saying little, she took out a pen and paper to scribble down some details: "Yes, yes," Rebekah said, "I will get straight onto it." She put the phone down and fixed a look at Sharon, who finally made to leave, half closing the door behind her.

Rebekah tapped her pen on the paper: "And so it begins!" she said: "We have finally managed to persuade the Bill Committee to have an evidence session about getting broadband into rural areas. Not the most exciting piece of work to come through this office but it's a good policy, has generally been well received, and it maintains the government's satisfaction rating which is what they want. Anyway, it's our job to get the right people in front of them to give them evidence about how it's all going."

Rebekah looked at Josephine, who tried and failed to hide her blank expression and began to stutter: "Broadband in rural areas. Yes. A DCMS policy?"

Rebekah smiled: "Yes that's right. The Ministers are keen to ensure that broadband is rolled out in all rural areas, but there has been pushback from the telecommunications companies who don't want to install a fiber network due to a lack of return on investment. Hence this meeting which will hopefully show these companies the impact of the decisions they have taken."

Sharon had her head on one side, her desk not being far from the half open door. She had told Patrick she wanted to "feng-shui" the office, but of course that was not the case. The reality was that the positioning of the furniture lent itself perfectly to ensure that she could listen into the conversations happening in the adjoining offices without being detected. This way she was forewarned of problems and could protect herself and those important to her.

She sighed. She knew the danger it could bring if other people had all the control. After all, she had grown up with the memory of the family's farm being forcibly taken under new rules of collectivisation. It had meant longer hours for less money and that she had to grow up quickly as her family's future became more reliant on events they could not influence. She would not let her life be so ruled by other people's whims again.

Listening to them discuss the meeting next week, Sharon was content that she wasn't missing out any juicy gossip and brought out her diary file so she could start responding to the dozens of requests for Patrick's time. She didn't dislike Rebekah, even though she represented everything that Sharon disliked about the privileged class, those that often seemed to take advantage of those beneath them to move up the ladder at the expense of others. However, she seemed to be a genuinely nice girl, and no threat, just big teeth and lots of youthful enthusiasm.

Married to her university boyfriend, she had a purity about her that was unusual in the world of politics Indeed, Rebekah's unavailability was obvious. The massive emerald engagement ring on her finger - a 3 carat stone surrounded by a cluster of diamonds - made that clear. Sharon gritted her teeth. Well of course, she had such a massive rock. Like had found like, and her and Sam were peas in a pod. She had come from a long line of very eminent lawyers, whilst her husband was true blue aristocracy with a family estate down in Somerset.

Being the third son meant Sam was not in a position to just work on the family estate, even though he wanted to. Instead, he had come to London and become a journalist. Having an easy manner that seemed to engender trust meant that he was credited with several good stories having often been able to disarm those he was interviewing. He didn't have that killer instinct though, preferring to take a more supporting role. The nice guy. It suited him. He didn't seem to want to bring anyone down really, he just wanted to have a comfortable life that allowed him to have a Parliamentary pass and close enough proximity to Rebekah so that he could surprise her with flowers before taking her in his arms and making her giggle by whispering in her ear - something she always seemed to be equally embarrassed and delighted about.

She pursed her lips, Sam always seemed slightly dopey, if not a bit childish for a man whose hair was now speckled with grey. A man who still lived in his favourite Armani Jeans, a monochrome blazer made by his own personal tailor and a pinkie ring with the family crest on his left hand. However, they were both kind and Sharon thought about how Rebekah seemed to feel guilty about her privileged upbringing meaning she worked hard in a way that many in her situation would just not bother.

Sharon stood up and moved back towards the water cooler at the edge of the office suite. Slowly filling up a plastic cup, she thought about the two girls, comparing their style. Rebekah dressed classically with freshly pressed shirts under tailor made suits that were modest. Josephine, however, had an edgier style as if she had something to prove.

The cut of her suits betrayed their brand heritage, but she gave them a more modern edge by accessorising from the high street. She was shorter in stature and naturally petite, her slim waist highlighted with the use of wide belts. Maybe more like herself, enjoying the cut and thrust of politics, a girl who saw this more of a lifestyle than a job.

She may have only just arrived in the office, but she had the manner of someone who would just go for what she wanted. Tutting to herself Sharon concluded that Josephine needed to be watched. Just at that moment, she now heard them laughing now as they cried, "2 in the bag!" The room then went quiet, but Sharon's phone rang before she could get in a position to be able to hear any more.

From inside the office, Rebekah continued: "So we have both sides of the argument now, a lobby group of residents, and a selection of communications companies. Not bad for your first day as it should make sure we have all the perspectives and information we need during this session."

"Yes," responded Josephine, "So the question is: is there anyone of interest who we need to keep a particular eye out for? Anyone we think is of interest outside this particular issue."

"Well, of course this is a special evidence session and it has escaped no one that the Leader of the Commons is making an appearance. Patrick feels that it will give those appearing the feeling that they are being taken seriously. Of course, Charlie is happy to oblige with the election coming up," started Rebekah. She moved over towards Josephine's desk, quickly clocking that that Sharon was safely on the phone so unable to earwig for the time being. She knelt down and began to whisper, already feeling an element of trust towards her new workmate: "Anyway, get used to that name coming up a lot in the office. Sharon used to work for him and there is a lot more of a backstory there than she was letting on."

Josephine's eyes widened as she realised quite what she was being told: "I did see the look in her eye when she mentioned his name. The question is, were they actually involved or was it fantasy on her part?"

Rebekah nodded conspiratorially: "Well the rumours would imply it wasn't just an imagined crush. Plus, I did once find a photo that left an image I would have rather not pictured." Shaking her shoulders to cleanse herself of the memory she continued: "Of course, by all accounts it was a long time ago, but it's good to be aware because he does pop into the office, and you need to watch what you say about him in any public forum."

Putting down the phone, Sharon moved towards Patrick's office and put the note she had written in the top draw of his desk. She noticed the door to the girl's office was now open, but they were silent. She cursed. She caught a glimpse of a smile between the two girls along with a couple of conspiratorial nods that seemed to generate giggling, but nothing more. She wondered what they had been discussing so soon after meeting that could possibly create such a reaction and made a mental note to make finding out a priority. It was obvious that a firm bond was already forming in that side office even though Rebekah kept most people at arm's length. She reassured herself though, she was a master of the political arts. Make no mistake.

Chapter 3

The room was buzzing. The Members of the Bill Committee were all carrying draft copies of the new legislation on broadband and were chatting conspiratorially in huddles whilst they enjoyed their free tea and biscuits. Sharon sat at the side of the room, her hazel eyes gazing over the room. She was still waiting for Rebekah and Josephine to arrive, but she was glad of the time to watch the members of the committee establish their alliances. Everyone needed friends in this business. No one was immune to the backbiting that came with the territory, and no matter who promised politics would become kinder, it never did.

Suddenly, the big wooden door creaked open, and within the crowd, Sharon could just catch the back of his head. Quickly everyone moved to take their seats. Sharon coolly watched him from the corner. She was pleased that for once, she was finally getting free of his hold.

She had met the Leader of the Commons many years before. She was young then, but at the top of her game already having perfected her style of classy sass. A time when his prowess was an open secret, his partying legendary and a job for him was like gold dust. He worked hard, played hard and she savoured every opportunity she had to learn from him. Soon with late nights and early starts there was soon a blurring of the lines, and as he found ambition, she became the trusted sounding board for his plans.

Of course, all this came with a downside and her affection for him grew, though she hid it well for many years. Eventually though, it got too much, and she left his employment implying that just wanted different challenges, but nothing could have been further from the truth. Instead, she knew she had to distance herself so she could cope with the relationship they had compared to the relationship she wanted.

She smiled to herself. It may have taken a while, but she could now look on their liaisons with the detachment she needed to. An itch that sometimes needed to be scratched. She watched him approach the main table, carrying papers in his hand, introducing himself to the witnesses simply as Charlie. She smiled. Not even a surname, no mention of his position within the party or his contributions to the election manifesto. He knew how to make sure everyone felt at ease.

He finished his lap of the room, and caught her eye, fixing her with his ice blue eyes. He smiled slightly, one edge of his mouth rising, exposing bright white teeth, faultless except for long canines. It was that look he had often given her before when they had carried on their private business. She sighed inwardly, determined to maintain her initial resolve as he looked her up and down, a smile of appreciation playing on his lips, that special and unique look reserved between those who had shared a bed.

Their gaze was broken as Big Ben chimed and the door opened again. Josephine and Rebekah slipped through and Sharon took the opportunity to roll her eyes at them and look at her watch, softly chiding their tardiness. They approached her with apologetic looks. Sharon looked around to see how much of a disturbance the girls had caused and couldn't help but notice that Charlie's eyes were flitting between the two, watching them with a mixture of interest and amusement.

Sharon looked down and she closed her fist. She had done so well and now her blood red nails were pressed deep into her palm. She breathed deeply, determined that the work to control her emotions over the years would not be in vain. However, as she looked up, she witnessed Josephine's surprised expression as Charlie looked over at her and smiled and her eyes narrowed. It could be a long meeting.

The Chairman of the Committee, Mitch Fairhope cleared his throat to introduce the session. He started to speak, and his broad Yorkshire accent betrayed the northern roots that he had polished up nicely, taking great care to clothe his broad physique in as expensive a suit as he could afford.

He quickly turned to Charlie and gave him the floor. He had wondered how wise it was to undertake this evidence session. It was the perfect opportunity for the Government to influence the procedure, but no one could ever quite know what a session like this would reveal and sometimes it could reveal a diamond.

Charlie took no time to start addressing the assembled crowd, his voice deep and strong. He spoke with authority and resonance: "Welcome to this Special Public Bill Committee session and thank you Mr. Chairman for allowing me to speak so early on in the proceedings. I may be part of the Government but today I am working cross party to ensure you know we want to bring on all stakeholders within our plans and it's with this in mind that, in front of the Parliamentary Council, this committee wants to hear from you, about what we need to do to make sure that no one is left out of the global communication age." There were nods of approval around the room. Charlie looked back over towards the girls and smiled, noticing their thoughtful and concentrated expressions.

He took the papers in front of him in his hand for further dramatic effect and fixed Josephine's gaze. She blushed. He saw Sharon's expression harden but continued, his professionalism his priority for now. "The Office of the Parliamentary Council have spent a lot of time making sure that this legislation is based on a solid grounding, so hopefully it speaks for itself. However, it's important that we ensure everyone has their say and it is with that all in mind that I beseech all of those who are going to be part of this legislative process that we leave politics at the door, and that we listen to all sides of the arguments, and co-operate, viewing all those groups involved or affected."

Rebekah and Josephine looked at each other. Charlie's reputation had proceeded him - the rumours, the speeches, the filibustering in the Commons - but they had never heard him speak before, and his voice was baritone in pitch, measured and authoritative, with the slight hint of a Welsh accent. Cabinet Member's didn't often speak except to answer questions at the dispatch box, but when he could be persuaded to do so outside the Chamber, it was a thing of beauty.

Josephine looked at him closely. He knew about presentation. His morning routine was like clockwork. He swept into Parliament on his bike at exactly 7am before heading down to the gym for a run. It was no surprise that membership had gone up.

"Hear, hear!" came the cry as Charlie finished and sat back in his chair. He nodded back to Mitch. Mitch looked at the witnesses in front of him and welcomed the guests, a slightly forced smile on his lips: "I want to welcome all our witnesses today. You will help shape this legislation, not just by highlighting the issues and exploring how the policy can actually be enacted, but by helping us understand what issues need the most time when this Committee meets in the future to discuss the legislation in detail once it has come before the House."

He slowly looked around the room and settled on a small, slim lady with grey hair tied up in a bun: "Let's start with Mrs. Chaplan – welcome!" She was immaculately dressed in a blouse and skirt that she had purchased many decades earlier. Polyester lasted and she prided herself that she could still wear the same clothes all these years later. Thinness was next to godliness in her eyes and she prided herself on never indulging herself more than she would have been able to during rationing. After all, who needed any more. She did not care that the ruffled collar of her blouse gave away her age, she kept herself well and she was pleased that in a world full of change she could at least keep some standards.

"Mr. Chairman," she piped up, her raspy voice betraying a slight Midlands accent that she had taken great care to conceal over the years through extensive voice training. If it was good enough for the Queen, it was good enough for her: "We have no choice that the world is changing, but we should have at least some choice in how it affects us. Instead at the moment, the communications companies have chosen to overlook any extra needs we might have, and just focus on their own bottom line."

Emphasising the words, she wriggled slightly in indignation and looked over at Kasper Bernard, who was there representing ComTel, a massive communications carrier that had recently refused to install any new telephone exchanges in rural villages. He deliberately ignored her look and admired his perfectly manicured nails.

Charlie, however leaned forward, resting his head on his hand and nodding intently. She was enjoying herself, making the most of her moment of fame and Charlie knew that it was best to let her talk. After all, it was important that Parliament was seen to listen. He watched her as she continued talking, unperturbed by the snub or completely oblivious. She looked back over to the man she blamed for her problems: "So, companies like them want us to do more online, whilst not providing us with the basic tools to do so. We are left to fend for ourselves, paying extra for the privilege."

She stopped for a second, taking a breath to savour her important task: "Now, I pride myself on knowing how things work, and of course it therefore came as no surprise that I was voted by the Women's Institute to represent the village in these matters. But not even I could persuade our local community that it's fair that we have to pay for the exchanges to be put in whilst those in the cities don't have to. Why should we pay the same tax when we are paying again to get the basic rights that profit obsessed commercial organisations won't give, instead choosing to put their shareholders ahead of us." She sat back in her chair, giving a little jiggle of satisfaction thinking about how well she had done.

On the other side of the room, Josephine watched Charlie with curiosity, admiring the attention he was giving Mrs. Chaplan. He was in such a position of authority, and yet he was so keen to ensure things were done correctly, that no corners were cut in the process of delivering their promises. She didn't notice that he was returning the favour. He had her firmly fixed in the corner of his eye, until he made his move, and held her gaze for 5 seconds.

Suddenly she felt very self-conscious, and breaking his gaze, she chided herself. With one move she had suddenly exposed herself. She fiddled with the ring on her right hand. Not one for excessive fuss, she had was very surprised when her long-term boyfriend, William, had given her a friendship ring a few weeks before. They had been together for an age, but there had never been any mention of the future, it was more of a rolling contract neither of them broke, so it had taken her a while for her to get used to putting it on each morning. This morning though, she had seen it glinting on her bedside table, smiled, and put it on quickly for luck on the most important day of her career so far. However, now already, she felt that she had betrayed it's meaning.

She had met William at the local riding club whilst she had been in her final year at university. He had graduated a few years before in sport science that had taken on a part time role as a riding instructor and groom to support his various sporting ambition whilst he tried to break onto the Modern Pentathlon Circuit. Josephine only rode for fun, but she was a natural horsewoman and they quickly bonded, and he made it his job to teach her everything he knew - in and out of the saddle.

She was away from him now, away in the bright lights of Westminster where it was different and new. She had always been attracted to the entire physical nature of his personality, a strong force, but over the last few years he had been more in her shadow, choosing to support her more than blaze his own route. Now she was in the company of people that still strived like she did, and Charlie piqued her interest, she knew that for sure.

Rebekah gave her a jab in the ribs and Josephine startled suddenly. She straightened herself up and gave herself a swift talking to about the job in hand. She would learn nothing by day-dreaming, and it was down to her to make sure the legislation was balanced and without unintended consequence. Patrick had told her this morning that he was going to be increasingly involved with the Serjeant at Arms initiatives to engage with other Parliaments around Europe leaving her to her own devices and forge her own path. He had trusted that she would be able to be left to work on her own initiative and she needed to prove him right. Now firmly resolved, she listened whilst those on the Committee questioned the community representatives.

Sitting to the right was Kasper Bernard. His shirt was struggling to contain the paunch of a man who spent a lot of time sat at the lunch table being entertained by shareholders. His thinning hair was made more obvious by the slight mist of sweat that sat on his head as he was sitting under the bright light. All he felt was increasing indignation that he had been called to this committee, as if he didn't have better things to do with his time. Nevertheless, he was keen to set the record straight and show that his company had everyone's best interests at heart.

Mrs. Caplan finally took a breath and stopped speaking, allowing him to respond. Speaking in a whiny and shrill voice that was made breathless because of the weight of his jowls on his neck, his pudgy fingers pulled at his papers so he could bring his pre-prepared speech out. He wanted to make sure he stuck to the script. These politicians were crafty buggers, and he wanted to give them no leeway in apportioning any blame for the current situation to him.

"I am sorry that you don't understand why it's important that we keep shareholders happy. Shareholders buy into the company to provide us with important funds that allow us to do our work. Yes, they want to be rewarded through profit, but it's not only for their benefit you know. More profit means more tax paid to the Treasury which helps ensure you get your pension."

He sat back, pulling on his belt to relieve some of the pressure on his belly. He pushed out his upper lip slightly, wondering what experience any of those around him had to give them the authority to question his methods of working. All he knew that he was working hard and Mrs. Chaplan of Burton in the Wane or wherever she was from just wanted him to spend more money so she could free up more of her pension for bingo and biscuits.

He screwed up his mouth, congratulating himself on having proved the point that he was on the side of people like her, he realised that Mitch Fairhope MP was preparing to speak, and he suddenly felt nervous. He looked him up and down. He knew Mr. Fairhope by reputation, and that he made no secret of the fact that he firmly and openly supported the underdog.

Looking at Mrs. Chaplan, who was fiddling with her papers as if it was her knitting, Mitch suddenly saw his mother in her. His father had never been the same after he finished working in the mines for the newly established big corporations that expected long hours in poor working conditions for no more money, and it had left his mark and a deep distrust of men like Kasper Bernard. His father had been retired early on ill health after a long fight, but this didn't matter in the end. He still collapsed in the park, unable to be revived, leaving him and his mum to cope on their own through the most formative years of their lives

"Mr. Bernard," he started: "I understand your point that increased profit means increased taxes, but we need to make sure the points and considerations of the ordinary people are in the legislation and that they benefit from the services they pay for. With that in mind, I recommend that The Office of the Parliamentary Council draw up documents highlighting the issues that have been repeated by those affected today, the points of which have been ably explained by the other witnesses and work out how this dreadful imbalance is rectified."

He looked around and room and continued: "In addition, I am going to recommend to the Speaker that this particular part of the Bill is debated on the floor of the house to ensure that great consideration is put on the implications of the Bill. After all, it is not just the constituents of those MPs on this committee that are affected, it is every other community too, especially those more isolated and more vulnerable."

Kasper couldn't quite believe what he was hearing, his jowls moving with a mind of their own. He opened his mouth to remark on his own testimony but before the words came out, a bell rang out signifying the start of the Parliamentary session.

Mitch looked at the monitor and closed his notes with a firm smack: "Unfortunately we are out of time, but least we are further forward than we were. We know which direction we need to take." He looked at Charlie for any final comment, who turned to look straight at Josephine: "Thank you Mr. Chairman" he began, "and all those that have given evidence today. I feel we will be in good hands with the OPC who will work hard to ensure they are in line with the findings of the committee."

With that he rubbed his two fingers around his mouth and smiled. He stood up, moving towards the door along with the other MPs keen to make their way to the Chamber for Prime Ministers Questions. Josephine who was still seated as he left, following him with her eyes.

Rebekah looked at her as the room cleared. "Well that was a success - a mention from the Leader is quite something. And of course, I am sure it hasn't escaped you that a few of those in this committee have questions on the order paper today."

Josephine looked up and smiled. She glanced again towards the door whilst delving into her bag for her make up case. Having got hold of her lipstick, they both moved quickly towards the door smiling as she quickly applied it before saying:

"Of course, and I think we should go into the gallery to watch them work." They both giggled and left the room, pulling the solid door behind them, and strode off down the corridor.

They didn't notice that a shadow appeared from behind one of the glass doors of the back offices around the corner, smiling to himself. He brought out his notebook and black pen and thinking briefly he scribbled down a few words before placing the book in his pocket. Tapping it protectively, he waited until they were well out of sight before he came back into the light, closed the door and made his way towards the Chamber.

Chapter 4

Josephine rubbed her eyes and looked at the clock high on the wall. She had been in the Department since the crack of dawn and the only thing keeping her awake was the strong Columbian coffee in her hand. The Bill Committee Chairman had been succesful in his request that the debate on funding should be held on the floor of the House and MPs of all parties were on a three-line whip to vote on the clauses. Josephine's email had been beeping rhythmically all morning as MPs prepared for the debate by requesting information or clarification, and she had been thorough and quick to respond to each in turn.

Now though, the job had been done and it was time to wait. She knew that as an Officer of the House she was supposed to be completely neutral, looking at all sides of an argument evenly. However, she knew in her heart that she would feel that she would have achieved something really important if the House passed discretionary help for those that needed to install broadband themselves. She steeled herself feeling righteous in her thoughts: little old ladies should not be out of pocket if they just want to communicate with the outside world.

Josephine noted that even Patrick had taken more of a personal interest in this Bill than was usual for him. He seemed to make it his business to check the briefings and then disappear with a pile to the Members Tearoom so he could watch where the alliances were forming without anyone thinking anything of it. He was so logical that everyone always put his actions down to his perpetual ability to think ahead and prepare. He hardly ever took a day off, and never missed an opportunity to gain more information about how a debate was developing in order that he could fully understand the political atmosphere around the Bills that passed through his office and ensure that he could effectively advise the Government on how to improve their message.

Josephine looked at the live feed on her computer screen and clenched her fist without thinking. They were reaching the final clauses in this session. This was it. This was the moment she had been waiting for. The MPs were coming to the crux of the issue and this one debate would represent whether or not the work she had done would be a success or failure.

Her phone was ready in her hand to tell William the news: good or bad. Their weekends together had been rare of late and she knew that it was hard for him that she was so far away stuck in her office often unable to speak. However, she had been looking forward to this trip away for a long time and she knew when she got onto that train and was headed out of London, she could really relax and get away from the hustle and bustle of Parliamentary life. Plus, this wasn't just a usual trip home. Instead, they were off to Scotland and she smiled as she thought about the wild landscape. No angles, no intrigue and no alliances to protect or form.

She watched the screen. Time was running down. The lobby doors closed before the tellers returned to the House of Commons Chamber to officially announce the result. The chamber fell silent. The result became clear. Ayes to the right - 326, noes to the left 319. Josephine exhaled loudly, a palpable relief in her gut. Her first success.

She looked at her phone and slowly tapped into it, not quite believing the words she was able to write: "We did it! The clauses are officially part of the Bill! Celebrations here, but I will make a quick exit as soon as I can."

She finished typing and the doors opened. In stepped Patrick. Josephine gave him a big hug, surprising herself as much as she did him. She had no idea how much she cared and how much effect this work had already had on her: "We did it!" she said, and he enveloped her slim fingers with his own gargantuan hands.

He looked back at her, holding her gaze, and spoke slowly and intently: "No you did it. You made this happen. Don't forget though - the hard work starts here. We need to ensure that the money gets to where it's needed and that no details are lost when the Bill is rolled out."

Suddenly the door opened again. Expecting Rebekah, Sharon and the rest of the team to enter the room, Josephine was less prepared when Charlie walked in. He was followed by his large entourage, who hung on his every movement. Always busy, they carried papers and checked their phones to see what was going on that could possibly affect his standing and position within the party.

He came towards Josephine and fixed his eyes on her. His eyes sparkled, and he smiled. She wondered if the look was just for her, or if everyone saw it and she was just being drawn in to his circus. Despite herself, again she felt intrigued. Charlie put his hand on her shoulder and she felt her heart flutter slightly as he made contact: "Congratulations," he purred, "I know how hard you worked on this, to ensure these clauses had passage." She looked at him and thought how much older he was, but how he kept himself in remarkably good shape. She had seen him fly in through the gates on his bike, the policeman used to him flashing his pass as he whizzed by, hardly slowing down.

He continued: "We will need to remain in close contact now so we can work out all the ins and outs." He accentuated his words vey precisely and pointedly maintained eye contact as his staff buzzed about. They stood there, meshed together in their gaze and Charlie stuck his arm out at a firm

90 degree angle. Quick as a flash, a young girl - all legs and arms - passed him a heavy Edinburgh Crystal glass with a large slug of 15-year-old Lagavulin. This was his signature drink of success – but it had to be the 15-year-old bottle. Any older and it was over-aged. Any younger and it was just too immature. He threw his neck back and swallowed the contents of the glass in one. Signally quickly, it was obvious he wanted a refill.

This time Sharon approached with the bottle. No one had noticed her enter the room, or move into position to be able to offer the drink, but he accepted her proferring in a flourish. However, this time, he was different with the glass. He was now looking for a longer experience. He took his time, sniffing the aromatic smokiness of the spirit that sat smoothly in the glass, a hint of camphor deep in its foundation. He seemed lost in the scent, silently admiring the drink, his eyes closed as it brought back memories unknown by those around him.

Sharon juddered slightly, unable to stop herself. She was outside her comfort zone, unable to read his mind. Indeed, she wasn't alone. Josephine felt slightly uneasy as she couldn't help but watch him either, lost in his own world. It felt like he was making them all wait. Josephine looked quickly at Sharon and seeing her look of desperation and confusion, quickly resolved that he would not have the power over her that he obviously had over those others around him.

She would not be drawn in, instead making sure she remained an enigma so he would wonder what made her tick. With her new plan of action in place, she moved away from the crowd and signalled to Patrick that she was going to leave. He raised an arm and nodded her head towards him in daughterly affection. Charlie spotted the move and he held his drink up to her with a cock of his head, but her resolve was hardened and she only quickly nodded back before she turned away to walk out the door.

She took out her hairband, allowing her golden hair to tumble down her shoulders, relieved that she had already explained to Patrick why she wanted to try and leave in a timely manner. She ruffled her hair as she walked towards the door, a wry smile on her lips as if she could sense Charlie watching her, and she was not wrong. His eyes followed her out the room, unable to help himself. She was different. Young certainly, but she had a confidence that was unusual for someone so new to such a stressed and pent up environment.

She closed the door and breathed an unknown sigh of relief, pleased she had held herself together having released the stresses of the day from herself in a physical sense, and got her into the mood for the weekend. Her phone beeped as she moved into the corridor, and she brought it out quickly. She saw the familiar number pop up:

"Looking forward to seeing you darling! I have a surprise for you!" She was pleased. She was about to go back into the arms of his safe haven, her William.

She sighed and wondered what it could mean. William didn't have much money, but he was certainly inventive. She thought about trying to find out and then decided against it. In this day and age it was nice to have a surprise, especially a simple and positive one, put together with thoughtfulness and care. There was little that surprised her nowadays. She hadn't been long away but she was already seeing signs that people were happy to push their own agenda no matter what.

She thought about all the conversations they had when they were alone, about how simple it all was for him. He wouldn't play any games, and he didn't want all the answers - he was just happy to live life for now. There was no side to his comments, there was no ulterior motive. Of course, Josephine knew that in London away from him, there was a danger that she could get sucked in. Even in her excitement about their weekend away, she had wondered momentarily if it had been Charlie with a message of congratulations, one final contact before she left. She grimaced slightly, finding her concern for him distasteful but there was no doubt, politics was addictive.

She smiled. That's all it was. It was nothing to do with Charlie. She was doing an important role in a beautiful building with important people. She was aware of the dangers but she was there to help people, to build on the work she had previously done and to make use of those exams she had taken. Even William's parents knew that her heart was in the right place, even though they were politically opposed to her on most issues that they had ever discussed.

Josephine wound her way down the corridors to her own office, her coat and suitcase standing by her desk ready to be collected before she headed off to the station. She entered the office for the final time that week, and closed the door behind her thinking that she didn't really want to travel in a suit. Whatever William's surprise it was likely to be mucky, and she much preferred her jeans and flat boots anyway. Laying her jacket on the desk, she opened the case, bringing out her travelling clothes. She pulled off her skirt and crisp pink shirt, folding them both properly. The shirt may be going in the wash but there was no need for unnecessary creasing.

Standing there in just her pants and bra, she suddenly became aware of the main office door opening quickly and slamming shut again. As soon as the door had closed, a voice penetrated the walls of the office, the distinct accent thick with anger and frustration: "I saw the way you looked at her, the new girl with her attitude, as if she was the one who voted the clauses through."

Josephine was shocked. She realised that it was Sharon spitting venom, and she couldn't help but slightly gasp. She heard a fist slam on the table. The shouting moved slightly further away from where she was standing and she opened the door ever so slightly, thankful that her office was in the new building, meaning there was none of the heavy creaking that came with the old doors in the older parts.

Soon a male figure came into view, followed by a sigh. Tired and unimpressed that the evening had suddenly made a turn for the worse Charlie approached Sharon, putting his arm out to try and appease the situation before it got out of contol. He slowly started talking: "Josephine was pleased and rightly so. She worked hard." Josephine slightly straightened, not quite sure how she felt that she was being attacked, and also defended.

He continued, pacing up and down the room, his breathing rhythmic as he tried not to react to the stares he was facing down: "All we were trying to do was get the right result for the little old ladies. Do you remember what that is? Teamwork for the greater good? No, I don't think you do. You can't with such a reaction like this. Remember Sharon, I am my own man, and I just do my job trying to bring everyone along together."

Sharon humphed and walked away from him, striding around the office like a lion on the prowl: "Yes well it's all well and good having these young things come and work for us but I have seen her laughing and giggling with Rebekah making notes and being presumptive in her manner."

His voice then hardened, and Josephine was taken by the difference of his soft and enticing tone from just a few moments before. He growled: "Don't blame me for your own insecurities Sharon. I like to play fairly and I just do my job. If you feel she's got ideas about her station that is up to you to deal with. Don't bring it to my door."

Looking at Sharon, he saw she was not backing down. He tried another tactic: "She's so young. She is just immature. She wants to play with the big boys but she isn't sure how and maybe she is just looking to engratiate herself. I don't think she means anything by it and would probably look to you for guidance if you gave her a chance. She sees how you have it sorted, she just wants a piece." He pouted: "And who wouldn't want a piece of your ass."

Sharon briefly stopped, taking deep breaths, but then she felt that anger rise once again a guttural instinct that had been lit: "That little bit of stuff was flirting with you!" her eyes flashing angrily, "and you embarrassed me by responding."

Charlie sighed again: "I embarrassed you? You were the one who decided to play mother by taking the bottle off Anya, so new to the team and with little knowledge of the dynamics of our offices. Christ, Sharon, I know you like to assert your authority but sometimes you take it too far. You will soon be saying that I am playing around there too."

Before he could finish the sentence Sharon couldn't help herself, the red mist rising: "I bet you are. I bet you are flaunting it in my face without me even realizing it until now, not caring about how I feel, the one who has been with you for so long and through so much. You didn't even notice I was there until I poured your drink. How else was I going to get your attention? I saw your look. Caught out were we?"

Charlie approached her again, this time unwilling to compromise. He had planned a nice surprise for her, but he didn't like being backed into a corner like this. He didn't like to be shackled: "I don't know if your blind rage is supposed to make you more attractive because trust me it isn't. I was surprised, yes. Caught out, no. But to you it wouldn't matter what I said. Unless I am on your leash outside the bedroom as well as in, you aren't happy. Well, I am sorry, I will not have you embarrassing me like this again. That's it. I just can't do it anymore." He then strode out the door, throwing his arms up in complete dismissal of both her and the situation, leaving Sharon alone and looking lost in the middle of the room.

Josephine was quite shocked by the turn of events and the anger her presence had obviously created. The fact that Sharon and Charlie's relationship had been so current shocked her. She had had no idea, and the fact that it was partly down to her that it was over now, was not her intention when she joined the office. She looked outside the office, unable to decide if she should try and explain to Sharon that she was not intentionally causing trouble, but she decided against it. Anger and frustration were still coming off her in waves. She could could easily react unpredictably and that could just exacerbate the situation.

Sharon wailed, her mascara beginning to run, her head down on the desk. She sobbed, and her shoulders heaved, heavy with emotion. Josephine couldn't bear to see any more and quietly closed the door shut, moving away to her desk to try and get herself together for her trip away. She realised that in the shock turn of events she hadn't actually dressed yet and quickly pulled on her clothes, listening for noise on the other side of the door, keen to make her escape. Hearing nothing, she tied her hair back up in a loose ponytail, before she approached the door again.

She slowly began to open it, but suddenly became aware of two softer voices talking, and the distinct sound of a lock snapped shut. She saw a different figure with Sharon, sharing a much more tender moment, having drawn her back from the brink. His back was to the door so Josephine couldn't see his face, just a mop of black hair. Sharon's head was on his shoulder. Her sobs were fading into whimpers, and her eyes were closed. Her heaving physique slowly quietening down into regular, soft breaths.

They whispered together, initially too quiet for Josephine to hear what they were saying. The stranger put his hand over the side of Sharon's face wiping away her tears: "Don't worry about anything" he said, raising his voice just loud enough for Josephine to hear. "You can rely on me." He then drew her close, and pulled her into a deep kiss. Sharon couldn't help but respond. Weakened by the rejection from Charlie, she wanted comfort, and she knew she her reputation preceded her. Jack was a new MP, young and unmarried. He had got into Parliament in a shock by-election, having won because of his vanilla attitude on most things, whilst his wish to get along and not bother anyone pleased the higher echelons of the party. Young men weren't her usual type but Sharon knew it was her best option tonight and she wryly smiled as he kissed her. It seemed he had more spark than she had originally thought.

Behind the door, Josephine quickly realised what was going to happen and thanked her stars that she wasn't going to have to sit at that table tomorrow. She closed the door sharply. There were some images she just didn't want in her mind. She sat down with a silent plop and then it occurred to her that she was going to miss her train. She brought her phone out to tell William the news that she had been delayed. All she could do was wait it out, and hope he understood.

Chapter 5

Josephine lifted her head from William's chest and looked at him, their bodies clamped close in the one sleeping bag. She sighed contentedly and ran her finger across his collar bone and down towards his muscular arms, and yet he still slumbered, tired from their evening of catching up. It had been a few months and they both needed the release.

His manly chest rose and fell, his breathing melodic and deep. She moved her finger slowly across his body, across the downy blond hair on his chest towards his broad shoulders, that were ever so slightly bruised from his hard daily slog carrying around the waste from the gardens he tended whilst he waited for his sports injury to heal allowing him to train again.

Of course, as the years went by, his chances of professional success decreased but he was still the same person she had fallen for all that time ago. The strong silent type that rarely became flustered by mishaps or drama, no matter what the situation - just using his intuition and wit to get through.

She looked around her and back to him. He had found a campsite overlooking her favourite view of Loch Lomond in the grounds of Boturich Castle. She remembered how much she had gushed about the location when they were last walking this way on one of their long treks. At the time she thought that maybe her affection for the lcoation was just due to the memory of how they had fallen lustily into a field, tearing at each others clothes. She giggled at the memory. It was only afterwards that she realised she had lost a pink bra that day.

Looking around now though, she knew know that was not the case. This was a truly beautiful location. It was just like she had remembered, and he had obviously done his research to secure such a perfect backdrop for their weekend of celebrations.

She climbed out of the tent, just wearing his t-shirt, her bare feet on the soft green grass. It was still damp from the downpour they had been protected from by the canvass as they huddled together in their own world. She moved quickly towards the edge of the area of cut grass towards the unkempt pathways that surrounded the campsite and lead back onto the main estate.

She passed the pans still lay sprawled by the little camp cooker which had provided a simple but wonderful meal from the vegetables he had brought from his own vegetable patch. A wonderful change from the limited and bland tasting offerings she was faced with at the cramped local supermarkets in London.

Soon she reached the edge of the Loch, and she marvelled at the light blue water down below her. The view beyond was outstanding, the rugged land scattered with a plethora of trees, just below the clouds that were lifting over the cool mountain view as the morning took shape.

Josephine looked at her phone and saw just a couple of bars of reception. She was enjoying being far away from London but it was always good to keep in touch. Then, as if responding to her thoughts, the phone suddenly beeped and an unknown number popped up with a text message. Used to spam messages from PPI firms using unknown mobile numbers, she was just about to press delete when she noticed that this message might be important: "Josephine, good work. I have a project for you guaranteed to whet your whistle: CC." Before she could stop herself Josephine took in a sharp intake of breath and looked around, unsure of what she felt.

She chided herself that Charlie was disturbing her weekend and thoughts, but she had done nothing wrong. She hardly knew the man and she had not given him her number. He must have picked it up from the general information sheets given out to all those on the team, and it was just a work text. There was nothing personal disclosed and he was one of the most powerful men in the country. It made her smile that he valued her work so much that he should think of her. She turned back to the view and ran her fingers through her hair. The calm of the view was what mattered now. The man who had picked out this spot just for her.

She walked back towards the tent, annoyed that she had been pulled off track so easily, impressed by power and presence, over kindness and consideration. She looked once more at her phone and put it on silent before throwing it into her bag in the corner of the tent. She knew that William would feel as if someone else was intruding in on their alone time if he realised she was communicating with people he didn't know in London, especially as she hadn't invited him to come and meet anyone yet. However, she reassured herself that he hated London anyway and that this way they were both entirely comfortable when they caught up.

Poking her head inside William was still asleep, but had moved onto his front. His arms stretched out exposing his strong gnarled hands with the ingrained dirt under his short broken nails and the new ink that snaked all the way down his back. A wolf stretched out clawing its way down his spine towards his pert bottom, there was a lot of detail. The wolf was poised ready to jump, its green eyes flashing, claws extended and fur standing on end.

When she had first seen it, he admitted that it represented how he saw her, a force to be reckoned with, dealing with life as it happened, relentless and strong. A constant reminder that she was alongside him, even if she was far away. She used her finger to draw down the length of his spine. He yawned loudly, exposing his teeth and making her jump. His eyes still closed, he looked like a lion with his curly mane of wavy blond hair on the pillow.

She imagined what the office would say if she turned up to a black tie function with him on her arm, his tattoos hidden under a smart black jacket, but the wildness still obvious for anyone to see, and the straightforwardness of his nature difficult for many in her new world to understand. She heard the words in her head, and saw the whispers in her mind that they were moving apart, but she couldn't let go of him. Not yet.

He then opened his eyes and turned to her. He looked straight at her and seeing her thoughtful expression, he jolted upright. "What's wrong?" he asked, worried;

"Nothing," she replied. She was telling the truth, nothing was wrong. Even though it would never be perfectly right, it could never be perfectly wrong.

He pulled her into his arms and held her close, his musky scent enveloping her. "This isn't the end of your surprise you know. Of course, if it was down to me we would never leave the tent, but I know there is something else you enjoy." He sat up and threw her a bag that he had concealed behind the first aid kit and she looked at him with her eyebrows raised: "Go on," he said, "open it!"

She unzipped the small sports bag and pulled out her jodhpurs and chaps. She smiled, quickly unzipped her jeans and sat on the sleeping bag, pulling them on quickly. "Oh William!" she said, zipping up her riding gear: "you are amazing."

He smiled at her, pleased that he had again made her so happy. She brushed her hair, humming a gainful tune that he couldn't quite place. He turned his back to her and opened his wallet. The money he was about to spend on this treat meant that he would have to take the work offered the care home at the weekend. He sighed with acceptance. She was worth it, and she did seem genuinely impressed with the way he had pulled off this weekends activities. However, a hack around the Scottish countryside wasn't much compared to all the fancy activities she could get up to in London. There she would have a range of things to do at her fingertips, and willing partners no doubt.

It was this that made William worry about her. Like him she was a country girl at heart and so far she had only had victories in her work, and admiration from those around her. She had been taken under the wing of her boss and colleagues, and was being protected and helped to establish herself. However, even William knew there was a darker side to politics. The way in which colleagues briefed against other party members, the aggression of Prime Ministers Questions. He only had a small window into her world and he didn't see anything kind. No prisoners were taken when things got rough. There seemed to be no protection at all when the knives were out and the daggers were drawn.

"Ready!" she called out, smiling at him broadly: "Let's go and find our steads."

"Hang on," he replied, "I need some trousers. I don't want to give the horses a shock." Looking down, she realised he was still in his briefs. Admiring the view for a second, she chuckled and threw him his jeans. A professional rider that had started riding on his fathers farm, he preferred jeans like a cowboy when he was riding for fun. He found competition outfits stifling and wouldn't give anything similar any quarter during his downtime. Soon he was ready and, moving slowly round the tent to gain an advantage, he set off with a start. "I'll race you!" he yelled and ran off ahead, his powerful legs striding towards the stables.

Startled for a second, Josephine saw her phone flshing again in the corner. Another message: "This project will help you influence the way the entire country is powered. The Energy Bill. Patrick wants you to be in it to win it. CC." She thought for a second. He was obviously keen to have her involvement and she knew she was qualified having created such a formidable network within the industry through her various placements through university and beyond. She thought about not responding but was unable to help herself. She quickly typed back: "Yes, back in on Monday. Shall we meet first thing?" She threw it back where it had laid, silently buzzing in her bag. She pondered for a second about whether or not she should take it with her, but she knew there wasn't an excuse. This was not London. She closed her mind off. Now was not the time to think about work, or Charlie.

She saw William slowing down in the distance with a mildly quizzical look on his face wondering where she was. She thought quickly, and called out: "I needed a pee!" He smiled and raced off further, slowing down when he came to a concealed entrance. She ran to him and he caught her in his arms. He whispered in her ear: "Daisy, Daisy, give me your answer do. I can't afford much, but I can saddle a horse for you." His ridiculous ditty made her laugh and they approached the stables, him still holding her fast in his arms. Suddenly they became aware of a stern looking instructress brandishing a whip.

As they approached William whispered in Josephine's ear: "Ooh, strict nanny!" and Josephine looked him straight in the eye and kissed him deeply. The instructress cleared her throat, and rolled her eyes, stopping them in their tracks. Camilla was wide set but obviously very fit. She had obviously spent many years outside in all weathers whilst perfecting her craft and her hair looked like it was made of straw having been blown by harsh Scottish winds and scorched by the sun in equal measure whilst she looked after and tended to the horses.

"You must be Josephine?" she said, eyeballing her two guests: "William said you were an accomplished rider."

"Yes" said Josephine: "I did have a horse when I was younger so know how to handle myself."

"That's good," Camilla continued, "Would you be ok with taking the horses out on your own?" Josephine couldn't believe her ears and squeaked with delight:

"Yes!" she exclaimed "I promise you we will take good care of your beautiful animals."

She then put her hand over her mouth, realising she was talking over her as Camilla slowly slapped the whip against her chaps, impatient at having been interrupted. Camilla continued: "Well, we have a staffing problem today, I think that might be best. I knew it might have to be an option because we have had issues with staff over the last month, but William was desperate for me not to refund his money, so here we are. Anyway, you can't go off the estate, because there are security cameras at every exit to protect the animals, so now the floor is yours for the next hour and a half."

Josephine squealed again excitedly, and the three of them turned towards the stables. For the first time Josephine took stock of the beautiful animals kept in the rustic outbuildings. She was motioned towards a beautiful bay mare standing at 15 hands. The beautiful beast had big brown eyes, and watched the new riders intently as they approached. Josephine instinctively put a hand out to her cheek, brushing her fingers along her soft mane as she made contact over the bridle: "Shhh" she whispered "I will take good care of you."

She opened the stable door and expertly took hold of the reins to lead the animal towards the mount. "This is Sophomore," explained Camilla: "She is very kind - a bit frisky but has not got a malicious bone in her body." Josephine drew alongside her and quickly mounted. She knew they didn't have long and she wanted to feel the wind rushing through her hair as she explored the rough terrine.

Quickly sorting out her stirrups and girth, Camilla signalled: "Right, off you go, wait over there," and turned round so she could help William. William, however, had already mounted, choosing to leap up from the ground. Sorting out the tack himself, he was riding a Chestnut gelding called Base. Base towered over Sophomore, but it was obvious the horses were good friends as they whinnied together excitedly about being let out into the fresh air: "Their first ride of the day," Camilla smiled, and Josephine and William looked at each other with a smirk before they headed straight off along the bridal way, waving goodbye to Camilla and the stable block.

Keen to pick up the pace as they reached the soft tracks, Josephine kicked Sophomore on - an energetic trot quickly turning into a hearty canter. Keen to not be left behind, Base quickly matched her pace and soon they were both flying along the paths with mud being driven up through the quickening horses hooves. Josephine's breath quickened as she felt Sophomore's smooth gait underneath her, and it she felt she had never been out of the saddle. They made good progress through the countryside and finding themselves by the edge of the Loch, William and Josephine slowed the horses down in unison to take in the beautiful view.

The rugged hills were a mixture of green and brown where the grass and heather met and entwined, whilst the trees provided ample hiding place for those animals that called the Loch their home. "It's so beautiful!" Josephine exclaimed, and William slowly pushed his horse next to Josephine's so they were side by side. "Hello pretty lady," he smiled. He pretended to doff his hat: "What's a pretty girl like you doing in a rough part of the countryside like this."

She smiled coquettishly: "Oh, I am lost. Was so taken in by the beautiful view that I am totally disorientated. Can you tell me where to go?"

He nodded again: "Well I can show you what you need, but I think you'll have to get off the horse first."

She felt her heart rate quicken and silently swung her leg over Sophomore's back. She dropped down onto the path and taking the reins up in her hands approached the nearest patch of grass with a well used hitching post. She quickly tied Sophomore to it in a Highwayman's Hitch and looked straight at William, who quickly copied her actions. Base and Sophomore looked at each other and whinnied, taking this change of events as the perfect opportunity to dip their noses into the cool wet grass, pulling it up with their teeth.

Josephine approached William and exclaimed: "Oh sir. I hope the horses will be alright. Will you show me how to get out of this mess?" William slowly approached her, pushing his body into hers slowly but determinedly. "Oh yes," he whispered, biting her ear softly, "I will show you the way out, I have a fancy it's this way," and he guided her out of sight of the horses. His lips moved to the nape of her neck as she softly sighed, his lips brushing her skin. She could feel his cock rising in his jeans, and she felt the throbbing deep in her core.

He lifted her up, undoing the zip of her jodhpurs with one hand, and smiled as he realised she was going commando. His cock was now desperate to escape from the restrictions of his trousers and she quickly helped him on his way. He entered her with one sure thrust, pounding her against the tree, their bodies gelled together in a mixture of tight clothes and hot appreciation. Totally lost in the moment, he pushed even harder, his teeth biting her lips aggressively, his cock hard and thick in arousal. Her back scraped along the bark of the tree, and Josephine exhaled quickly, the heady mixture of the sharp pain of the bark against her back.

Almost animal like now, they toppled over and fell into the mound of overgrowth next to the tree. The rhythm unhindered, William quickened up the pace again, his rough hands pulling her bottom up against his pelvis. Now totally taken over by the fierceness of their corresponding desires, a deep growl broke from his throat as he could feel his orgasm building. She bit into his neck, overtaken by shattering pleasure, and she came hard and fast in unison with him.

Deep in the aftermath, they slowly moved, their heads giddy, and the endorphins hindering their movement. She tried to stand but her legs ached with a post orgasmic throb. William helped her up. She looked down and suddenly became aware that the green patch they had been lying on had been completely torn up into muddy folds of earth in their exchange. She straightened out her clothes as much as she could, or as much as she could be bothered. She pulled her shirt straight and realised she was missing button and smiled. She always lost something when William was about.

She brushed the mud off her trousers, and ran her hand over her head and torso as she realised she had half of the landscape deeply engrained in her hair. William softly pulled out strands of grass from her pony tail, letting them fall back to where they had originally stood proud and unbroken. Their kisses were soft and tender now, their aggression spent in the hot moments of their love making.

"We should go," Josephine started, not wanting the moment to end but knowing that Camilla was probably wondering where the horses were. They approached the horses, who had managed to prune back an entire area of grass and they both mounted in silence, a warm sense of satisfaction passing between them. "I hope that wasn't private property!" Josephine joked as they looked to identify where they were and what the quickest route back was.

William pulled out his phone and found a signal. Josephine put her hand in her pocket out of habit. The phone shaped hole in her pocket shocked her slightly, but she felt relieved when she remembered that she had left her phone at the camp in case of unwelcome interruptions, as opposed to having dropped the phone where they lay. William soon had the way, and she looked at him fondly. He always made her feel safe, and now was no different. He had lead her through to ecstasy and was safely seeing her through the other side.

William was the first to make the horses find canter, but Josephine quickly followed, the animals enjoying the sprint back home. Both the riders knew that time was of the essence and neither of them cared whether or not their passion was obvious to Camilla. They had taken good care of the horses. Soon the wooden blocks came into view and they slowed the horses down, taking a final few moments of private time. They held hands and led the animals through the yard, his thumb stroking her hand. Neither wanted the weekend to end, but Josephine couldn't help but look at the clock, noting with sadness that each tick of its hands were now just leading them back to the reality of separation.

Chapter 6

The train pulled into the station, and William looked at Josephine with a mixture of affection and sadness. She opened the door of the train carriage, and they stepped on. Allowing others to pass them, she turned around, held his hands in hers and she promised: "I will see you very soon."

He looked at her fondly, knowing that the train was about to leave, but wanting to just enjoy the closeness they had had during the last few days for a little bit longer. She had always been different from the other girls. A lot of them had settled in the area after finishing school or university, taking work teaching or in the family faming businesses but that was never going to be enough for his Josephine and he loved and hated her for it in equal measure.

He maintained his contact with her, but he could see in her eyes that the pull Josephine had to London was enormous. He let go of her hands, giving her what he knew she wanted. She held her hand to his cheek and he moved into her touch as she stroked his eyebrow with her thumb. He closed his eyes, lost in the moment, and pulled her close into one final kiss. He slowly opened his eyes again a few moments later and took each side of her face in his hands. In practical silence they said goodbye, the words unsaid as he stepped off the train.

Josephine turned and walked to her seat. There was a deep sadness within her that she was leaving him behind, but in her heart, she knew that it was necessary, and comforted herself that she would see him again soon. However, she wanted to make the most of the opportunity being placed in front of her. Charlie Connery had asked for her. He wanted her to contribute to this new piece of legislation, and she wanted to see how far she could push it.

She had only been sat down a moment or two when the train pulled away and she looked out of the window. William was still waving from the platform, and she watched him until he was no longer in sight. She pulled out her magazine and put it on the table, idly flicking through it, but utterly unable to concentrate. She looked at her watch and knew it was going to be a long journey back down to London.

Desperately trying to relax, she pulled her shoulders back and tried to get more comfortable in her seat. She looked at her phone. No bars of service. She sighed impatiently, turning it off and on again, desperate to see whether or not there were any updates on when they might be meeting, and how the project might fit together. Sighing in disappointment at no such indication, lay back in her seat and closed her eyes, desperate to make the journey go faster.

Her mind was finally settling when a bar

popped up on her phone and this in turn delivered a message. Hearing the beep of communication, she opened her eyes excitedly and silently cheered when she saw it was from Charlie: "The project is too hot. We need to catch up tonight. Where are you? CC." Tired and sore, her body urged her to put him in a holding pattern to ensure she didn't look desperate and to show that she was in control of the situation. Her mind though, was racing, and she felt the urgency she had felt in the tent when his first message came through, that there was a need to get the meeting locked down.

Her heart overtook her head, and she quickly responded that she was on the train to Euston and could see him soon. After she pressed send, she looked at the screen. It immediately acknowledged a message had been successfully delivered, but not whether or not it had been read. She told herself to stop being ridiculous. He wouldn't be sitting there like her, desperate for communications.

It felt like ages before she got what she wanted - confirmation that the meeting was going to go ahead. It was brief. A location and a time. More of an order than a request. She googled the bar and sighed. It was just around the corner from the station and given the tightness of the timings, it would be impossible for her to go home to change. Instead, she would have to get ready on the train.

She slightly cursed that she was so casually dressed in jeans and a plain shirt, but at least they were clean, unlike the rest of her clothes that had taken a beating whilst she had been away. She pulled open her suitcase and found a pair of boots she had taken in case there had been a need and pulled them on, thinking to herself that at least she had been able to improve her appearance slightly.

She drew her body out of the seat, stretching herself to get rid of the aches of the last few days and made her way down the train, which was now softly rocking from side to side. Reaching the curved door of the toilet cubicle, she stepped inside and lifted her arm to put her makeup back in front of the mirror.

In that brief moment, she noticed a scratch on her arm where she had caught the tree on the way down into the bushes. She smiled and fingered it fondly, thinking about how different the two components of her life were. She looked at herself in the mirror and suddenly wondered what Charlie would think of her slightly rough and ready appearance. He was always so immaculately turned out, and she always made an effort at work. This time though she was being caught on the hop, like she was going to somehow expose the real her, the one that only those close to her usually saw.

She looked at her watch. Just 10 minutes until the train arrived. 10 minutes to make sure that she was fit for purpose. She picked out her emergency foundation and eye liner, quickly outlining her eyes in a deep purple, a sultry look she felt was not too harsh for her slightly tired skin but gave her a bit of definition. She turned her head to one side and then the other.

She pulled her hair off her face to accentuate the feline shape of her face and the nape of her neck. She rummaged around to see if there was any perfume in her bag and drew out a small, square bottle. She smelt the sweet scent that she had worn for so many years now, the backdrop of so many memories where she had felt powerful and strong, and splashed it on her wrists.

Suddenly an announcement came over the tannoy and the train slowed down. She quickly made her way back to her seat to pick up her suitcase and coat before returning to the doors to prepare for a prompt exit. All the calm she had felt in the country was disappearing and she was getting impatient now. She didn't want to be late for such an important meeting.

The doors were finally released, and she came out of the doors like a bullet out of a gun. Racing along the platform, she suddenly felt a wave of heat, and her face redden. She slowed down to a walk. It was much better that she was two minutes late and not hot and sweaty, than on time and flustered. After all, this was a last-minute arrangement when she was just coming back into the city after a weekend away. She wasn't superwoman. She smiled to herself, well not yet anyway.

Soon after exiting the station she saw the doors of the bar, prominent on the corner of a busy main road, and next to a luxurious London hotel. She approached the bar and looked through the window. He was already there nursing a Guinness. A man's drink. She walked in nonchalantly, letting the beat of the background music dictate the speed of her steps, passing him on her way to the bar. This had obviously been an old-fashioned public house at one point, that had been redecorated to a more modern style. The traditional benches had been replaced with red leather sofas, and the tablecloths were a deep scarlet with faux fur animal prints.

Some young men were at the bar, and they looked her up and down as she approached. One of them, dressed in a green rugby shirt that was too well maintained to be a team top, let out a whistle, and Josephine couldn't help but smile to herself. "Well, hello. Can I buy you a drink?" he asked, leaning on the bar in front of her so she would have to give him due notice. She saw the eager expression on his young face and looked at Charlie through the corner of her eye. He had seen her come in and was watching what was going on with interest. Josephine softly whispered: "No thanks, but maybe next time you will get lucky."

The young men cocked his head towards

Charlie, who had suddenly taken an exaggerated interest in his phone as if he had been caught out, and asked "Who's that?" Josephine smiled and turned her back on Charlie so he couldn't see what she was saying.

"Just my friend." The guy looked between her and Charlie once more and said: "I hope when I am his age, I have a friend like you." Josephine smiled again, and quickly taking her drink she turned and walked towards Charlie's table.

She was pleased that she still had the ability to be noticed and that Charlie had been caught slightly unawares by his own reaction to the situation. She approached and he looked up from his phone. He smiled, pretending he had only just seen her. Drawing his fingers round the top of his pint glass, he drawled: "You made it!" She nodded in agreement and sat down, placing her bag neatly by her side.

"Been somewhere fun?" he enquired, his gaze flitting between her and her luggage.

"Yes, a quick trip out of town to see my friend" she replied. She cleared her throat: "boyfriend" she corrected herself, wondering why she was withholding the fact that she had a partner.

He smiled and continued to trace a circle: "That's good, it so important to have outside interests." She squirmed in her seat slightly and looked him up and down, confused at the changeability of his reactions to what she said or did. He was much more casually dressed than the last time she saw him, but his shirt was still immaculately ironed without a button out of place. There was an old black leather bomber jacket tucked neatly into the side of his chair, and he saw her looking at it, slightly confused at its place in the picture, and trying to piece it all together.

With a teasing look in his eye, he put his hand on it, and squeezed it firmly. His hands were unusually small for a man of his height, with perfectly manicured nails cut short as if reducing the temptation to bite: "Ah this old coat has seen me through many a storm. There are just some things you hold onto you know." Before she could react, he turned towards her and continued, "Anyway, it's really good to see you. We need to get this nailed," and he softly brought his fist down on the table "Security of energy supply. What does UK plc need to do?"

She responded, happy to get down to business: "Yes, it's imperative. We live in an uncertain world whilst traditional energy sources are on the wane considering the number of plants about to go offline. So, we need to find new types of energy sources to bridge the gap."

He looked at her and thought he was right to ensure that she was brought on board for this project. He nodded his head: "Yes, that is the reason for this Bill, and the reason why the Government is so keen to get this legislation

80

through quickly. Of course, it's difficult. Energy is now a commodity, and the energy companies will always charge their share. So, the question is: how do we keep the lights on and increase our self-sufficiency at the same time? How can we make sure that this Government, and any future administrations - after all, we may lose the election - have varied sources of energy and that there is a workable solution for whomever is in power?"

She thought for a moment, this was not a man who just wanted the credit for himself, he really did want to make a difference. She started: "Renewables. Heat, wind, water – all natural sources that can't be drained. There is a lot of imperative towards it, both within the industry and the public. If we find a way to securely store such energy, we will have a supply for the future whilst not increasing our carbon footprint."

"Exactly!" he agreed, "So let's take one at random - marine energy," he started: "Oceans have a tremendous amount of energy and whilst tides are cyclical, they occur with regular frequency at different times around the coast of the UK."

His eyes flashed, and Josephine pulled her glass up to her lips and finished it off. It was intoxicating to be with someone who seemed to so be so passionate about his work, and the wine suddenly took on a somewhat rounder taste as her excitement levels rose. Keen to keep the conversation going, she stood up and looked

Charlie straight in the eye: "What would you like to drink, another Guinness?"

He put his finger to his mouth in thought: "No. How about a cocktail. After all, we are breaking new ground here. Let's mix it all up! A Manhattan perhaps. There is just something so exciting about when it arrives, all fresh and new with a cherry on the top."

He looked her straight in the eye, his breath ever so close to her mouth and moved his body subtly towards her, his soft cologne filling her nostrils: "But it's just the one and so quick and it's gone." He spoke in such a dead pan way; she didn't know what to say. She looked at him for a second and then finding herself at a loss, made an excuse to go to the bathroom.

She walked through the black wooden door to the ladies and chided herself again. She felt ever so slightly drunk and brought her hands over her face to freshen herself up with water, leaning over the basin to gain a sense of equilibrium. She wondered what he was going to say next, and if she was reading too much into his body language and sentence structure. Maybe this was how these discussions took place, maybe there was nothing unusual. After all, he had told Sharon he was not interested, and his natural instinct - to care for a legacy beyond his own - would imply he was a man of integrity.

Unnerved that she had given it this level of

thought, she walked over to the long mirror to check her makeup and seeing that she hadn't smudged her mascara, she just applied some lip gloss. After all, no matter how her interest was slightly piqued, he was much more senior to her, and she didn't want to be seen to be making an extra special effort, just to be calmly professional.

Leaving the toilets, she approached the table once again, and bent over to sit down. She sat down and put her hand towards the nape of her neck. She realised she hadn't spotted that a wisp of hair was coming down at the back. She quickly moved to correct it, but without thinking Charlie put his hand out and laid it casually on her forearm: "No," he said, patting her on the shoulder "let it fall, it suits you." She immediately stopped and slightly shook at his touch. She pulled out the one clip that was keeping her hair in place and shook her hair out. He watched her before he sat back in his chair and broke off the physical contact: "Do you want dinner?" he asked: "They do beautiful food here. They really take care to provide a taste sensation.." He then leaned forward again and looking conspiratorial he continued "It's all organic here - so important for the environment. Of course, since I moved to London, I haven't had a garden but the first thing I secured was an allotment so I could grow some vegetables, especially tomatoes, my own little contribution."

She looked at him. The comments he was

making were just snippets of life, and all pretty irrelevant to anything, but she knew how hard he worked to control his image. He continued: "I do wonder about life beyond politics, and what that might mean. After all, I never wanted to have a family, I always liked the selfish nature of my life. But then I grew those little fruits and tended them, and I felt like I was giving something back to the earth." He looked her straight in the eye: "Maybe this is why this Bill is so important to me. We need to be respectful of the world, not just take from it without replenishing its resources."

Not realising he had ordered the drinks in her absence, Josephine was pleased when a cocktail arrived in front of her. Green and fresh, he had chosen her a mojito. He had ordered the Manhattan and he fiddled with the cherry and he put it quickly in his mouth before taking a swig of the orange liquid. She took a mouthful of the minty drink and swallowed quickly.

Suddenly, they both heard a shout from the bar. It was the young men who had spoken to Josephine earlier. The young man in the green rugby top was still there, eyeing her up, and she suddenly felt a combination of embarrasment and excitement. She wondered how she appeared to the outside world. She was sitting with a man much older than her, and what he said had obviously excited her. She wondered how silly that could seem to anyone watching them, but she wasn't there because he was a man of position and power. It was because he had soul.

She took another sip of her drink and he had turned the conversation to the inner workings of the political machine: "So, here we are, fighting to get legislation through at the end of a Parliamentary sitting, whilst we are gearing up for the fight at the ballot box. It all gets so complicated. Not least keeping our candidates in check and make sure they are following the party line. Especially those not under the wings of the whips, those who are fighting the other seats trying to break through."

He leaned back in his chair: "My favourite story was from an election 30 years ago. I had been selected for a safe seat but my neighbour next door just seemed to enjoy breaking ranks at any given opportunity, no matter what the situation. I don't think she even realised how fortunate she was that the PM was coming to her seat on his journey round the region and how carefully managed such a situation needs to be. Instead, she went totally off message about education spend on the local radio which meant that when he arrived the PM just got a barrage of bad press." He shook his head at the memory: "Didn't just threaten support in her own area but my own. The whips had to give her a proper dressing down. It's ridiculous. Honestly, I don't know why these people get selected."

Josephine knew who he was talking about by reputation. Roxanne Lawrence was still around the periphery of the party. Older but still not wiser. Her hair was also still jet black in colour, though it was suspected that it was more down to a bottle now. Always dressed in designer labels with massively high heels, she certainly had a reputation as being a bit gobby. Saying that Josephine had never had any crossed words with her so she went a slight shade of red, feeling that by listening to this she was being disloyal, participating in idle gossip she couldn't corroborate or deny.

He saw her discomfort, and spoke softly: "I have embarrassed you, haven't I? Talking about others in such a way. You are such a nice girl. I just can't help but trust you, and the campaign trail can be a lonely place. I just think, you obviously get what matters, and that's special." She looked up at him and pulled the words in like nectar. This was what she wanted, a seat at the table, to be trusted by the big boys, and that was all he was doing. There was no malice intended in what he was saying.

Suddenly the bell went behind the bar: "Last orders!" She sighed. She didn't want to leave but thought about her long journey home and that she wanted to leave on a high. Quickly finishing the drink, she said "Thank you for your time Charlie, I so appreciate your kind considerations. I will make sure I can do the best I can by you, and the country of which we are so proud."

He looked at her: "I know you will."

She then stood to leave. She picked up her

bag, she didn't realise he had moved himself closer. Their hands briefly touched as they both got up to go their separate ways. She smiled and walked out the door, briefly turning around to look at him, watching him watch her go.

Chapter 7

The young man sat hunched over his desk. His spectacles were perched on the end of his nose, and his complexion was pale and blotchy due to too many weekends at his desk instead of being out in the fresh air. He smiled a crooked smile, completely ensconced in his work, his thin lips parting whilst he concentrated. Finally, there seemed to a Government that understood just how important it was to develop new technology to solve the energy crisis. Of course, with an election coming up how this was to be achieved was bound to become a political football, but he could do his best to try and prevent that from happening by laying out the options as thoroughly as possible.

He drew his hand over his hair, trying to control some of the more wayward curls. It had been five years since he had worked with Josephine, but they had maintained contact. They had both taken different paths though, with him choosing to stay in the private sector and become more of a technical specialist whilst she had moved into the civil service on the fast track scheme.

He looked at his work and thought that the call had come at an opportune time. Whilst she was very specific to say on a Government line that this was just an information gathering exercise, he knew her well enough to read between the lines, and he had got the distinct impression that she was especially keen to hear about marine and wind, something he had been working to promote for a long time as a valued part of the fight against energy insecurity.

His mind was racing, his blue eyes focused intently on what he was doing, mapping and remapping his work. He didn't care that he had been sat in the same place for the best part of 3 hours, or that his awkward position in his small office meant that his suit was being bent out of shape. He twisted himself round to look at his work from a new angle.

He wanted to check that he hadn't missed out anything from his flow chart. After all, if the technology was to work, the strategy would need to be exactly right. Anything else could have devastating effect on the development and manufacture of one of these massive projects in real life. Plus, of course, Josephine had such an eye for detail he knew she would pick up on problems or weaknesses immediately, whether technical or operational.

Big Ben rang out from across the road and a knock came on the door – a knock he recognised instantly. He smiled. That particular combination meant that the person inside should be aware that the boss was on the other side of the door. It didn't give more than a couple of seconds to prepare, but it was always better than nothing. The door opened and in came Josephine, Rebekah, and Ed's boss, Frank Derby.

Frank had grey hair and a pudgy face. His watery brown eyes were framed by thick spectacles made larger by the strong lenses his optician had prescribed. He was casually dressed in a black and white shirt, undone at the neck that showed some whispery grey hairs on his chest, and blue jeans. He always made a point of wearing denims whilst insisting that his staff were all dressed in business attire. He felt that it gave him standing. The man who didn't have to care.

Like Ed, his face was blotchy in complexion, but it wasn't due to the studious intent of a youth wanting to impress those in his office and perfect his art. Instead, it was because of too many late nights over hard spirits. The three visitors came towards Ed's desk and Josephine held out her hand in affectionate greeting: "Ed," she said "it is so good to see you again. Thank you so much for taking the time to talk to us. You know that I always value your opinion."

Ed smiled and blushed. Josephine always seemed to know just how to make him feel good. He knew he wasn't her type. She always seemed to go for a more rugged type of man, but he still valued her friendship and she was genuinely affectionate towards him.

They all sat down, and Ed straightened his papers and put them in a pile to one side. He didn't have an awful lot of space because he was still not management, but he had worked in the industry for long enough to still be the main lead on all the new technical developments in the marine turbine industry for his company Blatt, Paddy and Cornelia – the go-to guy for advice on how things might work.

"So Ed," drawled Frank, his eyes darting between Josephine and Ed, annoyed at their obvious professional closeness considering he was the boss: "What can you tell us about how UK plc can increase their security of energy supply on an operational level?" He puffed his chest out: "Obviously I can talk more about the strategy side, but I think it's important that the man on the ground talks about the opportunities and issues regarding particular projects and how they might work within the scope of a Government Initiative."

Waiting until Frank had satisfied himself that he was still in control, Ed started, "Well, we all know that the Government has agreed to reduce the UK's carbon emissions by 80% of 1990 levels by 2050. So, the question is – just how is this going to be achieved? There is always nuclear energy, but it appears this Government is keen to distance itself. This brings us to renewables, though it's still relatively new industry with issues around storing the energy and we have no idea whether or not it would get the support it needs from the Treasury in the upcoming Budget."

Ed looked at Frank who was looking bored. Deciding flattery would bring his attention back to what they were discussing and away from his evening's plans, Ed continued: "Of course, Frank, you were saying to the Ministers just a few days ago, the key is finding a way to harness these sources in a more reliable way, and create a synergy between them." Appeased, Frank sat up and looked around, a smug look on his face. It was his choice to hand over the meeting to Ed. It was him who talked to the key people, at the key receptions and events.

Seeing the change in Franks body language, Ed smiled and laid out his plan: "So I present to you a strategy with marine at the centre, with other renewables being harnessed at the same time. Marine itself brings vast quantities of predictable, reliable and consistent energy. Tidal waves occur at regular times around the coast of the UK - and abroad. In addition, the introduction of the lagoons would mean we could start to reduce our reliance on dirty energy sources because we could then store energy. Plus, there is always the possibility of harnessing the wind and biomass energy that can be produced naturally through these sites too."

He began to feel his theme and brought out his designs with a flourish: "So on the technical side, what you need are a series of smaller turbine devices with smaller rotors. Of course, to create such a network would take a lot more financial and operational support than if it was just a single build.

We would need to train our workforce with a new set of skills suitable for such an innovative solution, skills that cost money and training. However, it would be worth it. Indeed, the industry can come up with the best prototype in the world - but if we can't get built, then it's irrelevant!"

He passed the paperwork he prepared: "However, if we can get the support we need, both through general policy commitments and actual sector support, then the benefit would speak for itself." He stopped for a second as he mused before continuing, "The technology could grow and develop into an end to end solution. Plus, if we could get co-operation from other countries, we could expand this into a network of international co-operation. After all, we are all in one world here. We should try and make this a world-wide solution."

Josephine and Rebekah looked at each other. They were here merely for the purpose of research, though Josephine couldn't help but think back to the conversation she had had with Charlie regarding marine. He had skipped over the option quickly, but it showed that there was interest in such options, and in fairness, it was that which lead her to Ed's door. The department needed information, and with both the Budget and election coming up she needed to be prepared for any eventuality in case the Government decided to move.

She started speaking slowly, with purpose, but with caution. "Well," she said, "This is all very good, and the Government is obviously looking to increase security of supply but at this stage we are just gathering information." Seeing the slightly disappointed expression on Ed's face she continued quickly: "However, I think that the Government is looking at using potentially greener solutions so any concrete plans the sector has would only speed up the process." She paused for a second before continuing, "especially as there is a Budget coming up, after which there will be an election and Queen's Speech in due course.."

Frank looked at Josephine: "Absolutely" he said, "It all needs to be fleshed out, but we do have a guiding principle and a strategy around how using marine might work, and you can count on us for more feedback if you need it." Josephine opened her mouth again, but Rebekah put her hand on her arm, counselling silence. Seeing Rebekah's move, Frank closed his file, knowing his time was up but not wanting to be the one to be closed down: "I need to go but thank you for your time." He strode out of the room, in a sweep of his own self-importance.

Josephine pulled her phone out and began to move away, whispering to Rebekah: "I need to tell Charlie that I think there was something in what he said about marine."

Rebekah looked at her and smiled: "Oh dear,

someone has a crush." Not noticing the longing look on Ed's face, a couple of feet away from them now, so only able to watch the two girls whispering, she looked indignant:

"I have not! But I care what he thinks, and he seemed so earnest."

Rebekah smiled and leaned into her: "Go on, tell him. You are right, and it's brilliant. But let's do the niceties first." Josephine looked at her feet, unbelieving that her concern for Charlie had meant that she had almost left her manners behind. She looked back at Ed, who was still looking at her, desperate for approval. Moving back towards him she took his hand in both of hers and looked him straight in the eye: "Thank you Ed. It has been so useful to be able to catch up and discuss this like we have!"

He sighed slightly to himself, disappointed that she didn't talk about catching up socially, but having braced himself for his usual disappointment he held out his hand to guide her towards the exit: "Glad you could spare the time and we could talk it all through. Let me take you back to reception." Nodding with approval at this plan, she eagerly waited for Ed to pick up his files, so they could all leave the office.

He left them at the reception, and moved away with a resigned smile, wondering what Rebekah and Josephine were now giggling about, but understanding he would never know. They soon approached the door onto the street, and Josephine unlocked her phone, bringing up Charlie's number. Stopping momentarily, she noticed a number highlighted in red. Several missed calls from William.

She sighed sadly. It had been a while, but she had just been so busy. Before she could respond to them though, she suddenly felt a presence behind her. She felt hot breath on her neck, and a throat being cleared of phlegm. "Josephine, Rebecca," the voice said, turning on its own unique charm. She turned around and saw the thin and scruffy physique of Lord Cole of Weston Abbey. It had been a while since they met for that first time in the House of Commons, and somehow, he seemed even more dirty, with his jacket even more scuffed around the patches.

He looked them both up and down, and Rebekah brought her papers up to her chest, with her ring finger in his clear sight. Josephine suddenly felt slightly exposed. She hadn't put her ring on this morning. Lord Cole looked her up and down and came further into her space. "So, what's a gorgeous girl like you doing in an office like this?" he started.

"Just talking to sector professionals regarding some work I have been asked to undertake," Josephine replied, not knowing how much she was allowed to say, and not wanting to get into too detailed a conversation with the man.

"Oh, you are a clever girl. I should write

that in my whips notebook," he replied and moved towards her to stroke her arm, leaving a small trickle of sweat on her beautiful black jacket.

She felt the bile rising in her throat and smiled awkwardly. "I really have to get on," she said, trying to get away from him but he matched her movements, and came close to her again:

"Well, remember I can always help you out" he smarmed, "After all, I have a lot of experience, and could really help open you up, sorry open up opportunities for you." Rebekah shivered and Josephine stood there quite shocked, not quite able to breath and struggling for a retort she felt would show quite how low on her list he would be. At that moment though, a voice called out: 'Oh Bernard, you are an old goat. Not everyone understands your sense of humour."

Charlie moved into view, approached the group, and stood immobile whilst Bernard worked out what to do. He smiled at the interloper but felt a bit aggrieved. He had been lusting after Josephine since they first met and was just getting underway with his modus operandi. He didn't want to marry her, he just wanted to taste her, and this reformed charmer was now getting in his way, as if somehow his new lofty positions within the party gave him some authority over him, a Lord of the Realm. However, he knew the game was up, for now at least and conceded, "Of course, it's only a little bit of fun. No one could ever think I was serious." He looked at his watch, "Anyway better get back to the office. Serious business calls." With that he shuffled off, unsatisfied.

Charlie looked at Josephine. Seeing the relief on her face, he approached her slowly, careful not to seem that he was taking up her personal space. Rebekah looked on, checking the situation before she saw imperceivably a nod that showed Josephine now felt that it was all under control. Taking the lead Rebekah nodded and giving her a hug goodbye went out to get herself a cab home.

"Come on," Charlie said, "let's get you a cup of tea to sooth your nerves." Josephine nodded and opened the door, checking he was still behind her so she could follow his guided care. She was shocked at how relieved she was that he had happened to be passing. They walked and Josephine became aware that he had taken such a protective stance around her that she could smell his aftershave.

They stepped quickly into the pub across the road. Keen for some privacy, she moved quickly into a booth, and Charlie followed her. He was about to sit opposite her when he saw her look at him, her hands gesturing for him to sit next to her. "I am sorry, I don't want to impose but..." she started. He nodded and looked her straight in the eye, saying nothing as he slipped in beside her.

A waitress came over to the booth, and smiled at Charlie, silently acknowledging his regular attendance and he looked at Josephine: "Cup of tea?" She silently nodded, and he quickly ordered so they were soon left alone again.

"So," he started, "What did they say? The technical wizards that is. Not that lecherous old goat."

She laughed and nodded: "Yes, I was just about to text you before he arrived on the scene. I don't think you could have quite realised how accurately you hit the nail on the head when we last spoke. Your random suggestion regarding developing marine energy is further ahead than we thought. There are organisations already looking at new technologies and solutions, and I therefore thought it might be worth developing a paper that could flesh out some ideas."

"Ah right," he said thoughtfully, thanking the waitress with a nod. He poured out two cups, he looked at her: "That's a turn up for the books!' he exclaimed: "So you think that it's one to watch then? One we should research?"

"Oh yes," she continued, "and with the Budget coming up next week, we could capitalise on the current appetite for more unusual ways of solving problems, especially now there has been some positive news about the economy."

"Well, yes," he smiled: "This is the last chance the Government has to lay out its pitch ahead of the election, and you are imperative in making sure the right impact is made so any information you gather could be key to not just this policy but the whole direction of the country."

She lowered her head slightly, completely delighted at his praise, and ran her hand through her hair, slightly preening herself. "Thank you," she said, and as she looked up, she noticed his body was ever so slightly closer to hers than it had been when he sat down originally. She began to think back to Sharon, and how unreasonable her behaviour must have been to make him so upset. He was always so calm and helpful. She moved half an inch towards him, taking in his soft aroma. They danced towards each other, each soft slight movement almost undetectable, but then, his shoulder was soon pressing against hers.

To try and keep control of himself, he tightened the muscles in his thigh, but he was unable to hold back, and he pulled his hand over hers, gripping intently. He had a sudden urge to take her in his arms. He knew though, that he would be moving very quickly, and he wasn't quite sure how she would feel. He was a lot older than she was, and, considering her reaction to Bernard's advances, she wasn't easy like some of the girls who started working in politics just keen to get closer to powerful men, no matter who they were

He looked it her. She was not moving away from him. Josephine felt his grip and her heart started pounding. She was excited at the turn of events, but she was also very confused. She wanted to move away, she wanted to view him like she viewed all the men she worked worth with, like Bernard, but somehow she couldn't. There was no mistaking what he wanted, and despite herself, she was locked in.

She looked him straight in the eye, his gaze intent, and then his heart overtook his head. His lips fell on hers, and he pushed her back into the privacy of the booth. She gasped slightly as she fell into the moment, shocked at quite how much she had been unwittingly wanting him to touch her.

Outside a forlorn face looked in. He didn't see much, but he saw them disappear out of sight, emerging a few minutes later, hot and flushed. William had his phone in his hand, and a message half written: "In London, near you somewhere." He had his trusty rucksack with him, stuffed with a few hastily packed clothes as his decision to come and see her had been so last minute.

He looked down. He didn't know who she was with, but he knew that he was being left behind. The glass window between them now, a permanent barrier. He slowly scrolled over his words and retyped, a single tear making its way slowly down his cheek: "Been trying to get in touch but you seem to be very busy. I hope it all works out for you. Take care." With that, he closed his phone, wiped his face, deleted her number and slowly walked away, his head held high.

Chapter 8

Charlie and Patrick headed up the stairs towards the Prime Ministers private office. The massive rabbit warren of corridors meant that extra security around his office was unnecessary as it seemed like any other office housed in the main parliamentary building, the most senior man in the country hiding in plain sight.

The men approached the door, and neither expressed any excitement at having been called in. It was not unusual for the Prime Minister to have at least a dozen members of his trusted inner circle come to his office to fire questions at him on the morning before Prime Ministers Questions.

The main office was silent except for the tap of fingers on keyboards as social media was tracked, retweeted and commented upon with official lines to take and authorised press releases. The five figures sitting at their desks briefly looked up, and then went back to looking at their screens just as quickly. They were used to interruptions. Nodding a hello to them en masse, the two men walked past in silence and towards the side office where the Prime Minster was sitting.

The Prime Minister's broad mahogany desk was full of paperwork that he had retrieved from the open red box by the side of the sofa. Alongside the red box sat Old Stripy, the black box with a red stripe that was kept for highly confidential papers and remained firmly shut whenever there were visitors. By his side sat his trusted adviser - a sounding board and his most trusted ally. Together they sifted through the paperwork, whispering together as each piece of paper was addressed one by one.

Patrick and Charlie were used to the grand environment that lay in front of them, though not many of the offices in Parliament were quite like this. It had intricately carved stone walls, with large thick curtains in deep rich colours. On the walls were several paintings, magnificent in their large golden frames. Neither Charlie or Patrick were particularly interested in art, but even they couldn't miss the exquisite nature of the pieces, and Patrick couldn't help but wonder the value of the collection contained within these four walls.

Briefly standing to welcome his guests, the Prime Minister beckoned them both over to where he had been sitting. They walked over and the special adviser stood up. He handed the Prime Minister the paper he was holding and walked towards the door, closing it silently behind him. The three sat down. Charlie and Patrick wriggled slightly. Usually more people would join a meeting like this, not leave. Instead, they were the only ones in the room.

Unlike his guests who were both formally dressed in suits, the Prime Minister was casually dressed in jeans. His suit was hanging up nearby so that he could slip into it quickly when the bells sounded to bring everyone to the Chamber, but for now he just wanted the comfort. He was ageing quicker now than when he had been in opposition, his eyes slightly sunken from broken sleep and his hair taking on a silvery hue at the temples. He was also slimmer, a side effect from the stress he was under and the lack of opportunity he had to have regular meals.

The PM looked at the two guests and sat down. Clearing his throat, he began: "Thank you for coming in. I just wanted to give you a heads up regarding the Budget later. We both know the usual press interest on this kind of occasion, but we are really planning on creating excitement in the press lobby, and I wanted to make sure you were both fully briefed. After all, you Patrick are the lead on the specific piece of legislation, and Charlie, you are a key member of our election campaign team who needs to know everything that is going on."

He looked the two men straight in the eye, watching their reactions, and continued: "We all know that green issues are a priority for the younger members of the electorate, and that they are an increasing sizeable chunk of the votes we need to retain and further develop. We want to help this happen by addressing the issues that research has shown to be most important to them, and therefore the Chancellor and I both think that concentrating on renewable energy supplies would help this and put a clear distance between us and the Opposition."

Charlie smiled to himself and looked at Patrick. He was pleased that he had pushed Josephine into developing her thoughts into a proper strategic research piece, and that he had made sure it was slipped into the Secretary of State's red box to be raised at Cabinet at that opportune moment. Remaining silent though, he let Patrick take the glory: "Thank you Prime Minister. I am pleased," Patrick started, "Following the Government's excellent lead, we have been working hard to ensure that what we are proposing can stand up to criticism and scrutiny. This is also why we have laid out some options for you to pick from."

The Prime Minister nodded: "Yes, well, it will be important to get this right and that's why I asked you to come in. The information you have provided, along with some quiet polling we have done shows that marine seems to have the most to give. It's for that reason that this Budget will be looking to push this up the legislative agenda and provide the support needed to ensure we can maximise this policy area."

He brought out a piece of paper to consolidate his thoughts before continuing: "We have therefore developed a financial incentive to aid technology and skilling. This should provide the technology and jobs we need. However, it will be down to you to prove that this action is a new and innovative solution instead of a risky move from a government that's heading towards an election."

He paused before continuing: "but is not a free for all." Patrick and Charlie remained silent. It was unusual that the Prime Minister would take the time out of his busy schedule to relay such a message personally, and they both knew the enormity of this conversation. The Prime Minister was properly invested in this as a key election-winning strategy, and it was down to them in their reflective roles to help him.

At that moment, the bell rang to call everyone for prayers before the Parliamentary session started that day. "Anyway," the Prime Minister continued, closing his file and smiling broadly, "I just want to thank you personally for all your work, but the bells are calling so we better get ourselves organised for the onslaught." Understanding this was the cue to exit, Patrick and Charlie both made their way towards the door.

Once they were out and it was closed behind them, Charlie couldn't help but give Patrick a slap on the back as they made their way down the green carpet away from the office. "This is going to be the big one," he grinned. They reached the narrow staircases towards the Chamber:

"Well let's see what's actually said by the Chancellor, so let's chat later so we can discuss what should happen next!" opined Patrick. "After all, it's Prime Ministers Questions next and who knows what can happen in that!"

At the same time that the two men separated, a lift opened down the corridor. Josephine and Rebekah stepped out. Chatting quietly amongst themselves, they soon found themselves at the anteroom that lead to the galleries above the Chamber. The room was busy as the policeman scanned the tourists that were lucky enough to secure tickets to watch the days business from the Gallery. The two girls passed the line, flashing their pass at the doorkeepers to bypass security and enable them to head straight towards Strangers Gallery. Passing the crowds this quickly guaranteed them a seat at the front and they walked through the archway towards the Gallery.

Falling silent, Josephine stopped to admire the view. It didn't matter how many times she had been up here, she always found it breath-taking. From here it was possible to see the entire House of Commons Chamber. The Chamber never had enough had seats for the entire Parliamentary body, so it was not unusual for many MPs to stand beside or in between the green benches during the busiest of sessions, able to watch but not participate in formal proceedings. However, prayer cards already marked the territory of some keen attendees that wanted to secure a seat so they would have the right to catch the Speaker's eye and ask a question.

Josephine looked at her watch. There were only fifteen minutes before Prime Ministers questions would begin, followed swiftly by the Budget. Realising the throng of tourists was now coming in behind them both, Josephine and Rebekah started to make their way down the steep steps towards the old-fashioned wooden benches. Their heels clicked on the floor as they walked towards the end of the front row and they sat down. Below them, the Secretary of State for Scotland was beginning to wind down from his turn at the dispatch box, acutely aware that his session was on the final stretch.

He never enjoyed his time answering parliamentary questions. Being responsible for all aspects of life for the people of Scotland meant the opposition enjoyed exploiting the range of subjects they were able to ask him. Today they were focusing on the plight of the Scottish youth and local housing issues. He chewed on the side of his thumb, determined to bite off the hangnail he had loosened. Feeling anger in his gut, he bit down hard, only realising afterwards that he had drawn blood.

It was not his fault that house prices were so high. It wasn't like these young people were trying to get on the property market in London, unlike he had been forced to when he became an MP. He sighed. Why was it that these young whippersnappers out of school felt they were entitled to massive properties with no deposit and little income! Of course, this could never be said so he just stuck to the party line before sitting down to see who was asking a question next.

He continued chewing as an MP opposite him stood up to have his say. He watched the young man brandish a piece of paper in his direction, citing the inability of young people to access activities and how this drove them to use drugs through boredom and lack of structure. He sighed again. This boy castigating him didn't even seem organised enough to have a haircut. If he was their representative it was hardly surprising that any of them had any motivation to be self-sufficient at all.

He stood up to answer, a saccharine smile crossing his thin lips: "I understand why the Honourable Member is so concerned about drugs, a scourge in our society. That is why I am encouraging all our councils to encourage our young people to get together and make use of the great outdoors by organising activities in our parks like runs, walks and nature trails. It's fun, distracting, and free."

He sat back down as the Prime Minister and Chancellor both walked in. They moved towards the dispatch box and he moved over slightly, just as the Speaker called for order. His time was up, and he loosened his tie. "Questions to the Prime Minister: Freya Wright," the Speaker bellowed. A young girl rose, her broad Cornish accent filling the room: "I would like to ask the Prime Minister about how the UK are focusing on ensuring that the lights stay on."

The Prime Minister rose, a sly smile crossing his face. "I would like to thank my Honourable Friend for such a pertinent question. It really is an important issue. So, whilst I will leave the details of our strategy to the Chancellor, I can confirm that having a clean energy supply that's secure in these ever-changing times is a key priority for this Government."

He sat back down, and a brief nod went between the two men. Josephine and Rebekah smiled to each other, unable to believe their luck. Freya Wright represented a coastal seat near Cornwall. She had been part of the new intake at the last election and was brutally aware that her seat was often a bellwether seat for the election outcome, so often concentrated on real issues that had resonance locally.

Josephine mused to herself. There was clearly a movement towards providing real incentives for clean energy development. She leaned over to Rebekah: "It's hold onto your hats time I think!" she smirked. They both giggled, and then looked up to see a doorkeeper in his starched black uniform raise an eyebrow. It didn't take much, and the girls fell silent. The racket downstairs played on, the questions becoming more aggressive as

Opposition Bench Members had their say.

Soon enough though, another half an hour had passed, and it was now time for the Chancellor to rise to his feet. Shuffling his papers, the Speaker made way for his Deputy, the Chancellor rose when he was called. "Mister Deputy Speaker," he began, "It is now the final Budget before the election, and I am sure the House will agree that this Government has worked hard to make life better for its people during our second term of office."

There were murmurs across the benches. He slightly narrowed his eyes and continued: "This has meant that we have had an element of leeway to develop innovative solutions that can provide us with the security we need in this ever-changing world, ensuring out self-sufficiency for key elements of infrastructure. Infrastructure, like energy. We must move towards a cleaner supply for future generations, and we all know how easily energy sources can be disrupted by events beyond our control. With that in mind, we are therefore committed to creating a clean energy supply that we control here in the UK.

"It is our conclusion, Mister Deputy Speaker, that marine energy ticks all the necessary criteria. Tidal waves occur at regular times around the coast of the UK, and this provides us with the ability to harness the energy at regular intervals. It's clean and it's ours. I can therefore announce today that within the Energy Bill there will be provision for organisations that develop plants and/or technology that help develop technology that can harness this source, from the original capture to storage."

Josephine grasped her papers in her hands. She knew that her musings were only the start, but it was so serendipitous. The Chancellor continued: "We will provide tax breaks to companies that provide real solutions to help them with their essential costs, to allow them to focus on reinvestment and future development, to make their propositions work. After all, we must not forget the purpose of this endeavor, or the reach that this could have. We live in a global world. It could mean that we could provide best practice to other countries considering we all face the need to harness green power."

He continued: "We will also not forget the manpower this will take, Mister Deputy Speaker. The development of this new sector will provide a host of opportunities for organisations and individuals to develop new skill sets, which can only be good for our work force. It is vitally important that those who work within this sector are highly competent individuals that are motivated to stay and develop their careers within this sector. With this in mind, the Government also pledges to provide tax relief so that not just those running the businesses reap the rewards but the workers and investors too."

The Chancellor stopped to an uproar of cheering on his own side and he took a sip of water. He looked around the room at the opposition. He had managed to keep most of the details away from the press so that the opposition would have to make their response with little preparation. He liked the odds. He was a statistician by trade, and he knew that it was likely that they wouldn't be able to pick much apart in the time frame they had been given. He took a deep breath, he was on the home straight now and there wasn't much more to be said. The initial costing of the project was actually pretty reasonable, and there were always people that wanted to get into new technology at the beginning as that's where the big money was to be made.

Up in the Gallery Josephine and Rebekah couldn't help but smile. They looked down to see the Chancellor briefly discussing funding in terms of return on investment. They knew that the financial details would be glossed over at this stage, but it all seemed pretty simple. Tax relief in return for commitment. Rebekah nodded at Josephine and they stood up. The main event had now passed, and it was time to go.

Josephine's phone beeped: "Did you see the Chancellor give your work the go ahead? You must be very proud. Do you want a drink to celebrate?" Josephine looked at the phone shocked and turned it to Rebekah so they could both look and take the message in.

Rebekah smiled: "Well you are both professionals, aren't you? He just has the power to make things happen." Josephine felt her impulsive side rise, not quite being able to agree with Rebekah that it was just his authority she was looking for. Her look said it all. She texted back: "Yes, sure. Where?"

They headed out the Parliamentary estate, Rebekah stopped Josephine and looked at her friend: "I know what's on your mind." she said: "He's heady and exciting. But you are on the cusp of something really big here, and it can't be clouded by emotion." Josephine, looked down, understanding what her friend was saying, but her lips still buzzed from the kiss they had shared just days before"

"I know," she said finally: "This is too important."

They soon reached the nearest pub, The Celtic Welcome, and were keen to enter its warm glow. A country style pub in London, the wine was served with a smile and the food was good but nothing too fancy - just comforting portions that used lots of old-fashioned ingredients. They piled in, and giggling went into one of the booths. Ennis was Irish, friendly and keen to please. He had twinkling eyes, and an open manner. He knew them well enough to put a bottle of Merlot on the table, leaving them quickly to their girlish chatter. Josephine quickly poured the liquid into their glasses, clinking them as they smiled at the friendly pub landlord.

They finished their first glass, and the phone that Josephine had laid carefully on the table between them beeped in earnest. "How about the Celtic Welcome? I can be there in 45 mins." They burst into laughter, and Josephine quickly responded:

"Yes. I will see you there." Looking up at Josephine, Rebekah exclaimed:

"Right! We have 45 mins to down this bottle."

"Well," said Josephine, "that's a challenge."

They both looked at each other and smiled. Rebekah was long married but looked at her friend knowingly, remembering her own past. Charlie was not Josephine's traditional type, but Rebekah understood the strength of a powerful person and how that could turn someone's head. Such a presence could be intoxicating and energising, giving the world a more interesting feeling, something that could mask the danger of the situation.

Exactly 45 minutes later the door of the pub opened, and Charlie walked through. Luckily the booth they had chosen was away from the door in the back of the pub so they could see out, but not be seen. Quickly and deftly, Rebekah filled Josephine's glass to give the impression that a drink had only just been ordered and swiped the bottle and her own glass away around the corner. She winked at Josephine, just making it out of sight before Charlie made his way around the corner. Josephine caught his eye and smiled to welcome to him, nodding a quick and subtle goodbye to Rebekah as she headed out the door back to Sam.

Charlie immediately relaxed when he saw Josephine sitting there on her own, slightly relieved that she didn't have Rebekah with her. He moved into the booth and put his hand on her arm. "So, you were watching?" he started.

"Yes," Josephine grinned: "It was amazing, and I am so looking forward to being able to drive this forward. Imagine if we could create a new technology at the forefront of the worlds thinking. Our workforce starting a revolution in energy technology."

He looked at her fondly, "I know," he said. He looked her up and down. She was like young deer that had just learned to walk. He put his arm on her shoulder: "It's all down to you. The Prime Minister himself called Patrick and me in to thank us for all what we were doing. This is a key government strategy now, and we need to make it work. That now makes you key in driving the government agenda forward." She couldn't help but exhale deeply. He moved closer to her and put his hand under her chin.

Lifting her head so their eyes met, he stroked her cheek. She looked into his eyes and softly rested her cheek on his palm. He then lay her head on his shoulder and leaned into her. She felt herself drift off into a haze of happiness, as they just sat in their own world murmuring to each other quietly, snuggled together, physically at ease.

Too soon though, his mobile started ringing, interrupting them. Charlie grimaced, remembering that he had promised to meet Patrick after the statement so they could go through the practicalities. He sighed and looked at Josephine who still had her eyes closed. He pulled away slightly: "I promised Patrick I would see him after the statement, so I can't get out of it." He pulled the phone out of his pocket. She pursed her lips and drew his hand into hers. He looked her in the eyes: "I will come back for you," he mouthed, and then kissed the tips of his fingers before he put them to her lips.

Chapter 9

Charlie sat at his massive desk and looked at his screen. His hand loitered over the mouse, and his eyes were focused on a blank email. For once, he wasn't quite sure how to start. He was normally the master at being able to play it cool, but this time he was unable to stop himself - he just kept going back. It wasn't exactly unusual for him to be playing the game with someone younger than himself, but this felt as if it meant more.

He closed his eyes and concentrated on his breathing. He had even changed his daily routine so that he would pass her office. Normally he always took different routes around the estate to ensure that he would only bump into his various hook up's when he specifically wanted their particular taste of satisfaction but to ensure they were otherwise kept at arm's length, something that was even more important because of his new elevated position in the run up to the election. However, there was no doubt she was different to the average girl he met in this job. She may have been new to the political scene, but she was already self-assured, diving into the various tasks she needed to undertake with aplomb, and completely able to hold her own no matter who she was talking to, and what the situation.

He put his hand on his cheek subconsciously,

the memory of their last meeting bringing welcome relief to what had been a tough couple of days. He smiled. Another subtle change. Usually at this point he would have been down in the bar amongst the short skirts and giggly staffers, adding to his repertoire, and yet now it was this one girl that seemed to give him the relief he needed.

He was tired, tired from spending his time trying to keep Governments plans on track, talking to the Whips Office to make sure the MPs had the information they needed, and ensuring everyone understood the Government's instructions on voting to minimise dissent.

Charlie sniffed. He wasn't a fan of the Whips. Of course, he was Leader of the Commons and therefore needed to ensure that Government policy decisions and the subsequent legislation stayed the course. It was imperative that there weren't random Government defeats when their MPs all trouped through the voting lobbies, and he recognised that the Whips were intrinsic in making that happen. However, they often had too much power to make life difficult for those with the Parliamentary Party, a charter to scribble anything they thought was relevant to the "greater good" in their notebooks, often forgetting that they were often interfering in an individual's private life.

It unnerved him that there was a group of people that collated information about him that he could not control, information on which he could be judged by those who felt they knew best, even though they didn't live inside his head. His constituents were happy with what they knew. His seat was safe meaning he could direct his volunteers elsewhere, and surely nothing else mattered.

He chewed his pencil. Alfred Lawson. That was the name of the Whip that had given him all that hassle so many years ago, pouring judgement on the way Charlie handled his own personal affairs. It had nothing to do with him, or anyone else but Alfred was always on his back, picking him apart when he thought Charlie wasn't behaving properly. He was always gossiping that Charlie was in the bars too late, surrounded by young women that seemed to drip off his every word and action. It was him who had started that ridiculous rumour about his penchant for entertaining "guests" in his office and the meeting rooms. Charlie smiled. It wasn't totally unfounded, but he didn't need everyone to know.

He leaned back in his chair. Lawson reminded him of an overzealous RE Teacher. He was always slightly shabbily dressed, with patches over the elbows of his corduroy jackets. He never had a beard but was always slightly unshaven. The worst of both worlds, it just looked like he didn't really bother having any particular look at all.

A middle manager for a technical company, he never expected to win the seat he had been selected for at the eleventh hour, nor that he would hold it until he decided to retire. Of course, that's why he got the nomination in the first place - no one expected the swing on that night. However, he was a local man who went into politics to fight against big corporations and for the worker - a message that sat well with the constituents of Little Hampton.

Charlie snorted. What could someone who had been born, grown up and would probably die in the same little suburb know about how things should be done, and how the world really worked. Indeed, after 20 years sitting in judgement on those green benches, he just retired and went back to the exact same semi-detached house he had brought up his family in before they left home to undertake equally unremarkable lives.

Charlie looked around his office and smiled. Here, in his office, the stone walls were festooned with political cartoons from throughout the eras given to him by grateful rich constituents and businesses. Now this was the sign of his glittering political career, not a decent pension and a narrow boat.

Charlie admired a particular piece that had been crafted for him. A cartoon of him making a speech in the Chamber with various cabinet members sitting around him as he crushed his opponents in battle. He spent money on making sure it was perfectly framed and aligned, in pride of place above the mantelpiece, a proper piece of history to hand on to the future generations of his family.

Charlie moved in his seat and the hairs on the back of his neck bristled. Family. Charlie still couldn't believe that that Lawson's little runt of a boy had somehow got a scholarship at his school, Rossingham House. A massive stately home that had land backing onto the coast, it was usually the preserve of those like himself that came from money, those whose family had generations of tradition at that one school. In the spirit of a new focus on equality however, there were now exams allowing those that showed "promise" to attend even if their parents couldn't afford the fees.

He had often raced the boy down the beach and always beat him so there was no question that Charlie was superior. Leaving him for dust. But even then, he still seemed to manage to trail behind him, close enough that they ended up at not only the same university but the same college. Finally, their lives diverged but now the past was coming back again. He had appeared on the horizon again having joined the party, and like his father before him, was seen as an ordinary man and given a nomination for a safe seat. He sighed. Now he would have to face him in the hallowed chamber for years to come.

He sighed. That was a battle for another day, and he needed to get back to more pressing matters. He wanted to make contact with Josephine, but he just wasn't sure what to say. His brow furrowed slightly, and he moved in his chair trying to bring the words to life. He was confused. She unnerved him. He had already told her a lot about himself and trusted her with information about other people in the party. He didn't normally play the game this way. Normally he asked more of the questions, garnering information so that he could work out how to get inside his conquests head and align his patter and questions to their needs, their insecurities, and their weaknesses.

He put his hands to the keyboard and started writing: "It was great to see you. Keep smiling Bright Eyes. Don't burn too fiercely without me." Briefly, his hand hovered over the send button, and his finger slowly pressed down. Well, he thought, that's it. It's gone. He stood up and wandered around, slowly taking in the air. He looked out the large and ornate window. His office was large compared to those down the same corridor, occupying a discreet corner so no one could imagine the splendour inside the door unless they saw it themselves.

The main office contained a wonderful meeting area that he had furnished in deep blues and greens making any visitors feel they were being entertained in the drawing room of a country house. A comfortable room that he knew had helped him get to the root of a situation when he needed to. He smiled. Of course, it was through a second door towards the left where he did his work, and where he stood now.

Taking in the skyline of London, his mind worked over the possible responses that Josephine could make in return. He smiled as he thought about her, but soon chided himself. He had to calm down before his 2pm meeting. He approached the wall and stood opposite a picture of the entire Parliamentary Party. His eyes slowly made their way over the numerous faces and then fell on Phyllis. A rather rotund lady who had been an MP for the best part of 20 years, he felt his body soften as he looked at her. He sighed with relief. A technique that never failed.

He opened the door and caught a glimpse of Josephine walking down the corridor, in deep conversation with Rebekah. Seeing they were completed distracted by whatever they were discussing, he realised they had not spotted him. He quickly looked at his watch and noticed it was slightly earlier than he had thought. He put his coat on and quietly closed his office door behind him.

Rebekah was in her usual classic suit but unusually for her, today she had teamed it up with a pair of skyscraper heels and blood red nails. By her side, he noted that Josephine was even more beguiling than usual. She was always smartly dressed, but today she had seemed to make a more particular effort. Matched with her usual fitted jacket and camisole top was a delicate skirt. The skirt just skimmed the knees, hiding the top of a pair of black boots, newly purchased by their glimmer and shine.

Walking quickly in the opposite direction, he bent his head down to avoid them from seeing him before he reached the turn. The corridors of this building were so twisted that anyone could easily get lost, but when you had been around for this long, he knew how to make the corridors work and how to get away from someone. He knew that they were making this effort in preparation for the networking conference that was taking place this weekend, something he would not be able to attend until his last long and boring meeting was over. However, he didn't want to see them now. He didn't want Josephine to realise how much mental space she was occupying by knowing he was following her round like a little puppy.

Charlie cursed. Of course, he knew he wouldn't be able to spend much time with her whilst they were there. The entire event was an excuse to bring Parliamentarians and Officers of the House together in order to help create relationships between the two sets of workers and ensure smooth communication on the issues that mattered, and he was key to that relationship. However, least he would be able to make sure she was ok.

Down the corridor, Josephine and Rebekah were approaching their office, making plans for their trip away. Though the fifth year it had been held, it was the first time they had been invited.

Originally just an away day for a chosen few, the "team building" purpose of the event had been further developed to also encompass opportunities for networking and laughter, two ingredients that often seemed to helped programs to develop organically in a way that meetings that were normally vigorously noted and recorded, could not. Indeed, this was one of the few times that such senior staff really felt able to really let their hair down in the company of their colleagues.

They had both packed a range of outfits. After all, there were so many receptions, they wanted to make an impact in each and every one. Opening the frosted doors, they entered the room quickly, whispering quietly in case anyone was on the other side. Seeing they were alone, they sighed with relief in unison. "Did you see him?" Rebekah asked as she walked towards her desk to pick up her suitcase, putting it on her desk briefly to insert more files onto the top of her clothes.

"Yes, you couldn't miss him," Josephine replied. "He seemed slightly on edge, I wonder why he didn't approach?"

Rebekah smiled "Yes well, I guess the last couple of times you have seen him you weren't ignoring him quite so studiously."

Seeing Josephine's slightly conflicted expression, Rebekah continued quickly: "However, that was then - and this is now. We have a conference to go to, and people to meet. You were just caught up, and he is a powerful man with a lot of authority who keeps himself in good shape. That is all. After all, it's not like you are allowing your feelings off the leash or start wondering what's going to happen next or where it's all going to go."

Josephine looked at the Hansards lined up against the walls and started drumming her fingers on the shelves. Rebekah watched her friend: "Oh dear," she winked, knowing Josephine well enough to see that she was beginning to get emotionally involved.

"He told me he would come back for me," Josephine quietly repeated, her eyes closed allowing her to relive the moment in her mind. A couple of seconds later, she opened her eyes and looked at her friend, knowing how deep down the rabbit hole she was already falling. Josephine said simply, "although I do feel guilty about having these thoughts about him."

"William," they said in unison. Josephine cocked her head to one side. "Though I think those feelings were misplaced," she said scrolling back down on her phone. "I missed a few calls from him earlier on in the week and then I got this whilst I was out discussing business with Charlie." Swiping the screen, she opened her messages and pointed the phone back towards Rebekah.

Rebekah looked at her with an eyebrow raised, "Ah yes, you were very busy," she joked as she read the short text message. She looked at her friend and seeing the look on her face, looked at her friend sympathetically, realising that her friend needed her more than her jokes.

Josephine felt a sadness rise in her gut. "He was obviously calling to dump me anyway, so when he couldn't get hold of me, he thought he would just take the easy option," she said sadly, a slight tear in her eye. Rebekah looked at her friend, and seeing her pain, asked: "Are you totally sure you don't want to even try and talk to him?"

Josephine sniffed and took a breath in: "Yes, I am sure," she said flatly. "He would never have come to London anyway and he knew I wouldn't leave what I was doing. Not now. Anyway, he had obviously made his mind up and I am not surprised. Whilst we were in the same place it was simple, and we could forget all the differences and just focus on what we wanted to. However, as we started to move in different directions, it was always going to be harder. Now there is a proper schism really: different experiences, different choices, different friends."

Rebekah approached her and pulled her into a hug. After a couple of seconds, Josephine stepped back ever so slightly, her expression hardening. She looked again at her phone and re-read the message. "Well, there is nothing I can do about it now," she said and deleted both it and his number.

Exhaling a deep breath, she then looked at her hand. She pulled off the friendship ring that she

128

had only worn a few times. She held it in her fingers. Opening an unused pocket in her bag she slipped it in: "I don't want to lose it. It's part of my history, but it's time I moved on and it's not like any of this is really much of a shock." she said, looking at the desk one last time before putting the key fob back in her pocket. She looked at her friend: "Talking of which, what time is our train to Bristol?" Rebekah looked at her calendar, "The train leaves in two hours," she confirmed, "Let's have something to line our stomach when we get to the station."

They both giggled in anticipation of the long evenings and early starts. Indeed, an invitation to this event was still by recommendation only and was an honour. Neither of them knew who had put their names forward, but it didn't matter. They were going, and that was the important thing.

Josephine stood straight. This was the perfect opportunity for her to make sure she was taken seriously. After all, it was these contacts and this seat at the table that she had been working towards and it was vital that this was her focus now. "Right," said Rebekah, "Let me print out the last of the paperwork we have been putting together since the Budget. We can work on it on the train."

Josephine nodded and Rebekah leaned over her computer. The printer spat out page after page of writing and diagrams. She leaned into another drawer in her desk to pull out her business cards.

Rebekah could always bring things back under control easily, her straightforward manner always providing a clear and positive view of the future.

Josephine picked up her bag just as the printer stopped whirring, and Rebekah pulled all the papers into an ordered pile. Both together, walking in perfect stride, they pulled their bags behind them and headed to the door.

Rebekah went thorough first, pleased Josephine seemed so positive about the future. However, she was at a crossroads, a stable relationship just ended, and there was potentially fire ahead, fire that she might not quite see. Rebekah had been around a long time and she had heard the rumours about Charlie. He did seem surprisingly coy around Josephine though, so maybe his intentions were more honourable than they had perhaps been with others in the past.

Josephine looked at her friend, wondering what was going on in her head and felt surprisingly excited. Yes, she had lost William, but look what she was gaining. She was ready for big things and wanted to start on this journey as quickly as possible, grow and develop. Plus, she was lucky to have Rebekah to confide in. The sister she never had. "Ready?" Rebekah smiled;

"Absolutely," replied Josephine.

Walking down the corridor away from the office, they passed the office of Guy Richard MP, a very private man himself, but his staff were known gossips. A rather unfortunate situation considering he was seen as a safe pair of hands and was often seconded to bill committees by the Government. Josephine thought back to that first day when Sharon had got word that one of his female staff had managed to both throw her weight around and gossip about her personally, whilst drunk at a party. An unfortunate scenario to say the least.

The door of the office then opened, and a familiar figure came out. The girls looked at Rhiannon as she walked off in the opposite direction. She was defined by her short skirt and skyscraper stilettos. It was her usual uniform and it suited her perfectly. She may have been around the parliamentary estate for a good few years now, but she never seemed to age. She was always the same. The loudest girl in the bar. The last to leave.

She clacked away, unaware that she had been seen. The plastic bag on the top of her bright pink suitcase fell onto the floor spilling out a bottle of vodka and packet of cigarettes. Rebekah and Josephine stifled a giggle as she bent down to pick them up, her usual cut glass accent slipping as she swore. "Let's hope she learned her lesson and keeps out of Sharon's way," Rebekah whispered as they walked off in the other direction, keen to make sure they caught the train.

131

Chapter 10

Damien sat at the bar watching everyone enter and exit the main bar. He looked across the room, perched high on a bar stool. He made quick notes in his file of everyone he wanted to catch up with, and who was associating with whom. Of course, as a Special Adviser to the Secretary of State for Environment and Energy he could generally get a meeting with whomever he wanted but he felt he had to create an air of exclusivity at his office - no one should assume a right to pass into the inner sanctum unless expressly given permission.

He had only managed to secure the role after passing the developed vetting security protocol, and no one else should assume they should be able to bypass his own personal standards of security and clearance when they entered his domain. After all, it's not like he had a leg up like some of these public-school pricks. He had done it all himself. He had got to Oxford and beyond through sheer hard work. Many around him who felt he was in a position most of them dreamed about, but none of them knew the personal sacrifice, the loves lost because he knew what it would take for him to get to the top. He cocked his head. Tonight was his night, when he would bestow his good grace and create connections with those who were below him in the political pecking order.

It had now been six years since he was an activist on the front line after finishing his degree, his main goal to ensure the protection of the environment he grew up in and promote cleaner living. He was obsessed by politics, and it was not by chance that he took every opportunity presented to him to get to know his local MP Mary Greyflower and educate her on her local environment within the constituency. He had a noble cause, and he soon convinced Mary the importance of his quest.

It was therefore no surprise that once she got promoted to Secretary of State, she took her trusted right-hand man with her. He thought fondly of those early days, and how particularly touched Mary was when he bought her a Hepatica Taeka for Christmas - a reminder of the fragility of what they were trying to achieve, and how important it was. A small purple plant, it now sat in pride of place in her Ministerial office, cared for by Mary above anything and anyone.

He nursed his cider and looked around. Staring towards the door, he saw Patrick walk in alongside several his staff members. Damien and Patrick briefly acknowledged each other before Damien went back to scribbling his notes on the new entrants. He wasn't entirely sure who the two young girls with him were, but he felt that he would need to find out because they worked with Patrick, even though they didn't seem to realise that they were in the presence of a great mind like himself.

He sighed with a slight air of boredom and put a star by the reception taking place in half an hour in the Cromwell Room next door. That reception was open to everyone and he would make small talk with them there, leaving his time at the more exclusive events to commune with those higher up in the food chain. He thought about how much information he would be able to gather from them that he could put in the conference review that he and his four closest friends produced once the conference ended. Their own personal political almanac.

Patrick left the two girls chatting away excitedly to each other. They carefully thumbed through their invites, working out the best place to make the connections they needed. He walked towards Damien and sat down, signing to the bar to get him a whisky and to top up the near empty glass of cider sitting abandoned by the bar. "So here we are again," started Damian, "the yearly networking ritual."

Patrick nodded slowly: "Well I know you find it all a bit of a waste of time but it's good for my staff to see the lie of the land and to catch up with people, including yourself. After all, we are all in one place here, and it's good for team spirit when no one locks themselves away in their office."

Damien shrugged his shoulders, implying he had no idea what Patrick was referring to, "Yes, I am planning on catching up with your girls in the Cromwell Room later. After all, everyone should have their say."

Patrick looked at him sternly, "Now, now. They aren't my girls, and you should really learn their names. They will be the ones scripting the new energy bill my boy, and it might therefore be worth your while to make sure that you give them the information they need." With that, Patrick took his drink and necked it in one, before he signaled for another to replace it.

Damien looked down and nodded. Patrick looked at Damien with a smile. He didn't like pulling rank and Damien was actually a decent guy, but he specialised in feeling hard done by. Patrick looked over at Josephine and Rebekah, who had now been completely surrounded by others keen to make contact, and Damien conceded: "Well, they certainly seem to be making connections, and I promise I will catch up with them later."

With that, he popped off his chair and pulling his papers together, left the bar and Patrick alone. Patrick took the opportunity of a second drink to put his card behind the bar. He did this each year and it helped ensure quicker service. Pointing to Josephine and Rebekah, whose glasses were now empty, he signaled an instant refill for them before he made his way over.

The hotel staff knew to serve him quickly and that he wanted Josephine and Rebekah to be on

135

the list of those who should get the same service. "How's it going?" he said, approaching the group with Rebekah and Josephine now firmly at its heart.

"Fine," said Josephine as she turned around to face him and leaning in towards to whisper in his ear: "Lots of people to meet and not entirely sure where to start, but there seem to be a lot of interest in what we are doing."

At that moment, the drinks arrived, and Patrick handed them out. Before they could even say thank you, he then noticed a familiar face, and took Josephine by the shoulders quickly moving her round to face the group of men that had been talking just behind her. In front of her now, was Jeremy Lawson, a smile on his face and a large gin and tonic in his hand.

Josephine smiled in return and put out her hand in greeting. She had heard about Jeremy. His father had been an MP too - very much the local man. Jeremy, whilst having the same kind of appeal, had taken his local connections and evolved them into a self-made businessman, with a reach across the entire country. Indeed, before he had come into the Commons, he had owned a vehicle hire company that he sold for a cool £3m before taking his seat up on the green benches.

He was reportedly down to earth though and viewed himself as a publicly educated child due to the fortune of a good brain instead of just loaded parents. He had a social conscience who would help others. Indeed, it was not just the board who benefited from the sale of his company. He ensured a sizeable chunk of shares trickled down to more junior employees to ensure they knew the valuable part they played. Of course, such an act of kindness was unusual within the business world and, it didn't go unnoticed by the press. It was therefore no surprise that the constituency of Repton by Sea had jumped at the chance of making him their local MP. A local boy keen to give something back, as opposed to just adding to his own pile of cash.

"It's good to meet you at last," Josephine began, keen to make a decent impression on a man who not only had a business mind, but potentially a constituency she needed to sound out with respect to her plans. "Ah, so you are Josephine," he responded, looking her up and down with an evaluating eye, "Patrick has mentioned you frequently and the important work you are doing on green issues, and it has to be said I am glad to see you here so we can move that work on."

Josephine was pleased that her reputation seemed to proceed her but wondered briefly what could have possibly been said about her in such a short period of time. Jeremy continued, still watching her reactions and body language: "And I do believe that you are properly taking the bull by the horns though you would always be welcome in my office for a cup of coffee or..." He was suddenly cut short as his phone beeped with a message. He looked down and realised its importance. 'I am sorry I have to go so we can't continue to get to know each other here and now but here is my card in case we don't get to catch up later." A slight wink and he was gone, heading off down the corridor whilst she was left fingering his card, watching him leave.

Jeremy was soon down the corridor and out of sight, giving him the opportunity to look at his phone again. Recognising his constituency office's number he put the device to his ear. Looking up as he was listening to the message, he saw a familiar figure walking down the other side of the corridor, and he sighed. He moved slightly to one side to let Charlie pass, but Charlie was like a missile on a target.

Looking round briefly to check there were no witnesses he moved closer to Jeremy, nudging him slightly with his shoulder. He whispered: "Is it your daddy telling you to remember to clean your teeth like the big boy you think you are now you have finally joined us on the green benches?"

Jeremy took the phone from his ear and looked straight in Charlie's direction: "I won't be your fag now Charlie. You can't intimidate me. We are equal in the eyes of our electorate. In fact, Charlie, my majority is bigger than yours."

Charlie snorted, "Beginners luck, ginger boy. Everyone knows that swing was because you opponent was caught out." He walked off, aggression seeping from every pore.

Jeremy sighed. It wasn't the first time Charlie had singled him out and it wouldn't be the last. He looked at his watch and went back towards the doors of the main conference hall to see who was about. In front of him, he saw Rebekah and Josephine were still surrounded, and that Charlie was heading back towards them.

He quickly went into the nearest toilet, slightly irked that Charlie could still get under his skin. He looked in the mirror and smoothed his suit over his muscly physique. He was a very different person from the person he was when he had joined Charlie at school all those years ago on a scholarship. His slightly spotty skin had been replaced by the smooth appearance of a man who had matured into himself.

His hair was much darker than it had been - a flame red now instead of the strawberry blond that had made him the target all those years ago. His eyes were no longer hiding behind spectacles, replaced many years ago with contacts that highlighted the clearness of his green eyes. Of course, he was older, and Charlie was still taller, but that was just life. He was successful in own right. He had done what he had through sheer hard work, not family links, and that was what mattered - where you ended up, not where you started or even how long it took you to get there. Charlie was only fettered with the honours he was because he was always going to be in the right place at the right time.

Down the corridor, Rebekah and Josephine had finally got away from the crowds and made their mind up regarding their next stop. Heading off, they both felt a bit giddy from their first couple of glasses of wine and the general electric atmosphere as delegates got into the swing of the event. Making their way round the corridors, passing people whispering in corners, they soon saw the sign to the Argyle Room.

Entering, they saw Patrick again, this time surrounded by people. They approached and he moved away from the crowd: "Well, I am glad you are managing to make your way into all the receptions," he smiled at them, "It's important that people see you about."

"Yes," Rebekah started and opening her handbag, passed him the papers they had been working on: "I think it's really coming together. We have managed to make contact with some key stakeholders and will be looking to increase our knowledge of both political and all business stakeholders, whether manufacturing or consultancy, in the near future."

Just at that moment, Charlie approached to join the group. "Sounds like you are moving very quickly on this," Patrick smiled, "And it sounds like we may be able to skip the Green Paper and move straight into consulting on the primary legislation and the exact criteria of the financials."

Charlie nodded and smiled, "Oh that is good news, though we need to be careful to make sure that we are careful to keep those guidelines under wraps - the last thing we need is a leak, so that people can take advantage. However," he paused for effect, "I really think we need a drink to celebrate how far we have got so far." Patrick agreed and moved away taking Rebekah with him towards the bar.

Taking advantage of the fact that they were on their own suddenly, Charlie moved in close to Josephine, whispering in her ear: "I have missed you, you know, though you seem to be doing perfectly well without me now you have Jeremy to keep you company. Maybe he is more your type, the nice boy in the class."

Josephine was a bit shocked. She had not even noticed that Charlie had been watching her, "Well, no not really," she slightly spluttered: "Though he is charismatic and smart, and I don't know what you want from me." She looked straight at him and having had a glass of wine, she suddenly found more strength in her voice.

She straightened up and continued: "He doesn't seem to have any angles, but with you it's different. I know your reputation and I imagine some of it has some grounding in truth. What happens if you just want a torrid little affair which would then end as quickly as it started, leaving me open to questions whilst you move on - the macho stallion with another notch on his bedpost."

He met her gaze and smiled. She certainly had fire in her belly. A sharp mind and independence. She was becoming more and more irresistible every time they came in contact. Looking around, he saw that those around them were fully engrossed in their own conversations, and he pulled her in towards him, behind the pillar, so they couldn't be seen so clearly.

Whispering to her now, he started: "You know I care for you. That's why I was so pleased that I was able to ensure that you were being involved in this vital piece of work, which mustn't be put at risk because of hormones. However, the reality is…." He put his hand on his heart "when you reach my age you have a lot of history but that's nothing unusual. I work hard and play hard, and I told you ages ago that I had enjoyed every moment. However, I miss you and I want to see you again and I will be fed up all weekend unless you say I can see you again soon."

Josephine was pleased with his reaction: "You don't need to worry about Jeremy," she said, her brief attraction to him forgotten: "but it makes me smile that you now take me so seriously."

He smiled and their heads dipped closer together, "I have always taken you seriously."

Suddenly self-conscious, Josephine cleared her throat, and pulled back slightly, not wanting to give too much away. Charlie moved in slightly, keen to seal the deal, when Rebekah and Patrick moved back into view. Josephine spotted them just in time though Rebekah smiled slightly, seeing the slightly flushed looked on Josephine's face.

Handing her the glass of chilled white wine, she broke the slight tension: "Right, now we have a new drink shall we make our way round to the bar to see where we should be going next."

"Yes," Josephine answered, "Now we have updated Patrick we can look to see what else this conference has to offer."

Giving Charlie a sly wink as she passed, she was also pleased that she would be able to download these new developments to Rebekah and get away from the heat off the situation. She really wasn't sure how seriously Charlie took her concerns about what they were potentially getting into, but maybe she was overthinking it.

Leaving the two boys behind, they moved next door, able to pass those waiting on the door to judge who could go in with a smile and flick of their hair. Entering–it was like their dreams for some light relief were answered. The room was subtly up-lit, creating a more intimate atmosphere. The girls smiled as they were immediately presented with cocktails by the smartly dressed waiters and waitresses, who didn't seem to notice they already had glasses in their hands.

Walking round the room, Rebekah and

Josephine spotted a dance floor that was slowly filling up. The DJ was concentrating hard to create an atmosphere, and his efforts were being rewarded. They found a free table and sat down, their selection of drinks in front of them, whispering whilst they watched the few people became a flood, moving in a throbbing mass of one, like a wave in time to the music.

"It sounds like he has some integrity," Rebekah began as she listened to Josephine's update. "The important thing is that you don't get carried away at this conference. It would be very easy to end up upstairs. No doubt, he is in one of the rooms block booked and that's just dangerous."

Josephine nodded. She knew that she had to take her time on this and thanked her lucky stars that she had decided against bringing any of her nice underwear. The first time she was with Charlie she wanted him to come back for more, but she knew her baggy underwear wouldn't be a turn on. She relayed this sentiment to Rebekah who laughed, throwing her head back in appreciation as to the position Josephine had found herself in.

Rebekah's giggles faded. She took hold of her drink and was suddenly distracted by a face in the crowd. Dark floppy hair covered piercing blue eyes. The physique was unmistakable. Perfection in a tight, black, top and trousers, swinging hips were snaking along to the music, in beat to it perfectly. Josephine watched her friend, and glanced between her and this strange figure, shocked that Rebekah seemed so entranced by someone so different to Sam with whom she had been settled with for so long. Rebekah's gaze was now intense, fixed, as if someone had stopped time and she had become unable to move.

Just one word came from Rebekah's mouth: "Roberta." In a moment, it all fell into place for Josephine. Before now, this was a name that had only been mentioned in whispers, a friend long lost, but now it was obvious that this was a lover lost, lost in time but not in Rebekah's mind. The music slowed, Rebekah suddenly moved, and looking at Josephine whispered quietly: "I am sorry, there is someone I need to see." Before Josephine could even think of a response, Rebekah was on her feet, moving towards the dance floor.

For a moment, she was alone, and it seemed that her old lover had disappeared. Maybe she had imagined it. The lights then dimmed further, plunging her into near darkness. Suddenly, a song began playing, a song that took her back to a time long ago. Her eyes closed as she breathed in the music as oxygen, her chest rising and falling. Behind her she could now sense a presence, a smell, an enticing combination of cool citrus, honey and rum. There was no mistaking there was familiar breath on her shoulder. Rebekah sank back. Two bodies now just an inch away from each other, they slowly gave themselves to this moment.

No words needed saying. Roberta put her hands on Rebekah's hips, drawing her back so there was no more space, no more pretense. Rebekah's hand ran down the whole the length of her body, and finally finding where Roberta had hold of her, closed her fingers round her hand. Roberta sighed slightly. She dipped her head lower, kissing Rebekah's neck, her tongue taking in the soft salty taste.

The music drove their beat, their eyes closed. The girls moved as one under cover of darkness. "We could go back to mine," Roberta whispered, forcing herself to think about the fact that the song would soon end, and that the lights would go up. The DJ was doing her a favour by dimming the lights like this as she knew Rebekah, until this moment, long left this life behind when she had settled for sensible Sam.

Rebekah groaned. She didn't want this moment to end, but she knew she had made her decision a long time ago. She was now married, and she couldn't be seen in such a compromising position, no matter how tempting it was to throw caution to the wind. Reading her thoughts, the tempo of the music changed and Roberta, feeling the mood change let go of her grip.

When the lights went up, they were just standing watching each other. "I can't, you know that" Rebekah started, not quite able to look

Roberta in the eye, not wanting to say it.

"I know," Roberta said sadly, "And we may not have each other now, but we will always have that song." Rebekah finally met the gaze of her friend again, an understanding that what they had was unsaid and unfulfilled, but certainly not untrue.

Chapter 11

"I can't believe it's only been three weeks and we have come so far," said Josephine, looking up at Rebekah who was avidly typing away on her computer whilst a laptop sat open beside her.

"Well," replied Rebekah, continuing to type away, "We don't have long to consult with the sector to ensure that the rules around tax relief and procurement are clear. Hence my stop here," she said, pointing the laptop at Josephine. Looking at the screen, Josephine saw it was bookmarked at the webpages of the London Stock Exchange and British Chambers of Commerce.

"Yes," she agreed nodding, "It's so important that we engage with everyone that could help the government achieve their objectives. After all, the success of this policy will not just lie with those within the industry forced to adapt, but also on the shoulders of companies willing to develop new technologies - those with fresh ideas about developing clean energy that haven't been in this space before. The Chancellor is adamant that smaller businesses need to feel that they can enter the fray and not feel overwhelmed, and that this is to be the key message in the election campaign."

"Ah well," Rebekah sighed, "Least we have Government support. We both know how important it is for policy decisions to have backing if they are to have legs, and it's obvious from the conference that all eyes are on us."

Josephine smiled and winked at her friend, "Certainly some eyes were on you, you sly dog." She watched her friend closely, and Rebekah's cheeks slightly flushed as she stopped for a second and thought back to that dance floor in that hotel.

Rebekah cleared her throat: "I can't believe she was even there. It was such a shock. I didn't even know she was in town. About a year after we split up, she went back over to Ireland - angry with me that we had split up, and equally as angry that my next relationship was with a man. She didn't understand that when I fell for her, I fell for a woman, not women. She just believed that I had just been a straight woman using her."

Rebekah bowed her head, her body language clearly indicating this was still a sore point, "Of course, nothing could have been further from the truth."

Josephine put her arm out, keen to sympathise with her friend, and asked: "Is there anything I can do? Are you going to see her again?"

Rebekah's determined expression darkened her features, "No. Discussing anything with her is pointless. God, she was so demanding and intense, and highs were brilliant, but the lows were awful, dramatic and tumultuous. The reality is that I need someone much more relaxed, someone like Sam who just goes with the flow, and trusts in himself and us. Someone who I can talk to about serious or difficult things without a plate to fly at my head because I raised something slightly contentious. I just can't think about anything else."

Josephine smiled at her friend, maintaining the contact that had been reciprocated without hesitation, before she pulled her chin up so she could look her in the eye: "It doesn't mean you can't look back fondly. You have now found the love of your life, but no matter where we end up, our history is always part of us. Look at William. He wasn't right for me in the long run, but he is still part of my past - an important part. I just know that he won't be part of my future, something I totally accept now even though it was a bit of a shock at the time when I got that final text message. Anyway," she concluded, leaning back in her chair and breaking the contact: "Maybe I can find the love of my life like you did. Someone who makes me feel complete as well as alive. Someone who totally gets me."

They both sat in silence for a second, individually thinking about the paths that had brought them to where they were now and what the future might hold. Rebekah clenched her fist before breaking the silence, whispering: "Talking of which, what's happening with Charlie? Have you seen him since the conference?"

Josephine couldn't help herself and smiled broadly. "Yes," she said, and she started strumming her fingers, "He got so jealous when I was talking to Jeremy Lawson, he has been absolutely rigorous in contacting me. I couldn't even show you the messages they have been so filthy." She smirked, "And though it's been interesting trying to synchronise our diaries between the three-line whips, late night votes and random meetings we have still managed dinner. I must say, I don't know if he is Mr. Right, but he is certainly fun."

Rebekah looked her in the eye: "There's your tell again." They both looked down. Josephine's hand was still tapping away on the desk: "So, gory details?"

Josephine sighed, "Well, it's quite strange really. Even with the messages – which are almost all him, not me - when we get together, he suddenly becomes quite the gentleman which is a bit unnerving." She looked down at her lace top and straightened out her skirt. "He holds my hand and gazes into my eyes. I would have thought we might have sealed the deal, but I don't want to make the first move. Maybe I am just a bit of late-night relief. I really don't know." she pouted.

Rebekah raised an eyebrow, "He would have to be mad not to want to. Maybe his reputation is only guff and nonsense, or for those he doesn't view with respect. He talks to you about stuff, doesn't he?"

"Oh yes," Josephine replied: "It's certainly been interesting to hang out with him. Obviously when we chat he makes it clear that he is trusting me and that he is bound by the unwritten rule of professional discretion, but just by dint of being so close I am beginning to see how Government and opposition works, and obviously when we are looking at our diaries he will mention any particular interesting meetings which gives me an insight into who needs to be involved to get Government work done."

Rebekah shrugged her shoulders, "Well, even on the most basic level that gives you an instinct that others won't have, an edge that's worth more in the end."

Josephine sat back and smiled, "Well, that's all very well and good - but it's still been a while since Scotland, and a girl has needs." The both laughed, and Josephine smiled. Maybe he didn't want to rush it. Maybe he saw her on an equal footing to himself. She looked down at her work, an extra drive to prove him right and maximise the ringside seat she had managed to acquire for herself.

About half an hour had passed when Rebekah suddenly gasped: "Woah!" Clicking further into some company details, she quickly printed them off and walked round to Josephine's side of the desk. Josephine looked down and saw immediately what had caught Rebekah's interest. On first glance, a perfect company to involve in their discussions: "Agents involved in the sale of fuels, ores, metals and industrial chemicals as well as technological development," but then came the rub. The Connery Trust. Headed by Edgar W Connery, it was there, in black and white.

Josephine's jaw dropped: "It can't be," she stuttered-flicking up the Debretts Website to try and find out some details regarding the family tree. Two clicks and there was the confirmation she had been looking for. Edgar W Connery. Charlie's father. She looked at Rebekah, who sat processing the information: "Well," Rebekah started slowly: "I suppose it could mean nothing. After all, it might have nothing to do with Charlie himself, and these classifications are always so vague. It will be interesting to see if any of the search engines provide any more information."

Josephine started flicking through webpages, disappointed at the results not giving any more information about the family tree: "Well, nothing seems to be coming up, leaving me with the option of asking him, but I don't want him to think that I am being nosy."

Rebekah frowned: "This is not down to nosiness. This is about you doing research in line with your job. So, this is what I can see on the Debretts website. Charlie's father set up an oil trading business overseas, trading off the land the family owned in the Middle East. Of course, officially he eventually retired, but we all know that it's not uncommon for men of his means to keep a finger in the pie so it's no surprise that he's got business interests, and that's where the Connery Trust comes in. No more details after that."

At that moment, the door opened. Charlie walked in, his usual air of confidence oozing from every pore. "You rang my ladies?" he smiled as he approached the desk, the look on his face giving away nothing. The girls looked up towards him. Neither had had any idea that he was about to arrive, and both were concerned that he had entered the main part of the office without them even hearing him come into the office. He sat down, lit up a cigarette, and closed his eyes, inhaling the smoke and putting his feet on the desk as he took his first drag. "So, what do you need?" he said after he exhaled. His eyes were still closed, and he let the silence linger in the air after his open-ended question to accentuate the fact that he expected a response.

Josephine started, thinking there was no time like the present: "We are just looking at companies within the energy market in order to ensure we understand the market and understand how to engage with them. After all, we need to get a picture of those who might decide to enter the market to ensure that any rules around relief and procurement are flexible enough that smaller businesses have the necessary support they need to ensure that the giants don't hoover up all the contracts just because of their size or who might be involved in leading the venture."

She finished talking just as he opened his eyes and looked straight at her. Josephine quickly cast her eyes in her friends' direction, and Rebekah stood up and took her phone out of her pocket, "It looks like I have a missed call or two. Would you excuse me?" Josephine nodded, Rebekah walked out the room typing into her phone, leaving the two alone.

Josephine waited until the door had closed before she continued: "So I was looking at the different companies within the sector and have found The Connery Trust, is that anything to do with you?" She looked at his facial expression, hunting for clues, but he gave nothing away. She pulled out the paperwork that had been printed off and cleared her throat: "I was just wondering because I am sure you said your father was called Edgar, or maybe it was your uncle. Anyway, I am not being nosy and asking for no reason, I am just concerned that we are working so closely on the policy around future energy solutions, and I don't want anyone misconstruing your family links into the industry if it's all a complete irrelevance. I am sure you understand that my concern is merely around making sure that the legislation has a clear run and that there are no hold ups, it's nothing personal. It's nothing to do with you, and me."

She stopped for a second, keen to stop talking before he could get the impression that she had been looking into his family's history and getting ahead of herself regarding their brief encounters. She chastised herself, she really cared what he thought of her, and she realised at that second just how much she didn't want him to think that was the case.

Charlie turned away from Josephine, his expression slightly darkening. He didn't like intrusion, and he didn't like where this was going. He hadn't told her anything about his family, so she must have hunted the information down. However, he couldn't really blame her in this time of social media, and it wouldn't take much considering so much of his family history was in the public domain. After all, he had checked out her social media sites too.

He turned back, looking at her, just as she was finishing speaking, watching her stumble over her final sentence. He thought for a second, trying to keep a benign look on his face, and he saw the relief on his face as he moved towards her, taking her in his arms.

He cocked his head towards her and began to speak slowly: "It's my father's company. We had land in the Middle East that we could use to mine oils and fossil fuels. It made him lots of money and created the legacy you read about now. Of course, eventually he retired but the business has nothing to do with me."

He stopped for a second. She didn't seem any more relaxed. He was expecting this would be enough, but she still looked questioning. He sighed. He knew she was thorough and was just doing her job. Indeed, that's what he liked about her. However, his father had made the trust blind for a reason: "So you know what, I have no knowledge of what he is doing, though knowing the old dinosaur he is still using downhole drilling motors. In his mind, the only diamonds go on my mothers' hands. You will see that alternative energy sources don't quite fit the bill either. Wind, marine, all a bit flighty if you get my drift." He leaned forward so their heads were almost touching, and he was now close enough that she could smell his muskiness: "So now you know none of it is influenced by anything I do, say or feel in any way."

He put his hand on hers, and the sudden physical contact, along with the reassuring words he spoke made her feel mesmerised. She was getting a window into his personal world - a world he had obviously grown up to be very protective and private about and not unusual when someone came from wealth like this, especially considering this day and age of oversharing and social media.

She was frozen to the spot and could feel his breath. He whispered: "So none of that concerns us now. That's a history that we can't touch and can't touch us. Nothing can influence anything in the brave new world that you and I are building together." He ran his hand over her thigh and his hand found the boots that he had admired before they went to the conference. She felt the hair on the back of her neck rise in excitement as his hand moved slowly upwards. She arched her neck slightly, her eyes slightly closed as his fingers made circles over her skin, edging higher and higher. She felt her insides weaken and letting out a small groan she moved towards him, their legs touching. His free hand softly stroked her back, pulling her top out of her skirt so he could find her bra, which he undid with one swift movement, then moving his hand over her chest, stroking softly.

He put his lips on hers, and she smiled. It still felt like the first time. He stood, his lips still on hers as he picked her up with him. She wrapped her legs around his waist, and he laid her softly onto the floor of the office. She soon realised his reputation and prowess were not underrated. She had known the touch of an experienced rough man through William, but this was something different. She pulled him in as deeply as she could, keen to get every inch, to savour every drop. As each moment passed, she gasped ever so slightly louder, and soon she was so far into their own world that she almost tempted the gods to make this a truly exhibitionist activity, to allow someone else to come in and catch them, catch her making the Leader of the House this excited, this passionate.

Soon any semblance of coherent thought left her, other than the number of times he brought her to the brink and over, before they sank into each other, sated and breathless on the floor. Spent, they stayed locked together for a good few seconds afterwards as if it had taken everything out of them, neither speaking, their chests bound together whilst they caught their breath back.

Finally, she pulled away, desperate to stay close but her more sensible nature returning. She smiled and ran her hands through her hair. She drew her skirt back down, realising what had just happened, and what that actually meant. She had succumbed, and she didn't care. She took a deep breath, the release deep and heartfelt - a frustration that had been long in place finally gone. Putting her hand underneath her head and turning around towards him, she winked, "Well I didn't expect that when I woke up this morning."

"Nor me," he said, and he turned onto his back.

She looked at him, and he had a slight smirk on his lips, the expression of someone who had felt all his Christmases had come at once. She knew that she was good. She didn't realise she was that good. "So, what happens now?" she asked.

"Well," he said, "we could get on with some work, or we could go out to dinner and then retire to mine for rounds two, three and four." She didn't need to say anything, he knew what her response was going to be. Her hands locked over his, they rose together, and walked towards the door.

At that moment, a knock came, and the

words: "Cleaner!" was shouted from the other side. Quickly the two new lovers released their contact, just as the door opened. In walked the cleaner that they had both seen so often, but who was completely oblivious to the delicious badness that had just been taking place near where she was now standing. Briefly acknowledging her, Josephine breathed a sigh of relief that her passionate prayers had not been answered. After all, it would have put a dampener on things if they had been caught in such a way, and all she knew was she wanted to feel that good again. He had woken a need within her. A need that would need to be sated over and over.

Once they had exited the office, she couldn't help herself. She drew him into a side corridor and pushed close to him trapping him unseen by those walking between offices. He cupped her face in his hands and slowly moved his lips to hers, stopping just before they touched. "Come," he whispered, and he pulled her towards the lift.

She moved with him, and she couldn't help herself, replying: "Only if you play nicely."

He stopped, and he looked around briefly. He pushed her back against the wall again, keen to make her understand just what she was taking on: "Oh I don't know," he said, "I think it might be time to up the pace a bit." He affectionately bit her ear. His hands made their way down her body, more roughly than before. She gasped. A wolf in a sheep's clothing. She was even more intrigued, and all she could think about was not wanting to break the contact but knowing that they had to move location. He had reassured her in work, and he had reassured her in body. She knew that by tomorrow she would be tired through absence of sleep, but alive with passion.

Chapter 12

"Division, clear the lobbies!!" shouted the Speaker. The Chamber quickly emptied. The eight-minute countdown to vote had started. Aye or No. Josephine's heart pounded in her chest as the MPs raced towards the lobbies before the doors were locked. She knew it was a three-line whip, and that made it a bit more predictable, but she knew never to be complacent. MPs could change their mind at the last minute or decide to abstain, even though they knew they would win the wrath of the whips at a later date.

She thought back to the first time she had been in this position, how her heart had leapt as she watched the tellers line up. She sighed. This time she had Charlie in her corner. He had already requested a report on all those that had a reason to dissent and raise annoying issues in debate or amendments in Committee. Josephine looked at her notes on the important parts of the debate, with the names of relevant contributors highlighted. It wouldn't take long for the clerks to transcribe the proceedings for Hansard, but she knew that Charlie would be impressed with her thorough consideration of the bill so far. She might even get another present.

She smiled to her herself whilst she caressed the scarf around her neck. Charlie had bought it for her, and she thought back to when he first tied it round her neck. An erotic moment, in an ordinary location. He had waited until it was just her in the office, their discussion around the debate that was now coming to an end and then he came behind her and tied the light purple silk scarf in place.

She mused on the last few weeks. The liaisons had been frequent enough for her to be assured that he was only seeing her, but they were both still keen to be careful in these early stages, especially considering Sharon had still not got over her break up with him. Josephine always saw the look of slight longing in her eyes when he came to the office to see Patrick or discuss how the Bill was progressing. She tried to hide it behind heavy make-up, but there was a definite sadness for times past.

Josephine sighed sadly. She did feel sorry for her. During one of their late-night discussions, Charlie had admitted that their relationship had been going on for much longer than most people realised and that whilst he was honest that he hadn't wanted to settle down in the traditional way, he now realised she didn't believe him, thinking she could change him. Her look hardened. He didn't deceive her. It wasn't her fault that Sharon had waited for him to buckle, and then driven him away when he got sick of her jealousy. Monitoring his diary had been something he could live with for a while, until she made stupid comments that meant he ended up distracted and having to firefight ridiculous situations.

Josephine looked at her watch. The seconds counted down before the result of the vote was announced, and at that moment Patrick entered the room. She didn't feel the need to acknowledge his presence, as if any words would interrupt the tense situation in which they found themselves.

Soon enough though, the opposing tellers approached the dispatch boxes to face the Speaker and the ceremonial mace that lay in front of him in order to inform him of the result of the division. The Speaker sat in his Green Leather chair, his languid form resting towards one side, and his elbow resting on the plush green leather. His legs were crossed as he waited for the final tally, his ceremonial gown perfectly pressed, and resting under a figure taken well care of. He took his job very seriously, and he always gave the impression of calm authority. He was the focus point of debates and had been a Member of Parliament for 40 years before he was voted to undertake this most hallowed of tasks, and then dragged into the chair.

He looked up to the Public Gallery. There were always many people watching, keen to learn from him, and his blue eyes wandered over the crowd. He spotted the eagle-eyed students that were now a regular occurrence. He smiled and winked at a young woman at the front. She wriggled happily and smiled back at him as she ran her hand through her long hair. He had no intention of taking it any further. He had too much work to do to try and find her and he was happily married to Betsy, his childhood sweetheart. However, he knew that such behaviour added to the frisson of some of the more mundane debates, and he knew it was all part of the game. Part of the mystique that he, The Speaker, exuded.

Finally, the result was ready, and the aye teller started to speak. Josephine and Patrick looked at each other, both trying to maintain their poker faces, but their eyes danced as they realised that they had crossed the next hurdle, and that they were a step closer to making this law. Josephine half listened to the numbers, relieved that it had been a safe victory, but, of course, acutely aware that those dissenters were not going to go away, and that any one of them could be on the Bill Committee. For the moment however, she was just going to enjoy the victory of her hard work.

She wondered if she should text Charlie about the vote and what she had seen so far, or if she should wait for him to contact her. Just thinking about him made her breath shallower, as she knew they would celebrate in style. Patrick saw her smile, and how her breathing quickened. He knew how much tense a vote like this could be before coming closer to her and smiling: "This is brilliant news, but you don't need to be nervous." He started softly: "Though the real work starts here. It's all been pretty much routine to this point. However, I am sure that you and Rebekah will be able to carry on driving this through and weave it all together."

Josephine looked at him, covering up her slight confusion at his gentle and soothing tone, as if he felt she thought she was out of her depth. She knew that the job was nothing to do with it. She knew she was young in her role, but she was gaining in experience all the time. She nodded, "Yes, we have the initial clauses finalised for when the committee sits which is good, and we should be able to make informed decisions on the guidelines after that."

Patrick looked at her: "Excellent. Now, I have been considering what Charlie said about ensuring there is an even playing field for all organisations, big and small and I have come to the conclusion that the quickest way of bringing together relevant parties would be to form a steering group that can help us ensure the framework is right. It has come together somewhat quicker than I might have expected, and I have a quorum for a meeting tonight."

Josephine had been keen to capitalise on the success of the day with Charlie but had a definite sense of foreboding. Patrick continued: "So, as our policy lead, I think you really should go to the first meeting. It starts in an hour." He saw the look on her face, he thought for a second and said softly: "You don't have any plans tonight, do you?"

She smiled, keen to not make the mistakes that Sharon had by putting Charlie before work and replied quickly: "No, of course not, nothing that's more important anyway."

"Good, good, congrats again!" Patrick said as he headed towards the door, leaving Josephine's evening plans shattered.

She pulled out her phone and started texting Charlie to tell him the reasons why she wouldn't be able to quite make their rendezvous on time. A second later her phone beeped with his response. He wasn't surprised, in fact he was positively delighted, and reassured her that they would be able to celebrate after the meeting had finished. She was relieved. She didn't want him to think she was passing him over unless it was absolutely necessary, but she resisted the temptation of saying something too soppy and merely confirmed she would be with him at the house soon.

For Josephine his house was a particular favourite of hers, much more than her own apartment or any of the other locations they had claimed for their own. Of course, all were special in their own way, but she still rented with flatmates meaning it was difficult to get much privacy there, and that he had to be sneaked in. No-one she lived with had any interest in politics or would have any real clue who they were sharing toast with, but it wasn't worth the risk. Plus, meeting at his was private and showed that she had a real part in his life, a part that allowed her to go into his personal space.

He had bought his house with family money many years before he had entered the Commons. It was an old house, with a yellow front door and creeping plants, just over the river. Hidden away in a small residential square surrounded by shops and traffic, the tranquility was a complete contrast to its location just one side road off one of the busiest roads in London. A quirk that suited his personality completely. Of course, they still took the precaution of leaving and arriving separately, but he was always there first, welcoming her to his home with a new gift - some of which were for private use, others which were for plain sight.

She picked up her laptop bag, stuffed full of the relevant paperwork, Rebekah came into the office with a pile of papers. Smiling, she looked Josephine up and down: "Well, someone's looking like they are getting lots of exercise, and yet I never see you in the gym. Why is that?" she asked, already knowing the answer. After all, Josephine had told Rebekah as soon as she could after they had left the office that first time.

Rebekah could never have claimed surprise, not that Charlie knew that, but before Josephine could tell her of their expected rendezvous later that evening, Sharon walked in the office, her hair everywhere and a cup of strong coffee in her hand forcing the tone in the room to change immediately.

168

After all, Sharon's suspicious nature would never cease or compromise.

Josephine didn't miss a beat, and immediately focused on the meeting. "I really think the background we have come up with does the policy justice," she started and looked at her watch "but I guess the end of the vote means I had better head off to the offices of Swatch, Mungo and Fitch for this meeting. I'll catch up with you later and let you know how it goes." She gave Sharon a cursory acknowledgement. After all, she couldn't be openly hostile and give any implication that Sharon might have been right, but slipped Rebekah a sly wink before she left the room.

Heading to the toilet, she looked in the mirror and applied some lip gloss, before checking her mascara. She made her way to the lift to go to the meeting, tying the scarf around her neck tighter. She sighed slightly, a slight frisson in reaction to the silk on her skin as she thought of him pulling it tighter during their nights together.

Ten minutes later she was leaving the building and jumped into a taxi for the journey to the company offices. Arriving quicker than expected, she made her way up the ten steps towards the office and arrived in the reception. An enormous marble reception area, there were people milling about, waiting to be checked in by the lone receptionist. She was efficient and polite, and soon made sure everyone felt welcome as they headed through the barriers towards the lifts with their shiny new visitor's badges.

It was soon Josephine's turn and she was quickly guided through, ready to go to the top floor where the meeting was taking place. Moving through the gates towards the lift, she looked at those around her. She could already tell the city boys from those at the technical end of the industry. The loud shirts of the city favoured during the nineties and noughties had been replaced with a subtler look, but the suits were still immaculately made so anyone in the industry would recognize their ranking whilst it wasn't so obvious to the chattering classes just how much their bonuses were.

Pinning the badge on her lapel, the lift silently transported her. The doors soon opened to a room set out with one large table in the middle. She walked into the room and through the throng of people and looked around. A few of the assembled crowd were already seated, but many more were still milling around preparing themselves with a glass of wine from the refreshments table.

Spying the last glass, Josephine leant over and grabbed it. She quickly saw the frosted bottles of water and the waiter moved in front of her to take her order. A satisfied pop emerged from the bottle as he released the stopper and the bubbles tricked to the top and into the glass she proffered. She took a deep draw of the cool liquid and got him to refill her glass again. She had decided not to muddle her mind with anything alcoholic, feeling that she needed to be on top form tonight. Plus, she also wanted to make sure she was at her seductive best later in the evening.

She scanned the room and seeing a guest list left unclaimed on a seat nearby she moved quickly to pick it up. Looking up after taking it, and before she could sit down, she recognised the face that had just appeared in view, his notes firmly grasped in his hand. Damien saw her and smiled. He was expecting someone from the OPC to come that evening, and he had wondered if it was going to be one of Patrick's girls.

He approached her, his hand outstretched: "Josephine," he smiled, "welcome." She smiled, pleased that he had remembered her, and he beckoned her to sit next to him. He stacked his notes in a pile and commented: "So you must be pleased that the Bill has passed through to the next stage - though you must have been expecting it would." He looked at her and smiled. Seeing her blush slightly, he continued quickly: "Well, it's good that you are here – and I would like to chat, but I really should call the meeting to order."

She nodded in agreement as she was keen to not extend the conversation so that the meeting could start. "We don't want to hold up the process," she started, and Damien raised an eyebrow, unhappy that she felt the need to chivy him along. This was his meeting. He rapped on the table and the room quietened with those taking the last opportunity to fill up their wine glasses all finally coming to the table. "I think it's time we started the meeting now," he said, and the suits all took their drinks and sat down around the table.

Clearing his throat, Damien looked around and continued: "Thank you so much for coming to this event. I want to welcome you all here and say just how exciting it is to see so many new companies springing up keen to help the Government achieve their ambitions in creating an independent and sustainable energy supply, that also deals with that continued issue of improving energy efficiency."

He looked to his side and giving Josephine a side long smile continued: "I also want to welcome Josephine. She works for the OPC who have been key in putting the details together. However, we know that we can't work in a silo. We need to involve you, the sector, to ensure that we understand exactly what technology and infrastructure is needed in place to ensure that the sector can flourish for 10, 20, even 30 years. The Chancellor has already made a commitment to the industry, so it's down to us to make sure that help goes to the right place. So, with that in mind, I would appreciate any thoughts you have. Any ideas?"

Damien sat back in his chair and looked

around. A hand rose from a starched pink shirt and his eyes followed up the hand, to the arm, shoulder and face. He smiled. He hadn't seen Noah for a long time, since university perhaps, but it didn't mean he hadn't thought about him. He hadn't changed in all these years, broad but delicate facial features, and still wore his hair long.

Noah smiled. He knew he looked tired as he had been at a festival all weekend with his girlfriend, but he still wanted to make a good impression, and so he made sure his suit was freshly back from the dry cleaners. He had never returned Damien's feelings, even though he had briefly flirted with him, teasing him a bit when they were 18. He looked across the table. Resolutely straight, he saw the appeal of Damien's mind but not his body. Nevertheless, he knew that Damien was going to go far and could be useful in the future. He had ambition and wanted to maintain an audience approved position.

He leaned forward and pulled his cuffs straight: "Well," he started: "We know that the Government has made a commitment to renewables, that they want to make use of our own coastlines to provide us with the self-sufficiency we need. But whilst this is very exciting, I think it's vital that the sector has real input on the sector guidelines. After all, this will allow businesses thrive for their benefit and everyone else."

Damien thought for a second. "Of course,"

he said, "And how do you think that can be achieved?"

Noah put his hand to his chin, "If there was a system where we could, as businesses, submit technical amendments then the Government can ensure that the Bill truly reflects the needs of the sector. It would also provide a real opportunity for the Government to give back feedback on ideas and collaborate with the sector if it feels an idea needs to be improved or further developed..." Damien smiled as people in the room nodded.

"That sounds like a very positive idea," he said, "Can you show me how it could work in practice?" Instantly, a chatter broke out, and Damien looked over to the various groups, all keen to scribble their ideas on the paper that had been put in front of them that was then earmarked for the department.

Damien looked at the number of options pile up. This one exercise would put him in the perfect position to present the Chancellor with what needed to happen, whilst he could say that his views were driven by the sector. He smiled. It would set him up perfectly for a promotion after the election.

He watched Josephine, who had one ear cocked whilst she scribbled furiously, using a different colour pen in order that she could easily decipher her thoughts later. Damien started speaking, aware she was sucking on the end of her pencil, deep in thought. He began to speak, looking round the room: "I think your energy around this is amazing and thank you for spending the time you have to help us drawn on your experience. Of course, we need to work out the most realistic course of action. I don't know how you would all feel about us having a central coordinator to pull all this together, but I would maybe suggest Josephine would be able to undertake this..."

She started at the sound of her name and looked up seeing all eyes in the room on her. "It looks like you are already making a start...?" She looked up and smiled, nodding her head, unable to speak and hoping that this was enough to signal her agreement to her inclusion in his plans. A murmur of approval went around the room and Damien smiled, pleased that there had been no opposition to his plans.

Hearing Big Ben in the distance, Damien closed his file, wanting to keep control of the meeting until the very end: "Josephine, I am pleased you are going to be taking this role on. You have everyone's confidence! And on that note, I need to go but thank you for your time and look forward to seeing what you put together." He strode out of the room and quickly everyone else dispersed too.

Josephine smiled to herself, as she started picking up her own papers. Her conversations with Charlie had helped. They always made time for a little bit of work amongst the fun and he had laid it all out so clearly. Her understanding was increasing rapidly, and she was beginning to feel that she really was beginning to understand how to get things done in this man's world, how campaigns could be won and lost. Still though, she could have never expected this. She sighed contently and headed towards the door, checking she had enough money for a taxi to Charlie's house.

Chapter 13

She walked out of the office and the heavens opened. She sighed with relief when she spotted a free taxi and jumped in, keen to get to Charlie's house. She sat back excited at the prospect of seeing him, and as the taxi whizzed over the bridge her heart rate increased in anticipation. It had only been five minutes before they approached the door, she had become so used to in the last few weeks. Smiling at the driver as she paid him, she stepped over the pavement to the house. She knocked on the door, keen to get out of the rain and to tell him the news.

The sound resounded around the house and Charlie soon answered. Out of habit, he looked around to check that she hadn't been followed and rushed her inside. The heavy door closed behind her, she turned around to him and he put his arms round her neck. He kissed her softly and she melted into him. She cursed herself silently, trying to pull away and focus on the success she had just achieved at the meeting, but failing miserably. His smell and touch were just too much, and she knew to delay the inevitable would just make her more frustrated. He picked her up and carried her up the steep staircase towards the bedrooms, their eyes locked in silent anticipation.

Soon they approached his bedroom and he

pushed the door open with his back. She breathed deeply, her head now on his chest as she took in her surroundings, wondering if she would ever feel that these encounters were real and not just a figment of her imagination. She laughed as he threw her onto the massive unmade bed, and he quickly joined her, his intentions obvious. The thick purple curtains were open but because the master bedroom and ensuite took up the entire top floor of the house, the only view outside was back towards the Elizabeth Tower, high above any of the neighbouring properties, giving them privacy alongside the ultimate view.

An hour later they were lying sated, the duvet pulled up over their naked bodies. He stroked her arm softly. "Sorry about your back," she said smiling as her skin glistened. She lowered her head slightly, "but you just bring out my wild side." He smiled at her, pleased that after all these years he could still make such a pretty young thing that horny. She had been like an animal tonight and it had only been a couple of days since their last meeting.

"Well," he responded, "others have wanted me to be rougher with them, but it just didn't seem right. You, however, bring a very basic instinct out of me, one that's very hard to repress." He stopped talking, instead just watching the girl in his bed.

Most of the girls he met either threw their weight around, thinking that being a loud-mouth would be the key to getting what they wanted, or were complete wall flowers that believed being a mattress for a powerful man would make desire stronger. He smiled: "Well it has to be said, that was quite some work. There must have been some interesting thoughts going through your head."

She looked him straight in the eye, "Well, success is quite the aphrodisiac I find, and the meeting was rather positive even if I say so myself." She looked down and grinned, "and I do like being appreciated." Not expecting a response, but silent agreement, she leaned over towards the bedside table and poured water from the bottle that always sat by the bed. Her back was now exposed to him and he smiled - he had matched her scratch for scratch.

She turned back around to face him, and came to rest on one elbow, she saw him watching her, and smiled as she ran her hand across his chest: "So, Damien was expecting someone from the OPC to be there, but I don't think he wasn't expecting that the whole delegation of businesses would entrust the Department, no - me…" she stopped as she drew circles round his nipples "…to work with them to work out what key markers would help achieve the Government's objectives - whether that be technological developments or operations – through effective guidelines and legislation …."

She shrugged her shoulders in mock

submissiveness but stopped as she saw his eyes widen. She smiled to herself and settled back into the pillows, wriggling herself towards him, and interlocking her legs with his.

He quickly realised what she was saying. His protege was going to be so central to the entire policy that his legacy was set. No one could say that he was just another of those faceless politicians that come and go, part of a campaign that ended up being dismantled by the next Government. She smiled: "I know, quite a responsibility." Charlie looked down at her and smiled as he put his arms around her: "Darling it's wonderful," he started, "and it's well deserved."

Josephine smirked: "Yes, well I need to ensure that I keep pumped to ensure maximum payoff, and you will have to help me with that."

He laughed and squashed his body further into hers: "Seriously," he said, "This is such good news. We both know how important this is to the Prime Minister ahead of the election. God knows, if we get this right, we could have a template for the whole global movement towards cleaner energy. After all, it's not like it's not on the agenda!"

She looked at him and smiled, "Well, I think that might be a bit of an exaggeration, but still, I could not have done any of this without your help. You know that don't you?" He looked away slightly, suddenly feeling slightly bashful. He looked back at her, her eager eyes were watching his reaction, and he was torn. She was quite the siren - a dangerous combination of brains and beauty and yet she had already become to rely on him. He hoped that he wouldn't disappoint her. He had disappointed so many before. He cleared his mind. That was a thought for another time and feeling her body nestled up against his, he went in for a kiss.

Just at that moment, his phone beeped, and he sighed. Josephine looked at him sadly as he broke the contact and turned to address it. She hoped that it was something that didn't demand too much of his attention as she was keen on making the most of her time with him. He leaned over and picked it up, and she saw his expression become sterner. She quickly realised that his attention was now been drawn somewhere else and it didn't surprise her when he moved the covers off himself and pulled himself out of the bed: "I am so sorry my angel but an old work colleague is about to arrive at the house. He is only about five minutes away, and for him to drop in like this must mean he must really need my help."

Standing there completely naked, he was looking at her whilst holding the phone, his eyes darting between the two. She heard the slight impatience in his voice whilst noticing that he was still standing to attention and she sighed. She knew she would now have to move out of the warm bed, still fresh from their lovemaking and go back into the real world.

Her body slightly slumped but then she resolved herself to go out on a high. Throwing the covers off, she stood up, and bent over with her back to him as she pulled on just her skirt. She knew that would keep his attention for a few more seconds. She straightened up and turned to face him, still only partly dressed as she held her knickers in her hand, swinging them slowly. Silently she hooked them around his hand, smirking as she moved away to pick up the rest of her clothes.

It took Charlie a second or two to compose himself, and he cursed that he couldn't just pull her back into bed again. He walked towards the door where his abandoned clothes were lying in a crumpled pile, but he knew that time was of the essence. Quickly he dressed, and as he pulled on his trousers, he put the pants she had given him into his pocket. Josephine watched him through the mirror on the chest of drawers as she finished dressing and put on some makeup. She was sad that she was going but pleased that a small sign of her was left behind and would be with him through the meeting he was about to have.

Soon they were both making their way down the stairs, Josephine walking in front of him, but Charlie was close to her, whispering into her ear, keen to let her know that they wouldn't be apart long and that a repeat performance would be organised when he had finished dealing with the impending crisis that was about to arrive on his doorstep.

She couldn't help but push against him briefly halfway down. Moving two steps above him so they were the same height, she took his face into her hands, kissing him softly and deeply. At that moment, the door rang, and Charlie moved past her to answer it. She slowly made her way over to the oak table in the hall. Seeing the open wine bottle that they had walked straight past when she arrived, she quickly poured herself a small mouthful of the deep red liquid which she then downed. The shot of alcohol on her heightened senses gave her a rush and she turned around to see the two men already standing deep in conversation, the stranger standing with his back towards her. She watched Charlie's reaction to what he was saying, and eyed up the intruder, taking in his general persona as she overheard the occasional word. Carter, Hick, nothing that made any sense though.

Hearing her approach, the two men fell silent. The stranger had inquisitive brown eyes, a strong physique and brown hair cut straight and short. A jock, she thought to herself, as she noted the tattered old rugby shirt with the partially ripped number from the back, and yet this seemed too much more serious conversation than one might expect from a meathead. Briefly touching Charlie's trouser pocket in which her gift still lay, she purred: "Have fun, lover," quietly so only he could hear, then stepping out though the newly opened door and back into the fresh air.

Charlie closed the front door behind her and looked at his guest. Conor smiled, nodding his head in the direction of the door as he walked back along the hall towards the kitchen, picking up the wine bottle. He smirked as he entered the large kitchen and pulled a glass from the imposing drinks cabinet. He sat down and looked at Charlie before smirking: "Business or pleasure?"

Charlie looked at his old friend. He felt protective of Josephine and didn't like her to be referred to like an object. In slight internal retaliation, he looked at his guest and swiped the bottle before Conor would pour himself a glass, before putting a slug of wine into the casserole he had slow cooking in the Aga. However, that act was enough to state his frustration, as he knew it was unlikely that Conor could have been expected to know Charlie's growing fondness for the girl in his hall, and he placed the rest of the bottle in front of his friend before finally answering the question: "Both."

Stirring away at the meal he had prepared ahead of her arrival, but would now suit the new situation well enough, he started: "I have been working with her on the Energy Bill - a key piece of Government policy and I told you that the PM had entrusted its care between myself and Patrick. Anyway, in turn, we trusted some of the detail to her and I thought it would be an easy win to send her to the inaugural steering group meeting being held today. Of course, as is being increasingly proven, she is quite the little firecracker both in and out of the sack."

Conor took a drink from the wine in front of him. Charlie continued: "Damien was so impressed that he not only publicly praised her and the OPC at the meeting but the whole group approved her authority to disseminate the industry's wants into a fully functioning operational and financial plan to ensure that the right people thrive."

"Well," Conor said smiling "wouldn't your father be proud."

Charlie's expression changed. "He locked me out of the business long ago, deciding that my interest in politics could only sully his work - that I was just a dreamer that would never be able to take over the business and make it a success. He really didn't think I could add any value at all, so he just allowed Bertie to take over."

Charlie shuddered at the thought of his brother and his exaggerated way of behaving. Giving the family business over to Bertie even though he was younger, had made his brother an insufferable know it all. His large frame made his small eyes even smaller, trapped in the rolls of flab that had grown over the years from too many meals out with his equally rotund and self-satisfied friends. "Of course, Bertie has shown no imagination. I

185

tried to say the board should at least look at diversifying, and that renewables might fit in a balanced energy mix, but he blocked it before I could even present my ideas. Instead, the whole lot of them prefer to rely on the old boy's network and old trade agreements, no matter what new technology or developments or emerging that would have actually kept his business at the forefront."

He sighed and retrieved a glass from the drying rack and poured some wine for himself. He swished it round the glass, watching the legs of wine form on the side and then his eyes narrowed. "I have done all I can though to help them take advantage of the new world. There is nothing I can do if they won't accept that there is a new order, a new raft of energy solutions and a whole generation of skilled workers driving it forward proving that the sky really is the limit."

Conor smiled, "Yes, it's their problem now, and your interests can't be in their business now. After all, old sectors have to change, or they are just at risk of dying. Talking of which, I have registered my new business with Companies House, so have been looking at new premises. Turns out the best location at this stage is in Renton. It's quite a sizeable piece of land on the docks that would be perfect considering I will need space to grow quite rapidly. Plus, it always amazes me how cheap land is outside London, so it would have been silly not to think ahead. Of course, it will need some renovating to make it entirely suitable for the new apprenticeships, but as the local MP is always on the news talking about how there need to more initiatives to decrease unemployment, I can't see how there can be opposition from him or the Council."

Charlie nodded: "Yes, you are helping his local constituency after all. Just protect yourself mind, and make sure your courses reflect local needs and that you have undertaken all due diligence to answer any questions." Conor looked at his old friend and sighed contentedly, pleased that they had maintained their friendship over these years and that he could get some help to understand the nuances of the political world.

"It is such a relief that I have you onside to help me with all this. I have to say, your father's loss is my gain. How on earth he could have passed you over for that inward thinking sloth is just beyond me. He wouldn't know how to develop a big picture strategy if it came with a booklet and an apple in its mouth."

Charlie couldn't help but smile. Anyone looking at him would never think he had a lack of confidence in himself in any circumstance, but any mention of the family business and all his insecurities came back. He always appreciated when someone he trusted and valued told him he had effective business and political acumen. Enough people always wanted to see where the gaps were, where his life wasn't perfect.

"Well yes," Charlie said, "And I just don't think it's a time when any organisation can just stand still. Science has come so far, with new developments all the time being beamed around the world, reported and discussed. Of course, I seriously doubt that father has ever looked on the internet for new discoveries or used an online community to collaborate with others. Taking on board new trends was never his strong point. He always seemed to assume that the old boy's network would see him through and that the young needed to "learn" the old ways before they had the right to contribute. That was fine even ten years ago, when it really seemed to matter that someone had been at a particular university. Now what matters is someone's potential, and whether their businesses will overtake old technologies in terms of efficiency, carbon footprint and consistency. For God's sake, I don't think he even believes in global warming."

Conor sighed: "Well that's it isn't it. We are talking about a man who can't even get his mind around clean energy, let alone making headway regarding improvements in its efficiency. He is a dinosaur, and dinosaurs should be left in the past."

Charlie nodded his head in agreement: "Of course we need to make sure that the new sector is held to rigorous standards and real due diligence. So, I was thinking that it might be worth developing some real guidelines by which we can judge them, standards that are based on academic rigour. Plus, of course it could always help with skilling in this sector. We need to make sure the businesses have the people they need to bring their ideas to life. Conor smirked: "So, we need to get some young, bright minds onside to lead the way. Well, it just so happens that I have put the feelers out to a local university. After all, what better way to provide our young people with opportunities than to provide them with research opportunities suitable for a dissertation that could lead to a career in the industry."

They both smiled and Charlie stretched. The mental and physical vigour of the evening suddenly hit him just as his mobile went off. He was pleased to see that it was the whips saying that the adjournment debate had now concluded, and that business was over for the day. His body was aching, and he wanted to get back upstairs. He still played the game of a 20 year old man, but it took him out of him.

Conor looked at his old friend and smiled. "Anyways, on that note, I will leave you to it now. Thanks for everything and sleep well." He couldn't help but wink "sweet dreams," as he headed towards the door and into the cold night air.

Chapter 14

The Commons library was quiet, with just a few tables occupied. It was still one of the most old-fashioned rooms in Parliament with no computers on the immaculately maintained wooden desks - just newly installed plugs so laptops could be charged. The ambiance of the room had not changed in hundreds of years though, and it was still a location of quiet contemplation and work.

Josephine and Rebekah worked in silence, having positioned themselves in a corner for maximum privacy and so their occasional whispers would not be heard elsewhere in the room. Josephine flicked through the texts and research papers, her eyes drawn to a new piece of work by a local university. The development of marine renewables to include prediction technology so that it wasn't just carbon neutral but could also be stored for future usage. She rubbed her head. It had taken a long time to put all this together, but she felt so lucky. Everyone, including Charlie seemed so interested and supportive, guiding her when she felt she needed help. Still, it was her job to ensure that she knew all the details. If she was going to ensure it was moved from a nice idea to reality, she knew she had to make sure it actually worked and that it wasn't just a theoretical solution.

She looked out the window and saw the

night sky darkening, a stark reminder that she was here and not in Charlie's arms. Josephine leaned onto her hand, her mind wandering and her eyes glazing over at the thoughts going through her head. Suddenly she heard Rebekah clearing her throat, and as she looked up, she saw an eyebrow raised. Josephine mouthed sorry and looked back down at the text in front of her, her trusty flow chart by the side to help her make sure nothing was missed.

Still though, she couldn't quite leave her thoughts behind. Looking at her screen, his last message was still there, brutal on her senses, his desires clear. Their story was getting longer, and now that phones were no longer banned in meetings, it certainly made any dull sessions more interesting. She smiled a lot during those meetings, quite unable to help herself. It struck her that there was always a chance that someone would realise that she wasn't just smiling because everything appeared to be going so smoothly, but she didn't care and didn't believe that anyone would actually think someone would be so blatant, so bad in clear sight. To everyone else she was at her professional best. Inside she was passionate, powerful, loved and a beacon of energy.

She turned her attention to the team of MPs that would be discussing the Bill, those she was working to provide the briefing notes for. She started noting down emails and phone numbers for a new contact database, saying the names as she worked to ensure she spelt the emails out correctly. She flicked through the list and then stopped at the profile of a new MP she recognised. She tapped the desk with a pen to get Josephine's attention, and held up the picture smiling: "Ah yes," Rebekah said quietly "Freya Wright. One of the new intake. Very eager by all accounts. Keen to get to know everyone."

Josephine smirked, "Yes, and so keen to get in on the act. It was almost as if she knew what to say to encourage a smooth Budget announcement." She looked at the picture again "Didn't you say that Sam had worked out there was something going on between her and Guy Richard?"

Rebecca nodded, affirming what Josephine said: "Yes, Rhiannon was never good at keeping office gossip to herself and so it was never going to be long before it went around the press lobby. Of course, the main joke was that he had any spark in him at all and it didn't seem to be anything more unusual than a bog-standard office romance, so he just let it slide."

Josephine giggled quietly. Rebekah carried on: "Of course it didn't last long. She soon moved on when she realised that he wasn't a favourite with the whips, and was repeatedly being overlooked for promotion, or a better office. Or anything really. Don't know who she has her eye now though, but there will be someone no doubt, someone she feels befits her status!"

Josephine nodded and traced the photo of the young girls face with her finger. A finely defined face with golden skin, it was surrounded by a short dark bob with a sharp fringe. A look that seemed familiar somehow that she had seen before. She focused on the expression on Freya's face. Brown eyes trained to look soft and meek but with a hardness at the core, as if she was constantly preparing herself for the next opportunity, for the next big push.

Elsewhere, Freya's picture looked up from the desk at its owner of the image sat in her flat, holding exactly the same expression. Her grand plan was coming together. She thought over her rise so far and those naysayers that had tried to bring her down with rumours and gossip about her and Guy. The rumours had, for once, been true, but no one had proof so it could never have been substantiated even if it had reached the ears of the press gallery. Indeed, so much rubbish was circulated about who said what, or did what, that it was a perfect protection really. Unless physical evidence existed then there was no story and it soon became clear that she wanted more than he could provide, at which point she quickly managed to erase any sign of her presence in his life, even encouraging him to clean the bathroom just before she finished with him for the final time. He had thought it was foreplay with the latex gloves. He was so predictable.

At the end of the day it would never have worked. She wanted to be part of a power couple that could command the respect of everyone, that would afford her opportunities to go on foreign trips and mix with the elite, to build up her path towards her true calling at the higher echelons of the political world, and allow her to move away from the more dull elements that came with being a mere constituency MP. The late nights, the long hours, the tedious bill committees where she was expected to read a whole load of paperwork at the request of the Whips or ask set questions by more senior politicians to help with the party's reputation - even if such requests came from Charlie Connery.

No movie or TV program ever had the Prime Minister reading a whole load of boring paperwork - it was all decision making, War Rooms and strategic thinking sessions at large country estates away from Westminster having delegated everything else to those in more junior positions. It was for this reason that she insisted on taking off at least a month of the summer recess period without doing any surgeries or local meetings. She needed the time to rest, recuperate and plan her own maneuvers. It may not have gone down well with the Whips or her constituency officers, but she didn't care. They should know by now that she shouldn't have to obey the same rules as everyone else.

Of course, they thought she was softening and becoming more pliable having accepted their suggestion to be part of the Bill Committee for this Energy Bill, but she had left them waiting before accepting, and even she only accepted having seen how much coverage this one piece of legislation had got compared to the rest of the Government's election plans. After all, she knew that the Government's reform plan was all about showing how caring and kind they were, and how innovative the administration would be if re-elected.

She ran her hand over the paperwork. She would be able to claim that this innovative and life changing Bill only reached the statute book so smoothly because it had her vital input. This would mean that those at the top of the political tree would have to pay her the respect she deserved and that the introductions she craved so much would start falling into place. It was her destiny and she was determined it would be her legacy. It was still boring in the meantime though.

Soon Big Ben chimed and the bells outside the room rang to symbolise that the House had finally risen for the night. Both Josephine and Rebekah knew this was not their call to finish though. They stayed in their chairs, their eyes and brains heaving with technical information and complicated procedures. As they worked, their pace slightly slowed as a familiar figure came through the door, having been preceded by a very familiar waft of aftershave.

Approaching the desk, Patrick had an earnest look on his face. Josephine and Rebekah slightly straightened in their chairs, keen to show their most professional image. They may have had previous successes, and it may be late at night, but it wouldn't matter to Patrick. He would still be keen to know exactly where they were with their deliberations, and what still needed to be finalised.

This time, however, was different, and he was not immediately firing questions. Instead, he had a few papers in his hands that he laid down on the desk beside them: "A bit of light reading," he said, "It's important we know exactly what's being said in the press." He looked at his watch and seeing the time started making his way back towards the door, his voice slightly raised so they could still hear him: "Would love to stay, but Charlie wants a meeting on the other side of the estate in 10 minutes now that the House has risen. If there is anything important before our departmental meeting tomorrow just text me." Reaching the door, he caught the eye of Phyllis Waterbottom and he winked. She tutted at him, disapproving of the interruption. Charlie was right, he thought as he walked out the door. She really could flatten a man's good mood, even if she wasn't even touching you.

Rebekah and Josephine looked at the papers in front of them, and quickly divided them into two piles, technical details versus PR. Josephine quickly decided that she would just have to get up early and look at the technical details tomorrow but looking at the time knew she could quickly check for interesting press. Flipping through, she reached an article from which her eyes were unable to move. She looked at the picture in front of her, flipping to the text to try and find out why this piece seemed to stand out.

A minute later and it had come to her. He had been the man at Charlie's. He was the reason she was kicked out that evening. She carried on reading, clocking up the glowing words, referencing how his businesses were going from strength to strength, enabling him to grow outside the city and expand his reach. A philanthropist that had an interest in the new generation energy sector, he was looking to ensure that industry had the skills they needed to maximise the technologies of the future. Josephine was confused. A company in trouble would not be expanding, and she remembered distinctly that Charlie explaining that "for him to drop in like this must mean he must really need my help."

She frowned. She got the distinct feeling at the time that he seemed remarkably relaxed for a man whose business was about to go under, but it was a feeling she dismissed at the time as protectiveness for Charlie and the frustration she felt that she had to leave. However, now she wondered what it all meant. Looking for more clarity on the situation, she noticed the name of the journalist that had undertaken the piece and interviewed the man. It was Rebekah's husband, Sam. She was relieved. She didn't immediately want to confront Charlie. His view on a business's success might be different to hers but this means she could make some quieter enquiries.

She sat back and then leaned forward, pushing the piece of press under Rebekah's nose. Rebekah looked up and, looking slightly quizzically, Josephine was quick to clarify: "I am sure that I am being overly sensitive and silly, but I know that man. That's the man I saw at Charlie's and something just doesn't add up. The reason I was kicked out of the house was because he was supposedly in trouble but look: "An innovative businessman with a rapidly increasing portfolio of businesses that spans environmental technological and engineering concerns, he never makes a decision without due diligence and thorough planning."

She put down the piece of press, her heckles rising: "How can that be the case? How can his reach be increasing when I was specifically told that my night of passion was being curbed because of a bad deal gone wrong? I don't know. Maybe I don't know what constitutes a bad deal." She closed her eyes and pouted, completely torn about how to handle it, whispering to herself: "There are obviously different definitions of needing help that

I don't understand. All I do know is that they definitely went quiet as I approached, and that something doesn't fit."

Rebekah knew what she had to do and put a comforting arm round Josephine's shoulders. She whispered quietly. "Leave it with me." As Josephine's breathing slowed down, Rebekah made her way to the door to make a call, leaving Josephine by herself in her thoughts. Josephine closed her eyes again and let the situation wash over her, sure that she was overreacting, but glad Rebekah was taking control.

Breathing slowly and methodically, she didn't notice the figure approaching the desk, his flame red hair a candle in the darkening room, his strong, sinewy body twisting and turning as he approached. Suddenly sensing someone near her, she opened her eyes, and caught her breath. He was a good-looking man, and his green eyes were fixed on her. "Jeremy," she said: "what a lovely surprise."

He smiled, his white teeth showing a friendly affection for her. She straightened herself up and said, "It's all so exciting, it can get a bit too much," to explain why he had caught her with her eyes closed.

He nodded, "Yes, it's fun to be part of but no one would imagine the detail needed, or who might pop up." At that moment, his eyes spotted the papers on her desk and he pulled the picture of Conor towards him: "Him, for example," he started, "who would have thought when the three of us were at university together that he would be cited as one of technologies hottest entrepreneurs all of these years later when all he seemed to want to get in with the right crowd all those years ago."

Josephine's eyes widened: "Really? The three of you?" she questioned, unable to help herself if he could provide her with any extra information on this man who suddenly seemed to be so important but had up until now been hiding in the shadows, from her at least.

He sat down next to her, suddenly aware that he was breaking all the rules of the library but wanting to get to know this enigmatic young girl a bit more. She seemed interested in what he had to say, and he didn't know why but he didn't care. He had her attention now: "Oh yes. He was in the same year as Charlie and me. He came from money so had a lot in common with Charlie, though it was new money of course. Conor's father had private dental practices that he had bought over the years, whilst Charlie's family had built up their fortune from family trusts and old offshore accounts, but in the end it's all money isn't it. They spent it the same way, competing on who could have the most expensive bottle of champagne or the biggest car. How much money they could waste in a weekend seemed to be a sport for them in the same way most of us would kick a football."

Noticing that Josephine was straining her

neck as she looked at him, her tired eyes beginning to sag from too much work, he continued. "Anyway," he continued: "Charlie often boasted about how he was going to take over the family firm, saying that money beget money and that it was in his blood to follow on the family line. Of course, he then changed his mind and decided he didn't want a position in the family firm, so like a cat with nine lives, he got the safe seat of Ash Green."

His eyes slightly narrowed, "Conor, in the meantime, changed from his playboy type demeanour to businessman. No horizon too lofty - he decided he wanted to put his mark on society. It was this that set the scene for his interest in technology and the environment, the brave new world. Of course, at a cost, he would never do anything without getting paid well but he reconciled that with the fact that he is just being compensated for helping the world become a greener and better place, and I suppose it's not like he is now just spending the money like he did all those years ago. In that way he left Charlie behind, and their interests forked."

Josephine moved slightly closer to him and pushed the piece of press in his hand. Jeremy looked down reading what was now being reported: "I am not surprised he is hitting the headlines, and who knows where it will end. After all, he has just purchased a massive amount of worthless land that has never been developed before in my constituency. The plot is spacious and by the sea but just has shrubs sprouting out of broken slabs and potholes at the moment. He must be planning something big considering the money it will take to repair and restore but with the current focus on the environment through innovation, I wouldn't be surprised if he suddenly re-found his old network."

Josephine clenched her fists, wondering what this could mean and asked the only question she had on her mind. "Do you have many university reunions?"

"No," Jeremy shook his head, "It's a small world, but not a friendly one. I don't know about anyone else, but I prefer looking forward rather than backwards."

A voice then came from behind then: "And this is a library. You shouldn't be talking either." They both turned around as a small man holding a big pile of books wagged his finger at both of them. Smiling slightly, they knew their time was up and Jeremy took the lead. He left the room with a flourish, leaving Josephine sat in place, digesting what she had been told. It could still be nothing. It could be something.

She fingered her phone, a message from Charlie lying unread. She was beginning to get suspicious. Did he know what Conor was doing? Did it matter if he did? This time she decided to ignore his calls for her to meet him, texting him that she was still in the library because she had taken a break earlier in the evening. Not too far from the truth, she reconciled in her head. She looked around her with the paperwork and books scattered and suddenly incomplete. She wondered what kind of rabbit hole she was in. Nothing would tell her but time.

Chapter 15

Though many newspapers had moved to swankier offices as their readerships increased, the Independent Chronicle was still housed in the traditional sixties office block that had been its home since it was a regional rag. Rebekah approached the door of the offices and looked at her watch. She was ten minutes early so had a few moments to think about how she was going to get the information she needed.

She was pleased that Nick had taken her call so quickly. He knew that she would have never requested the meeting unless she had a good reason, even though she was Sam's wife. It had always been much simpler for them to keep their interactions to the purely social nature of the job, and even now the boundaries had been slightly blurred she knew that whilst he had accepted the meeting, he was a stickler for protocol. He would not just drop his guard and allow her unfettered access to the sources he used and his reasoning behind the piece he got Sam to write on Conor Black.

She pulled open the front door and was immediately recognised by the man at reception. He gave her a cursory nod as a sign that she could pass through before he even lifted the phone to announce her arrival. She approached the lift and stepped in. Pushing the button for the 10th floor, the doors slowly closed, and it rose up the building in its quaint and bumpy manner.

After a while, the doors opened and she was met by Nick's secretary, who greeted her with civility but had the same guarded body language she was expecting through this entire visit. They quickly walked together passed the grandmother clock to the ante room outside Nick's grand office. Nick was nothing if not particular about providing a full reception service and if someone was coming to see him, he would always make sure they were immediately received if he was not instantly available. True to type, ten minutes later, Rebekah was nursing a drink on a very comfortable red sofa just outside his office reading a flurry of confused text messages from Josephine.

A chime rang through the office to greet the new hour and Nick's head popped round the side of the office door and he smiled in welcome and beckoned her in. She smiled in return and followed his lead, quietly reassuring him that she had been adequately taken care of and did not need another coffee.

Seeing that the meeting was about to start, Sam crossed the office from his desk and hurtled through the door behind her before the door closed, quickly pulling her into a big hug before she had chance to sit down. She loved being near her bear of a husband but was always slightly embarrassed by his overtures in the office. No one else seemed to engage in such public displays of affection. However, nothing had been said and she could never resist that smile beaming down on her, before Sam smooshed his lips into hers passionately. Her professionalism soon kicked in again though. Pulling away, she whispered in his ears to wait for later, and they sat down next to each other in two brown leather chairs.

Nick plonked himself down behind his big oak desk with a file of papers in front of him. It may have been Sam's story but Nick always chaired proceedings in a situation like this. "It's great to see you Rebekah," Nick started, "You look so well, and it sounds like you might have a rather interesting take on a story we wrote. Tell me all about it." He then leaned back in his high sided leather office chair, bringing his hands together with his fingertips just touching.

He said nothing else, giving nothing else away. He concentrated his gaze on her, silently waiting for her to speak and open up about the reason she was there. Feeling his eyes on her, Rebekah started slowly: "Well, I guess I am here out of an element of curiosity, I guess. The election is close now, and the Government has been working hard to provide full transparency. It's with this in mind that we are undertaking extensive consultation processes on all pieces of legislation, ensuring that we have all the facts around what we are trying to achieve before proceeding."

She looked round at her audience to ensure she had their full attention before continuing: "A case in point is The Energy Bill. We have established a very open steering group for all those interested parties to ensure that no one can feel that they aren't engaged. What seemed curious though, is that with all of those companies out there that have made their intentions known and the nature of their involvement clear, you choose to interview Conor Black – on green issues. This is even though he has had, up to this point, no obvious connection to this policy and has requested no information from us. Of course, it could be nothing but he we were just wondering if it was just a puff piece or if he a real player."

Nick looked over at Sam, his face straight. He slowly nodded to Sam, giving him permission to speak. "Whilst some companies have already declared their hand, we wanted to look at a wider perspective, and that's what lead us to his door. I have to admit, we didn't know much, so it was a fact-finding exercise on an interesting person. It turned into such a human story - the man of privilege that has used his business acumen and background to help others and therefore started Carter, Johnson and Hickson."

He looked at his wife: "Of course, your interest is now sparking off other questions. Whilst it is only prudent that you take note of what the press is up to, it's unusual for the OPD to pay a visit to discuss the content of our pages to discuss one potential entrant in a field of thousands, even if the author is the dashing husband responsible for the article." Their eyes locked. Nick looked at them both and walked across the room. He wasn't sure why, but he was sure there was more to this than she was letting on.

Nick stood at the old-fashioned mini bar that had been installed when drinking during the working day was still fashionable, and he still refused to dismantle it on principle even though it never contained anything stronger than tomato juice now. He poured himself a drink and turned around to face them. He shrugged his shoulders nonchalantly and said: "After all, there have been puff pieces about this subject by many press outlets, on many different people that want the world to understand the good they are doing, virtue signaling if you like. So, I have to ask - why do you focus on him?"

Rebecca bit her lip: "Well, he seemed much more familiar with the sector than we expected, which was just a bit of a surprise. Plus, he wasn't always this philanthropic and open to helping others." Rebekah sat back slightly, not quite sure what she was saying. She knew that, even though Josephine would deny it, this entire investigation into Conor's business interests had merely started because Josephine had wanted to know more about the man that had spoiled her evening of lust.

Rebekah knew that there was no reason why Charlie should have to declare all his friendships. After all - like always finds like, and therefore a top businessman will always search out and befriend his equal. However, considering the fragility of public support and trust in those of power, there was still the question over why Charlie lied about the state of Conor's business. Why would he indicate there were problems, even though there clearly weren't?

She continued "Indeed, my sources tell me that he much preferred to associate and help out people like himself, which makes it all the more interesting that the Right Honourable Charlie Connory and him are old university friends."

Nick and Sam looked at each other but were still unwilling to completely show their hands. After all, they had asked the question about how his past had set him up for the future, a comment which he had dismissed thoroughly. Nick jumped in, keen to take control: "How interesting. Seems like he has completely turned over a new leaf to me, with no interest apart from doing good. He certainly didn't seem to have any interest in helping anyone apart from the disadvantaged."

Sam nodded in agreement and Nick continued to test the waters. He addressed Sam directly: "Didn't he say that he felt reborn after he went to university?"

Sam nodded as Nick continued, "It certainly seemed to me that he now firmly believed in helping others, and that an individuals' success should not be due to the old boys' network, but instead based on a commitment to do the best they can for themselves and their fellow man."

Rebekah knew they were just probing, but before she could help herself, she blurted out "I can't tell you how, so please don't ask, but I have a feeling that they have been in contact, and that it might mean nothing but…" She tailed off. The two men looked at each other, respecting that she was trusting them, and finally getting the confirmation they needed since her initial phone call. Sam approached her, his arms outstretched. He pulled her close to him and whispered how much he loved her into her ear.

Nick knew what he had to do. "Rebekah, you know how much I respect you. Not just as Sam's wife but someone scrupulous in making sure everything is above board, and we understand exactly what you are saying. It might not matter that they have been in contact, and we know it's a small world out there between business and politics but considering the indication that Conor had supposedly left his boys network behind, it's certainly worth exploring, especially considering the Government's environmental agenda. The question is whether or not we can establish if there would be any reason for them to discuss what was going on or if their contact is entirely social."

Nick left his seat and started to pace the

210

room. "I suppose the next question is what do we do about it. You know perfectly well that we are supportive of the government, but equally I can't compromise the values of the paper and we have always advocated that those in positions of authority should be scrupulous in their dealings, making sure things are done in the right way."

Rebekah knew what he was saying, and that was why she came to him. His first story was a personal one, and he had taken great joy in taking down the criminals that were trying to infiltrate his local boxing club. He had no problem in exposing their plans to get the young men he knew to throw fights, even when they had trained so hard to achieve their levels of fitness, and their personal goals of discipline. She looked determined: "We will need to find out more about his business and see whether or not there are any conflicts of interest. We need to know who's involved and what exactly he is looking to do. After all, there is finally an opposition that will pick up on any inconsistencies in what the Government are trying to achieve and will look for any way they can to derail it, especially considering the Government are using so much of taxpayers money to help the sector thrive."

Nick finally sat down again and started writing notes, nodding away to himself. He looked up at Rebekah to see if she had any more information that she hadn't yet told him, but she kept her own council. She had said enough and was unwilling to give anything else away. After all, Jeremy may have been loose lipped due to a feeling of bad blood and she needed to concentrate on gaining facts, not stirring up supposition. He might have got the wrong end of the stick and Charlie and Conor could be under suspicion for no reason at all apart from a bit of frustrated lust on Josephine's side, and bitterness from Jeremy who might just resent him.

She simply said, "Of course, I can't be any obvious part of any investigation, and personally it doesn't matter to me what businesses benefit as long as they make a positive contribution in return for the Government's help. However, I need to ensure that the process is fair and that no one is at an unfair advantage."

She fell silent and Nick smiled. "Don't worry. No one will know your involvement. Everything will be done through a third party. I feel one of our associates will be able to submit the relevant questions so that we will be able to get what we need which we will then be able to get to you anonymously." Rebekah looked at him, relieved and pleased he was going to help her make some official enquiries. It would just give both her and Josephine the peace of mind they needed.

Down the road, Charlie paced across his office, his phone stuck to his ear. He held the report in his hand. After five minutes he headed over to his desk, drawing out a pencil from one of the large wooden drawers, before sitting down at his desk. He quickly started annotating the document, covering the page with corrections and changes. He smiled as the conversation turned to pleasantries: "Yes, of course Patrick, thank you for calling. I think the consultation is a real positive way forward. It really validated what the government is trying to do and showed that there is an active sector that is really geared up to make it work. Yes, thank you. I will make sure I report back to the PM just how well it's all coming together."

He put the phone down and smiled. He looked at the piece of paper in front of him, putting it on his desk very precisely so he could admire it fully. Those academics had been very busy, and their efforts had paid off. The potential of this was limitless. He flipped to the back where the name of everyone that had contributed was listed. It was a name among many. Just like it should be. It just dovetailed nicely.

He picked up the phone and dialled a number he knew off by heart. "Good news." He began. "The consultation seems to have been all encompassing. No one can say that there hasn't been a full impact assessment of the technology and the benefits it will bring."

He laughed down the phone "Approval ratings will go through the roof as the Government implements its promises, and everyone wins." He stopped for a second, "Well apart from those that are unwilling to understand that a new world means new technology of course." He moved over towards the window, looking down into the courtyard beneath and the pass holders move around the estate below. It was getting dark outside but there was one figure he would always recognise by sight.

The click of her heels confirmed his suspicions and he smiled: "Of course," he smiled, "Obviously start up's like this always need help to make sure all the ducks in a row, and I have someone in mind who can deal with all the paperwork on our behalf." He paused for a second "Oh yes, she is happy with the offer and knows I am to be kept out of it."

Putting the phone down, he smiled, admiring himself. He went towards the mirror and looked at his new suit. He always prided himself in his appearance, but it had been a while since he had been able to be quite so extravagant. He ran his hand over the soft material. A deep blue, he matched it with a darker tie. A bespoke cut, he was keen to make this his new standard.

Josephine sashayed into the room, knocking on the door quickly. He didn't like her loitering outside the office in case someone spotted her, and she took great joy in the fact that she therefore had some freedom to enter the office of one of the most important men in the country.

There was always a risk that she could enter

when he was in the middle of a meeting, but she knew his signal that would indicate a liaison would be badly timed. He always made sure there was a note on the door saying that deliveries should be taken straight to the post office for him to collect later, innocuous enough for someone else to not recognise the significance but a clear indication for her. Tonight though, there was no note and she had made sure she was wearing his favourite scent when she dressed this morning. After all, it had been a couple of days since she had felt his hands on her, and she was keen to change that.

Her hair was down, and wafted down her neck, over her shoulders. She approached him and put her bag down in front of the desk. He had still not turned around, so she approached from behind him, she ran her hand down the fine material of the jacket and beyond so he couldn't misread her intentions. Running her hand back, she put her hands on his shoulders and turned him round as she murmured, "that's one fine suit!"

She drew her hand over the trouser leg. He closed his eyes as she went further up, enjoying her touch, and he knew exactly where he wanted this to go. He opened his eyes and smiled, "You didn't answer my text. Was it because you wanted to see my suit in person?" She smiled and pulled him round to face her. Turning, his eyes caught her bag, and the documentation spilling out of it. Not quite knowing why, he felt his lust wane slightly, and he

215

leaned down to get a better look, drawn to the papers even over her.

Josephine moved back slightly, shocked at the change of pace. She looked at him quizzically but laughed with relief as she saw he had just picked up the press coverage on Conor. He bent down and picked the papers up before looking at it and then her with a quizzical look on his face that she didn't quite understand. Unsure where this was now headed, but keen to get it back on track, she stammered: "Just a little bit of bedtime reading. After all, you were worried about him when he came over and I just wanted to know who I was fighting for you." She smiled, "Of course, you needn't worry about him quite so much now. His fortunes seem to have got somewhat better since you last met."

She saw him stiffen and he moved away from the desk away from her. "Well," he started "someone has been a busy bee." She opened her mouth, unable to quite process the tone he seemed to be using to her. She moved over towards him, keen to touch him again, tell him that she was just having a laugh, and move on from what she knew had just been jealousy on her side. However, she saw his mood had not lifted. Instead, he pulled away.

Josephine looked at him, and his eyes softened slightly. "I'm tired and I have a lot to do," he continued, "Why don't you go to the bar and have a night off. I will call, but I just need to check a few things out." She stopped, a tear pricking her eye, but she knew it was time to go. His body language gave her no doubt. She walked towards the door. Turning around to look at him one final time, he had not moved one inch to persuade her to go back to him. She opened the door before moving into the corridor. She stood shocked, alone, unsated and unsure.

Chapter 16

Jodie was used to dealing with situations like this. She had known blokes like Charlie and Conor all her life, and it was her job to make sure that their interests were maintained in the best manner possible. That's why she was paid over £1,000 an hour after all. She walked into the room, where the two men were already sitting talking quietly and conspiratorially. They stopped as she walked in towards them. She thought how funny life was, how people who had a history never really got away from each other.

She put her black briefcase and flask of green tea, specially prepared at home before she left for the gym, down on the desk. She sat down and they both watched her in silence. She opened her suitcase to draw out a set of documents and laid them on the table. She sat back and sighed. She knew they expected things to just run smoothly and she hated relaying bad news, no matter how well she had perfected it over the years. However, she knew that Charlie had asked the question and it was down to her to give them the truth, no matter how unpalatable.

The lawyer sat forwards again she began slowly: "I have some information you are not going to like." She laid some papers in front of the two men carefully, "It seems your hunch was right

Charlie. There has been unexpected interest in your businesses Conor…" Charlie clenched his fist under the table, his heckles rising. It should never have got this far. After all, what business was it of anyone's what a private company like Conor's was doing. He looked at her expectantly. Every minute was costly, and he just needed to hear what this meant. She continued: "This is why I told you no more pieces of press. It's not worth it at this stage. Directors, accounts, they will need to be public eventually but for now we have to be careful to protect the interest of the business."

Jodie looked at Conor's face wondering if he would see the concern, but there was nothing there. She knew the arrogance of men like this. They often felt that they could bulldoze their way through anyone else and it was her job to make sure that they knew that there could be implications. She turned to Charlie and saw that whilst there was no surprise, there was a lot of pent up anxiety.

"Who?" Charlie said quietly.

"Well," Jodie replied changing her tone as if she was talking to a young puppy, "It all seems to have been done under the guise of official press interest, and there is nothing unusual in itself in that, especially considering Conor's new found silence on what he's doing. However," she said, turning to Conor, "I have to ask you to make sure that you are very careful Conor. We don't know what other searches are being done, or why. We can only surmise. So, it is vital that you are forward thinking regarding how you organise your business interests and associations."

At that moment, Charlie stood and walked across the room, his teeth clenched. He looked at her, watching her systematically tear up a page of her notebook into smaller pieces. Her nails were painted a pillbox red, and he wondered if was worth a shot, but he quickly deciding against it. She was all muscle, and no matter how fit she was she definitely looked much older than her 43 years.

It was as if she had never quite known where to put herself with respect to both her work peers and personal contacts and had therefore felt she had to be different. By wearing very high heels, even though she was almost 6 foot, she would give out the subliminal message to everyone that she was not to be messed with, someone that wanted consistently to be the best and prove others wrong. He mentally clenched. Anyone pissed her off, she would break them in two, and if she didn't manage, she would die trying.

Yes, he thought to himself, there was definitely a balance between letting it all go and taking it all a bit too seriously. That was one thing about Josephine. She worked hard, but she enjoyed life, reveling in the ridiculous, and the knowledge that whatever anyone did no one would make it out alive. He sighed. He definitely missed her. She had an infectious laugh and had made the most boring situations interesting. She had enjoyed coming into the office with little more on than a skirt she had worn the previous week out with her friends to the "school disco" evenings that they held at one of the local clubs, her red lipstick in hand as she daubed his chest in mock ownership before.. before…. He stopped himself. That was then and this was now. It might all be coincidental. But it might not.

He was just about to speak but before the words left his mouth, Conor responded with a reassuring manner: "You don't need to worry. We have it all under control." Conor smiled and leant forward. "I decided a long time ago that nothing with respect to the business should come to the house, and that's where Charlie's expertise came in brilliantly. He made sure that we had an independent location for all paperwork, and a truly independent manager of all the regulatory paraphernalia to make sure no decisions that was statutory could ever be attributable to anyone benefiting financially from the organisation, isn't that right Charlie?"

Charlie nodded. He had worked hard to persuade Conor that was entirely necessary, but now he was pleased that he had taken such precautions. Jodie looked at the two men. There was nothing else she could do for now. "OK," she said, slightly dismissively: "Well, it all seems to be in order for now, but we need to be careful. Whilst there is nothing obvious that can be called into question at the moment, there is no escape from the fact that someone wants to know your business, and that in itself is telling."

She stood up and threw her head back. She always knew that these men would never have been her type, but still she felt slightly annoyed that he didn't seem to be in awe of her like so many of her clients were. Of course, she knew that it was in their nature to feel superior to pretty much anyone, but it always felt like she was back at college again, where she was never the cleverest or prettiest and was fighting to find her place. That's why she never let herself off the leash. She couldn't afford to. She always needed to be on top. No embarrassing scenarios for her, where she had done something inappropriate or out of place. She turned, "I'll be in touch with any developments. In the meantime, stay out of trouble."

She left the room, and the two men sitting quietly. "I need some air," said Charlie suddenly "Is there anything you want from the bar?"

Conor nodded, "Whatever you're having," he said and with that Charlie moved out of the door.

Walking down the corridor, he saw the doors to an office down the corridor. He stood, waiting, like a lion in a cage, desperate to pursue his prey.

On the other side of that door, an envelope had dropped on the floor of the office. The two girls pulled the paperwork out and quickly absorbed the information. "Well," said Rebekah, "There have been a lot of changes at the land registry, all of which seem to lead back to this one address. One address for 7 property charges in all. Whoever they are, they are obviously gearing up for something. The question is what? And even if they are, surely that's a good thing considering what we are trying to achieve?"

Silence filled the room and she thought back to the conversation she had had with Jeremy previously. "Isn't it interesting?" she started: "First we hear that Conor has bought a whole load of land in Jeremy's constituency at the same time he's in the news. However, then there is radio silence. No comment. No follow up." Suddenly Josephine's stomach started to rumble. She was never good when hungry. Her brain always tended to get slightly scrambled and she knew she could easily start reading things that weren't there. "I need some sustenance to get my head around this," she said: "Is there anything you want from the cafe downstairs?" Rebekah shook her head and Josephine stood up before she grabbed at her purse and headed out the door.

He saw the door open and Josephine come out. He bared his teeth slightly, noting her quizzical and ever thoughtful expression. He knew he should just leave it, that he should give more thought to how he might want to approach her, but he couldn't.

He moved towards her and Josephine looked startled. The usual welcoming approach was not there. She felt a sadness. The simple way of resolving all of this would be talking to him and for him to open up to her - reassure her. However, this reassurance, this kind manner seemed to be a loss to her now. She didn't quite know how to place herself but soon the answer was taken out of her hands.

Having nothing to lose, she looked up and smiled at him, hoping she was wrong, that she had read too much into his body language but then saw the grim expression on his face: "So," he started, "You couldn't leave well alone then?" She was taken aback, not quite knowing what to say.

She stiffened slightly and looked him straight in the eye, "I have no idea what you are talking about." She tried to sidestep out of his increasingly aggressive stance, but he blocked her from moving forward and she wasn't in the habit of knocking past anyone, let alone someone she had shared a bed with so recently.

"Really?" he said, his heckles rising. She had obviously not let anything go since their last chat when he had tried to warn her off nicely. Now, however, he had a feeling that her office was somehow now beginning to interfere and raise interest in Conor in a way that was most unwelcome. "So, I suppose it's just a coincidence that questions are now being asked of businessmen that happen to have been associated with me in the distant past is it? At the same time, I have noticed a distinct drop in your productivity."

He tightened his jaw and focuses his ice blue eyes on her, but in his steely anger they seem to almost be grey. "Yes," he carried on: "I would be surprised if Patrick hasn't noticed your change in pace either, that you always seem to be heading off somewhere or another, like you are now in fact." She stopped, knowing that for now at least she would have to face him off, but not sure what she had done to suddenly warrant such aggression from the man who had helped her do her job such a short time ago, someone that had been so interested in making sure the Bill came together so well, and ensure that she was able to present her findings so careful and positively to Patrick.

"I don't know what you are talking about!" she started, "I am going out for some food now because I have been in the office for hours doing my job properly and without interruption. It's not like I am spending time doing other things at the moment after all."

He straightened up, his hands on his hips. She looked him up and down. Normally she would take any opportunity to make a comment about the position of his hands but this time she felt that she had no right to say anything, that any real personal interaction would be most unacceptable.

225

"Well," he hissed, "All I know is that it's always better when people stick to the job they have been given, and don't rise above their station. It seems to me that you are beginning to get a bit too big for your boots. Not dissimilar to someone else who decided to throw her weight around and lost."

Colour drained from Josephine's face as she was transported back to when she overheard him so abruptly dispose of his relationship with Sharon. With that he stood to one side, letting her pass, but his face like thunder. She walked off, looking at her watch with tears pricking her eyes, but determined to not let him know that he had bothered her in such a way. She pulled her phone out and quickly texted Rebekah. She knew she would understand that such a confrontation left her massively confused and that she just had to get home. What was he saying? That she was being nosy and self-serving in a bid to get one over on him?

She raced down the corridors and soon found herself out of the building. Luckily, she had everything with her, and she bolted out the swing doors. She already had a taxi in her sights, running towards it. She leaped in, relieved that he had contactless pay, so she didn't even need to get to a cash point. Living so close to the office was a godsend on days like this and she wondered what she would do when she got there.

Five minutes later she was soon unlocking her front door and screeching into her study, looking at the paperwork on her desk. She stood there for a few seconds, but her eyes could not focus, and the words were just swimming in front of her eyes.

She felt the anxiety and annoyance inside her, swirling in a heady combination like a drug which afforded her no control of her feelings and actions. She spun back into the hall. How dare he treat her in such a manner. It was his unexpected reaction to her work that had sparked this turn of events. It was his suspicious behavior. He had encouraged her to engage with the sector and make sure they were involved. Why was this suddenly now a problem?

She ran through, turning quickly into the kitchen and reached out, clasping onto something she could take her anxieties out on. She saw a bottle of wine on the counter and clasped the neck tightly. Her eyes closed in frustration now, she brought the bottle above her head. She used all her strength to throw it at the wall, her eyes opening just in time to watch wine explode all over the wall and laminate flooring.

The relief was palpable, and she sank in tears on the floor. She sat there on the floor, her tights ripped from where she had fallen. She wondered just how many times he had done this before. Watched and waited, helping a young girl to achieve part of what they wanted, before pulling the plug, before he accused them of behaving in a manner that didn't befit her position within the political machine. All she wanted to do was her job. She didn't want to find what she found. She didn't even know what she had found.

She lay there for a few moments. Her breath stabilised and she began feeling a little bit less spaced out. She stood up, a determined look on her face, and ran into her bedroom, kicking off her heels. She pulled out some jeans from the wardrobe and quickly changed. She needed some proper space, and she knew that a small flat in Vauxhall would not suit the purpose. She needed to go somewhere that she could think.

She threw some things into a bag, and texted Rebekah. It was Friday now anyway, and she could take some time. She had not had a holiday since she had been in the job apart from the weekend away with William, and even that had been disturbed.

Looking around she locked up and made her way to the railway station. She looked up at the departure board as she always did when she happened to be here for other journeys to see when the next train went back to her safe place, a train she often longed to catch when moments became a bit harder. She didn't need to bother though, she knew when the train was going, and she knew that she had no time to lose.

She headed to the relevant platform just as the train was arriving and leapt on, quickly heading to a seat. It didn't stop for long before setting off and soon she was watching London fade into the distance as she headed West through the countryside. The landscape was getting wilder as the train travelled towards its destination.

It wasn't the quickest train, but she knew that she would get where she needed to be. It had obviously been raining hard, and the wind was raging now driving the water that had settled on the fields to pucker into little waves. Her mind was still trying to process everything. She knew it was vital that she tried to make sense of it all away from the hustle and bustle – away from mobiles and emails, away from prying eyes as she worked out her next move.

Chapter 17

Rebekah looked at the last text message from Josephine again. Charlie had got a proper bee in his bonnet and, she wasn't surprised Josephine wanted to get away. She mused that Josephine and Charlie had seemed an odd couple, but they had both been enjoying seeing where it might lead. However, now he was just being secretive and nasty. She looked down at her phone again. No further messages from Josephine and she hoped she was ok. Josephine had said she was going somewhere she felt at home, but nothing else.

Rebekah looked at the paper given her by Nick, and she knew she wouldn't be able to help herself. The address was on her way home. It would take her no time at all to do a walk-by. She wasn't sure what she what she would see but she looked up the address on her phone and started walking.

Musing on where Josephine could have gone, she realised that she had reached her destination. Before she could even catch a breath, she heard a drunken laugh. In the dark she could still see the mop of blonde hair and thanked her lucky stars that there was a dark alley next to the houses in which she could hide.

She recognised her immediately, and peered round to see what was going on. There she was. And so was he. Holding her up, Charlie was whispering into her ear causing her to smile before she pulled him into a kiss and pushed him against the wall of the house.

Rebekah was shocked. It hadn't taken for him to move on. Or back. The courting couple finally broke from each other and Sharon slurred, "What's mine is yours," and she brought out her key. Moving behind her, pressing her against the door. She laughingly pushed him back before they practically fell into the hall. She kicked off her heels and quickly removed his jacket. She then pulled him towards the stairs and that was it. They were gone.

Rebekah stood there for a few minutes taking in what she had seen. Forgetting the sexual politics of the situation, a more serious question rattled around in her head. It was obvious that he was a regular visitor to that location and whilst it wasn't conclusive, it was certainly suspicious that the place where key company information was being dropped off was the same place Charlie was using to knock off Sharon. She thought for a second. Maybe there was someone else at the address and it was a complete coincidence. Thank God for the internet. She typed in the website she needed and slowly inserted the postcode, holding her breath.

As if her phone knew how important the situation, it took it upon itself to slow down and freeze. Rebekah closed her eyes and she opened and closed her fist closing to try and keep her calm. A minute later, the website flipped over, and Rebekah saw what she was looking for. Sharon was the only person registered on the electoral role, and she had been there for a long time. There was no one else so she had to have at least given permission for the to use her place as a drop box for the company details. She had some involvement somehow.

She picked up the phone and tried Josephine's number. She hadn't wanted to disturb Josephine's thinking time, but she also knew this was important. She was relieved when it began to ring, but soon it reached the voicemail. Rebekah wasn't entirely surprised but she knew that time was of the essence and that it was important the message got across: "Hey Josephine," she began, "I know you are probably in the middle of something exciting, but I thought I would let you know that I have now located the new headquarters for Conor's company. It's obvious that Charlie and Conor must still be in contact. I saw him here. With her. It's the same place that Sharon lays her head. Not sure of the significance at this point but a bit odd no less. Speak soon!"

Josephine looked at her phone. Absolutely no signal. She had only been on the train for two hours, but she was already much more relaxed. She needed time to get away. She had no idea why Charlie had suddenly turned, but for now she didn't care. The bell pinged overhead, informing the few people left on the train that they were about to stop at the final destination. Josephine looked out the window and could see the seaside whizzing by alongside the tracks.

Soon she was stepping off the train. She stepped out onto the platform and looked around her. It was dusk but it was obvious that little had changed in this little place, this little piece of heaven. The station was sill unmanned and deathly quiet. She picked her way slowly along the street, moving down the road like she had never left. She breathed in the clean air and took a moment to take in the sights. Her eyes wandered down the road and spotted the ruined castle glistening on the hill in the distance. She had spent many a happy day and early evening sitting up there watching the waves go in and out, a bottle of beer in hand, gossiping with her friends. She knew she make her way up there whilst she was here. It had been too long. Life had been too busy.

Walking along the narrow road, it converged into the one main high street. A young girl hurtled out of one the houses, a student like she had been all those years ago. Josephine caught her eye and smiled. The girl was clearly drunk, tottering in her heels along the road, not caring that the dirty water on the cobbles lashed against her tights. Josephine had no choice but to follow her and soon became aware of the music blasting from one of the pubs. Outside the pub were two young men smoking rollups who welcomed the young girl fondly before

233

throwing their arms around her and pulling her inside.

Josephine smiled and headed down to the seafront. Soon she was soon on the pier. She walked to the barriers, partially mended after the last big storm and took it all in, her hand running along the mended brickwork. She couldn't help but feel the power of the sea as she breathed in the salty air and took succor from the noise of the waves that were pounding against the shore. The view around the bay was spectacular.

The multi-coloured houses along the seafront were mingled with halls of residence, and all showed the individuality of the owners. The gardens were all carefully mown, with well-kept borders. The flowers swayed in the wind, a plethora of blues, reds and yellows, planted with care and love and standing proud like they had done years before she first came here, and would do for years afterwards.

Watching some students emerging from her old hall of residence, Josephine knew exactly where they would be heading. The Old Bowling Alley where the drinks were cheap but in multiple supply. She smiled to herself. She remembered her own time in that bar and thought how different it was to the bars she tended to go to now. It still had a pull though. Later, she thought. At this moment in time, she knew where she wanted to be, and that was out in the fresh air sucking it all up.

She walked quickly towards the end of the pier, back towards the marina from where the boats never seemed to move. Away from the seafront now, the students were a long way away and the sun had started to go down behind her, her figure casting long shadows. Lost in her own thoughts it felt like moments before she was looking down into the old slate quarry and she felt a wave of exhilaration.

The many levels that had been worked over the years, stretched out in front of her, a wound in the earth. It was so far down from where she was to the mine below – one of the last mines still worked, and a rarity in this modern age. It's greyness standing out against the finely cut grass that lead back to the pier, the pubs and the rows of little cottages with their straight curtains and polished doorsteps.

The men down below were hard at work, not noticing the figure at the top of the bank, watching them carve deeper and deeper. They didn't care that it was nighttime and that the rest of the town was coming alive to enjoy the varied nightlife. They had a job to do. She watched them work, their muscular bodies working the earth.

Of course, like everything else, those in Westminster couldn't help but make mining a political football – something for them to argue about, but still these men just worked the land, as had probably been done for generations, their fathers before them. She looked at the grey slate piled at the side – a testament to the earth's evolution - and thought about small she was in comparison to the volcanic ash and clay of years gone by that had slowly compressed and lay silently in the ground until it was plucked from the earth by mankind.

Cut into the side of the mine, was a lone, winding access path, access to the site for those working hard in its guts. It snaked down the side of the mine, steep and narrow having been laid so long ago. The wind was picking up again now, and she pulled at her coat and took her first step. Her coat was already done up against the weather, but this simple if not useless action made her feel as if she was further protecting herself from the elements, from what was going on in the world.

She made her way down slowly at first. Some of the small white stones the path had been laid with slid slightly and she gasped. She soon got into a rhythm though and her trust in herself grew. She jumped further down the path to create more distance between her and the top of the mine, further and further from the winds cold and immediate touch; but taking her closer and closer to where the men worked, closer to distracting them with her unauthorised presence. The pull of the mine was great and here she was near dusk, exploring the uneven terrain, for fun, for kicks, going faster and faster. Soon she began not to care if she slipped, just needing to take the risk, to bet on black and see how the chips fell.

She was brought partially to her senses when some of the stones started to fly, their uneven edges scratching at her ankles. A voice in her head told her she needed to slow down, but soon she had reached the bottom of the hill. She was sure she had never run that quickly before, and she never felt so free. She looked back up the shaft and felt that she had flown down.

Lost in her own thoughts, she didn't realise that the shift in the stones had alerted the miners to her presence. It wasn't until a tall man emerged from behind her and put his hand on her shoulder that she realised what she had done. She stumbled over her words looking down at her feet, suddenly feeling very insecure in her actions: "I am sorry – I just needed to get away."

He didn't respond. She lowered her face, feeling embarrassed that she had invaded the space of these men, when she hated anyone invading her own. He slowly spoke having taken in her alien presence: "It's getting dark. It's not safe down here. My men might not realise you are there." She looked up, startled. She recognised that voice. She began to shake and moved round to face him, moving them both to bring his features into the last light from the sun, bringing out thoughts long lost to the back of her mind.

"Josie?!" whispered the voice. There it was

again, that voice. So sweet, so lilting, and so familiar.

"Richard!" she gasped. She remembered him now. Indeed, she never forgot. Their affair had been fleeting and no one in the hall had even known. She looked him up and down. He hadn't changed in all those years – a few more tattoos, but basically the same slender physique, honed by physical activity. His familiar white t-shirts showing off the strength of his body, under the battered old bikers jacket she had worn when no one else was around, when no one else could see. "What are you doing here?!" she stumbled. "Last I heard you were teaching!"

He laughed: "I was, but I was sick and tired of being unable to get on with the job. It seemed to come with so many distractions. Doing this I can see what I have achieved day to day and then leave it behind.." He paused for second: "Plus, of course, it's easier to get a space for the bike than in stinky old London town!" he laughed. "And what about you? You sick of London?"

She looked surprised. She had no idea he knew where she had been all those years and wondered briefly why he had never got in touch. He saw the look on her face and smiled, "Oh yes, Miss Josephine. I have thought and wondered about you. I wondered about getting in touch, but I never quite had the courage. You always seemed to be onto the next thing, the next project, never standing still. I never expected to find you here though, back in this place."

She laughed: "Just here to have a break. Spend some time up at the castle, go into our old hall, walk up those winding stairs and look at the dirty roof…."

"They cleaned it," he said, "things change, even here."

She looked straight into his big blue eyes, "Well how about a trip into the past? A game of Jenga. It seems fitting somehow." He nodded, and called back to his men, who had become distracted by the interruption to their flow, to their working day. "Don't worry about this one, I will make sure she gets off the mine safely," and with that he offered her his hand, "Time to go."

She clasped his hand, just enjoying the moment. They quickly made their way to the top of the mine, his long legs stretching forward with impatience. She knew at that moment that no matter what was going on in London, in her real life, she had made an impression here, one that couldn't be tainted by implication and gossip, and she wanted to savour it. It started to rain. They quickened their pace as the rainfall became more intense. He took his jacket off – and wrapped it round her shoulders like he had done before.

When she got to the top of the mine, she felt slightly faint and a bit giddy with excitement. She looked along the path back towards the civilised world and steadied her thoughts. The sound of the rain pounding reminded her of the rotor blades on a helicopter – one long whirring noise, a reminder again of the power of mother nature, and how like ants the human race were in its presence. Puddles of water sprayed up against her legs as she ran through them soaking her legs and getting into her shoes.

Racing back to the front of their old college, they were soon back in the town, in front of the faded blue front of the Bowling Alley. Richard opened the door and she quickly headed through, keen to get out of the elements. She looked around her. Its faded wallpaper stood proudly, a monument to the many young people who had come and gone. He took her hand again and she gasped inwardly. He led her to the raised sitting area and signalled to the staff. She wasn't sure what he ordered but she didn't particularly care.

They sat down together in the corner, the sound of pins knocking together prompting yells and sighs from the students playing. She saw the battered games were still there and wondered how many dates had been started at that very table. He reached down and pulled out the box just as their drink arrived. True to type, there was that caramel liquid that smelt so strongly of the charcoal filtered barrels it had rested in before being bottled. She smiled and took a sip. Still it burned the back of her throat as it went down, but it hit the spot: 'Right," she said, "Ready to be thrashed?"

"Always." he winked.

Just at that moment, her phone beeped into life. Josephine looked at her phone. A missed call. A message. She had wanted to find out what had changed, but she wanted to stay in the present, away from everything. Whatever Rebekah had to say would be important no doubt but was unlikely to make her happy.

At that moment the bricks crashed on to the table and she laughed, unable to stop herself from making an involuntary whooping noise. She looked at Richard and smiled. He sat there with a sad face: "I know I expected a whipping, but I didn't think it would be such a public spectacle." She leaned over the table to him and he took her hands in his. She marvelled at how rough they were, but how good that felt.

Her phone was still flashing, and she pulled away slightly: "I need to know what this message says," she said and breaking loose from his grip, she put the phone to her ear. Quickly she listened into the phone, listened to the message that told her that Rebekah was outside the new offices but that it raised more questions than it answered meaning they needed to regroup.

As the message unfolded her face went from confused to resigned through to determined. Finally, she sighed. How and why was Sharon involved, and what did this imply about her relationship with Charlie? Had they been carrying on for the entire time he had been seeing her? She wondered for a second, waiting for the pain of the revelation, and yet there was none. It was amazing how the heart was so strong, that it could protect itself when it needed to.

She just knew she needed to understand exactly what was going on, to bring common and decent goals back to the office. Everything else was gone. He had categorically denied that he had even been involved in the industry. Conor in turn, his friend, had an undisclosed interest in the industry and land that could be used to provide coastal energy. All this at the same time that the Bill was going through Parliament. A Bill that could be very lucrative for those that had an understanding of how to make sure the financial benefits were maximized, and one in which he had taken a great personal interest. Accident? Maybe. But not likely.

She looked at the clock and Richard's quizzical face. There was absolutely nothing she could do. It was far too late. Suddenly, she realised she had been sitting in silence for a good few minutes and smiled. She had come back here for a purpose. To find herself. She knew what she had to do. She was that mine, with all its crags, and all its depth. Not perfect. Not simple but strong and more imposing than anyone could ever imagine unless they saw it in the flesh. She could take strength from inside herself, feel confident in herself, walk her own path. She had a long way to go, and the path was treacherous in the dark, but she knew she had the strength to do it.

"Are you alright Josie?" Richard finally asked.

"Yes," she responded, and for once she knew she would be. "I need to leave tomorrow morning. But we have tonight," she said, a smirk dancing on her lips as she pulled him away from the table towards the door.

Chapter 18

They sat on the lone bench together underneath the station roof. The automatic indicator on the platform showed that it was fifteen minutes until the cross-country train would come through to take her back to London. It had been 24 hours since she first arrived at the little seaside village, and that time had been spent reminiscing about old times, a place she had felt safe. She hadn't told Richard anything about what had brought her there, not really, but she was grateful that she had found him, allowing her the perfect outlet to kick back and get some perspective.

The minutes ticked by and they sat in a peaceful silence, just enjoying the familiar comfort of each other until Richard told her simply: "I have no real idea why you ended up back here, but you must have faith in yourself. Don't let anyone wind you up or give you that red mist. Take the time to think it all through before responding to any provocation. No impulsive decisions."

She smiled. He didn't know how accurate he was. Charlie had tried to force her position, and she still didn't know why he had reacted to her like that when she was just trying to do her job. After all, it was in everyone's best interests to make sure there could be no way in which the department could be criticised.

"And what about you?" Josephine asked, turning towards him. She smiled: "I hope I haven't got you into too much trouble by interrupting your work schedule, pulling you away." She stopped for a second and took his hand, "But I can't even tell you how much you have helped me to straighten out my thoughts. You were just there, letting me prattle my nonsense." He smiled, sad at how transient it had been, but a perfect reunion, nonetheless. A perfect opportunity to get lost in their own world until the sun rose.

Her phone rang and she looked at Richard, knowing she had to answer it. She heard a familiar voice on the other end, and was just about to speak when the train pulled in. She quickly mumbled that she would call back in a minute and put the phone down. This was her cue, but she had a few more seconds to give. They stood and she pulled Richard close to her, breathing in his musky smell. Friends in the past, friends in the future, apart for the present.

She looked at him square in the eye and ran her hand down his chin, his slight stubble rough on her hands. The call came over the tannoy and she turned to take the couple of steps up into the carriage. Moving along the carriage to find herself a seat she looked out the window but there was no time before the train picked up speed and flew down the track.

She slowly brought the phone into her

245

hands and looked at the last number. She watched whilst the number slowly connected before putting the phone to her head and began to speak, pleased that there was no one in the carriage so she could speak freely: "Hi, yes, I am on my way back now. it was great to get away to clear my mind, but I am now ready for the fight. What have you found out?"

Rebecca took a breath. "I'm afraid it's all rather confusing," she started. "We have the address of the business but it's in the centre of London, and the last known occupant on the electoral roll is Sharon. Also, Charlie was there, and it looked like it wasn't his first time in the building. I am sorry." Josephine took a sharp intake of breath and sat back in her seat. None of this really made sense. Why would Conor change the address to a London location, and to Sharon's home address? It wasn't based where the work was happening, and she wasn't an entrepreneurial type having always wanted the security of a paycheck.

"What does this mean?" Jospehine stuttered "Why would she be involved - why would it even be necessary? Have you spoken to anyone else about this? Is there anyone we can trust?"

Slowly, Rebekah started speaking on other end: "I have no idea why business is being handled in this way but there is no way this is a holding address for a dormant company. The Council website shows there have been requests for planning permission, all of which are directed towards this one address. In addition," she paused for a second "it seems that there are numerous references to a pending patent. Of course, there is only a limit to what is public information, but I told Jeremy and he made some enquiries as the local MP. Turns out the changes are pretty dramatic."

Josephine paused for a second: "Are you sure we can trust him?"

Rebekah nodded down the phone "I think so. He seems to certainly share our concerns and that it's his responsibility to keep a watchful eye regarding what's going on."

Josephine found her voice: "Well it's quite simple, we need to find out what those changes are. Leave it with me."

Josephine put the phone down and looked at her watch. She knew where had to go. She pulled up the website of the patent office on her phone. A press release on the front page gave her all the information she needed about the new starter she needed to speak to. One she had been meaning to get back in touch with. It didn't matter that it was a photo, Ed's soulful eyes looked up at her. He had moved department about 18 months ago. A step up the ladder that was duly deserved. His office wasn't far away. It would take her no time at all. She stopped suddenly. He didn't even know she was on his way. She was acting on instinct now, but that didn't mean she should lose her manners.

She was pleased when he answered

immediately, and he told her to come to his office. Thank god for modern communications, and the fortuitous timing of a lunch break at the same time she was going to hit London. She still wasn't sure what she wanted to say, but she knew that this was a good a place to start. All she could do now was wait.

Soon enough, she was there. She was quickly allowed through, having a secure pass, and moved towards the open meeting area. Ed was already ensconced in a meeting pod in the main shared office space, an intense look on his face as he flipped through some papers. He always was so keen to see her. Nothing she asked of him seemed to be too much trouble. She hoped this good luck wasn't about to run out.

He stood up as she approached, and he looked her up and down. She was still the same, if anything ever so slightly more beautiful, but she had a slightly haunted look on her face. It was obvious that she had rushed over from somewhere. Always rushing and unsure what was driving her but driven, nonetheless.

She approached him quickly and took his hand. "Thank you for seeing me at such short notice, can we go somewhere with a bit more privacy? What we need to discuss is of a delicate nature," she started. She looked at her shoes. She hated asking for favours but knew he was her best shot.

"Of course," he responded, warm in his welcome and he took her over to a meeting room and closed the door. "From our brief chat, you wanted to talk through the technological patents that have be submitted for the energy sector? he started. "I am slightly surprised at the interest I will say. I thought the Government was actively encouraging further technological developments and would want it to be easy for projects to get through the process."

He looked at her expectantly. He was sincere in his questions, and she didn't quite know how to put her response. She had to be careful about how she phrased the questions she was about to ask, and what fears she could publicly admit to. "Oh, we are," she replied breezily, "so I am just undertaking due diligence really. Checking what we are doing is having the effect we are expecting and want." She looked at him again. She was trying to sound really casual in her tone. She didn't want to give too much away when she didn't know where this rabbit hole was going to lead.

"Anyway," she continued, "The Government wants to do a general assessment of what kind of things are coming through the system to check that we have correctly matched the support available with the types of technology that can be developed."

"Hmmm, true," he agreed. "No-one needs legislation that isn't fit for purpose, and that holds even more just before a general election."

She smiled, pleased that she had tickled his nerdy-bone, and tried to hide the fact that she was pulling herself slightly further upright as he pulled out the documentation and skimmed through it. He nodded "Right, we have three on the books at the moment in this area, all massive projects that will benefit the industry." He stopped for a second, "So, two of the projects adapt old technology to ensure that the energy source is cleaner by primarily using renewables but with the understanding that there would be a need for more traditional energy sources when it the wind doesn't blow or the waves don't come in." He then stopped for a second, "But I think it's this one that's the most interesting, and a clear match for what the Government is trying to do. It doesn't just look to make energy cleaner by introducing a renewable element. Instead, it uses renewables both the immediate source of energy – and the back up through efficient storage. The technology is very innovative in fact. Genius."

Josephine sat forward slightly on her chair. She knew that she was using a favour to eek about more information whilst she was here, but she had a feeling that this was the key to working out what was going on. Cocking her head to one side, she knew what she had to ask: "So.... who is the amazing entrepreneur who has created such innovative technology? The company name maybe. A contact?"

He looked at her and moving slowly forward towards her he brought his lips to her ear, he whispered: "Conor Black. He's the man behind the technology but he has a working partner based in East London at a company called Carter, Johnson and Hick and she is to be the main contact regarding paperwork."

Josephine took a breath in. The meeting at the house between him and Conor where he first heard those names. The lie he told her that Conor's business was in trouble. The fact that Charlie was seen at Sharon's house. The anger Charlie felt when he thought she was asking too many questions about his business interests. There had to be a connection.

She looked up and Ed was watching her carefully, slightly confused at her reaction. The picture was beginning to form in her mind, and she took Ed's hand and looked him in the eye, "That's perfect - that's all I needed." He looked at her, pleased that he seemed to be such security to her but knowing that look, he knew she had things to do. "Pleasure, as always, glad to be of help."

She took his hand "Bye, Ed and thanks." She really did mean it, and she didn't want to leave him stranded considering how honest he had been with her, but she knew that she had to fight this fight on her own.

Walking out, she wondered where she could take this next. Her last contact with Charlie had not been massively friendly, and whilst her and Sharon tolerated each other, she couldn't just turn up at the house. It would massively intrusive. Plus, they would wonder how she even got the address. She didn't need them to know what she was up to. If there was an unholy alliance going on, she needed to unpick it first before she went to anyone with her findings.

It then occurred to her. Bring in a professional. She picked up the phone and phoned the direct number for Nick's office. She had to balance how much she wanted to say but she knew that he was her best chance in finding a way of discovering what was going at that property without being personally liable. Plus, he was so very loyal to his staff and those associated - and she would always be Rebekah's best friend, so he may not ask too many questions.

The phone started ringing, and Nick answered tersely - a sign of his extraordinary efficiency in a 24-hour media age. She took a deep breath. "Nick," she finally said, "I need your help. It seems our hunch was right. I can't say too much but there have been some unexpected developments - an unexpected change in the confirmation statement and it would just be worth checking it out. Can I meet you face to face so I can tell you exactly what we need to do?" She smiled at the response he gave down on the phone and closed her eyes as she confirmed: "Can I meet you there? I will text you the address now." A second later, Nick's mobile beeped and he saw the address. He was immediately at ease. He could help her out whilst checking out his other interest in that area. Nothing really passed him by.

Chapter 19

Sharon came through from the other room with a stack of post in her hand. She offered it to Charlie with a smile on her face. She just couldn't help herself. There was no doubt about it. She had been more than slightly offended by his casual dismissal of her concerns when that waif had started at the office, but that was a long time ago now. He was there back in her house and they were about to embark on a most exciting project.

She knew how to handle him now, and he always came back to her. He needed her. Just in a slightly different way. She had told him about her childhood, that many of her parents' generations didn't care about how they looked or how they behaved. All they cared about was that there was enough money to go the pub. Their last thoughts of progression dying with the collectivization project – never able to start again. Her life was going to be different. She would have comforts they could only have dreamed of.

She viewed this as her security. She would do what he asked regarding the business and he would give her the life she craved. There would certainly be enough for her even after he had taken his cut from the dividends. The champagne she could never afford on her normal salary and the jewelry none of her boyfriends would be able to afford, even if they had the taste to pick it out. All she needed to do was set up another bank account but that was easy enough. Carter was an anglicisation of her name, and all she needed to think was another permutation.

She looked around at the flat. It still had the old-fashioned furniture and baroque style paintings on the wall, the faint smell of Imam bayildi deeply embedded in the walls. It was large for a central London flat, and a family home long before Sharon had moved back in when her mother died in order to take advantage of the peppercorn rent.

They had had many a night there waking up the neighbours, and now she wanted to be his kingmaker. He might try and persuade himself that she was just a nominal shareholder to protect his identity from prying eyes, but nevertheless, he was only able to do what he was doing because she was looking after him.

He took the post from her and sat down at the table. Opening each letter one by one he lay out the documents in order. He looked over them once he had finished. The patent was now underway. There was nothing that could be done to prevent Conor's company having a key technological breakthrough, whilst he could ensure that the operational and training tasks were undertaken by his company using his knowledge of the industry and the law to ensure that they got maximum benefit. He smiled, not that anyone knew that considering the fact that Sharon had now been confirmed as the nominee shareholder. It was genius. They would be able to charge what they wanted for their specialist services, whilst they would get tax relief under the new legislation which would help build the business quicker than would otherwise be possible, whilst Sharon took a cut before siphoning the majority of the dividends to himself.

He smiled again as she approached him. He knew what she was after and that she wouldn't be put off that there was anyone else in the house, but they still needed to be careful. There was no doubt about it - she loved passionately – open and without shame, and he was her biggest obsession of all. She put her arms around his neck and kissed him softly. Her hands started to move down his body just as he was picking up the paperwork. She made to scatter it on the floor but felt his body language slightly harden. He looked at her face and pushed a strand of hair out of the way. Her hair was untamed just like she was. "Not yet. Not with Conor here. We have to be professional," he quietly pacified her. "There is too much to do, but I promise you we will go away soon. Just the two of us. Find somewhere on 'www.I don't care where we go if the nights are long.com." She smiled.

At that moment, Conor walked in, pleased to see the scene in front of him. His dream team together, all there for different reasons, but for one result. Money. "So, do you have everything you need?" he asked Charlie.

"Yes, I think so," came back the reply, "and I have the mole problem under control, so I think we are done for tonight."

Conor looked at him, reading the cue as Sharon nodded, pleased that the evening had opened up again unexpectedly. She still had it. Confident in herself she knew the rest of the night was hers and she opened the door to encourage him to leave. Looking at Charlie, Conor saw he was slightly surprised at the chutzpa being used to head him out the door, but Charlie seemed happy enough. Conor turned to shake Charlie's hand before heading into the night's air, not noticing the camera click on the other side of the road.

Chapter 20

The noise in the pub was extraordinary. He would never have come if it hadn't been necessary to meet under such conditions, but whilst he was sure everything was continuing normally, Jodie must have something interesting to say if she was insisting on having a meeting outside work hours. Her huge pay per hour didn't change for consultations in the evening and she was always insistent that she was uncontactable unless an emergency once the sun was down. This time, she had been quite specific that they should meet somewhere that no one would think they would be.

She watched them finish their drinks and began to speak: "I know I have raised this before, and I know that you feel it's under control but I do wonder if you have just put in too many applications to the council and patent offices at the same time."

Charlie looked down the list of proposals. "Yes," he started, "there is no doubt that this is a big project but we know that the council is just interested in increasing their business revenue, and even if a local councillor did decide to take an interest, they are hardly likely to disagree with something so lucrative for the local area, not when they have their own elections next year and only have a small majority of control."

Charlie stood up. He knew what she was saying, and it was all highly irritating. He knew he was riding a thin line, but all he was doing was helping those with the potential to succeed to achieve the reward they were due. "Drink?" he simply said to the other two, and then walked to the bar knowing what they would want, it was nothing if not predictable. On his way, something made him start slightly. He saw that distinctive physique. Damn. He was not supposed to be seen, especially not by someone like him. It was just too irritating. He carried on walking towards the bar and stood right behind him. Getting close enough that his target couldn't escape. he coughed, knowing it would be enough.

Jeremy turned around and saw Charlie behind him, his eyes piercing, watching his body language like a hawk. That was Charlie's mode of operation. Make someone feel trapped, and pounce. Don't let them escape. "So," said Charlie, "here we are again. Never the twain shall meet, except we keep seeming to find our paths crossing again. So, who's going to help out whom out this time."

Jeremy straighten his back, "I don't know what you mean!" he said dismissively turning back towards the bar to order the drinks.

"Oh, I think you do," said Charlie cramming his body in beside the smaller man, "I know that you have a crush on that little newbie in Patrick's office, and I think you owe me."

"Really?" Jeremy repeated, "I don't know what you mean. I am just here for a drink, minding my own business." He hated that Charlie could still read him, but he didn't need to admit that was the case.

Charlie sneered, looking him up and down: "Of course, who says she would ever go for you, I don't think you would ever be her type, but maybe you can try and use the small amount of charm you do have to find out how their due diligence is coming along and if they have the all information they need."

Jeremy looked down, counting to 10 to stop himself reacting. "And why would you care? Why don't you ask her yourself? After all, someone of your importance hardly needs an introduction from someone like me."

Charlie rose himself up: "True, but you must understand that those within the department can be a bit intimidated by me and I don't want her to be liberal with the truth. The election means I need to keep an eye on what's going on, need to know everyone is onside in making sure the Government's legislative agenda stays on track.

"If you want me to spy on her," Jeremy retorted, "Tell me straight. Play a straight game." Charlie smiled, his mouth slightly opened and his eyes beginning to glint "Straight?" he said, "A straight game." he said, "I think that's a bit rich from you. I don't think you played a straight game when you were running for your selection. Always the good boy, huh? Not one iota of trouble in your rosy-cheeked life, nothing swept under the carpet in your race to rise above your humble beginnings."

Jeremy faltered slightly. He didn't want to think about it, but he couldn't deny an element of truth in what Charlie was saying, and he didn't like it. He didn't even want to think about it or discuss it.

At that moment, a group of youngsters approached the bar, and Charlie looked at them dismissively. All dressed in ripped jeans, they were typical of the youth of today and the type of people he was trying to avoid by not coming to places like this. One girl among them, with bright green hair stood out. He looked her up and down assessing her. She seemed more interested in her phone. As fake as her selfies.

Moving them both away from the noise, Charlie knew that he needed to make sure Jeremy absolutely understood what he meant. "You will find a way of making sure that they are on track, and you will make sure you keep me informed in that very honest way you do," said Charlie. "After all, we protect each other don't we. Remember, remember, the 16th of November, with doors that were smashed cos of pot."

Jeremy's face crumpled at the recollection. "You wouldn't do anything, and it's been far too long for it to be of any interest to anyone now," he whimpered. Charlie sneered: "Are you sure of that? One word from me and you will be recalled as quickly as it will take that young girl to do something stupid for her Instagram followers," he said flashing a look at the girl who hadn't moved from the bar as she hadn't got quite the right shot yet.

Jeremy knew he was right. No deed ever went unpunished and the older generation of his association members would have very little sympathy with mis-demeanours, no matter how small. Plus, the fact that they hadn't been told previously would drive them mad. Jeremy would be insane to risk it. "I can't interfere in department business," Jeremy said quietly.

"Oh of course not," Charlie responded, "but it's every Government MPs responsibility to help us win that general election." Jeremy nodded sadly. He knew that Charlie had him over a barrel. It was an expensive joint and one that won't ever leave his system at this rate. "Good boy," Charlie smiled. He patted him on the shoulder. "Now scoot!"

Watching Jeremy leave with his shoulders slumped, Charlie approached the table where Conor and Jodie had been sitting waiting for their drinks. Seeing their expressions, he looked at his watch. It was getting late, and he knew that they had been waiting for a while, but he had needed to make his point and he had. He put the drinks down. "Here you go," he said. "Are you not joining us again?" asked Conor.

"No," Charlie responded, "I don't think we can do anything else tonight and you have given me a lot of food for thought so I need to go home now to work out how to make sure all your concerns are addressed. I hope you understand."

The other two nodded. They knew that when Charlie was in a mood like this there is little that can be done. He had been edgy since he got the club, and his mood had not exactly improved, though he seemed somewhat more focused, like something had fallen in place in his head. Anyway, it didn't matter to them, he will have settled the bill so they would be able to stay where they were for a while, whilst Charlie went to do whatever it was that would give him release tonight.

Chapter 21

Patrick's parties were definitely the place to be, and the two girls made sure they arrived on time. Josephine and Rebekah entered the room, passing two doormen, each resplendent in their uniform of a black long-tailed coat, white bow tie, and a silver-gilt waist badge of office. They passed over the threshold and instantly drinks were thrust into their hands.

A massive room overlooking Whitehall, it had been given to Patrick as a special favour due to his career as a respected and senior officer of the House. The space was set aside for him to do with what we wanted. It was within his nature to make sure he spent his working life immersed in the department, but it didn't stop him for using the room to relax with his friends, and tonight was one such evening.

Josephine felt her gut slightly tighten. Even having had been in her role for a while now, she was always staggered by the opulence of her surroundings. Of course, Patrick was very particular regarding how it was furnished, making sure that the whips provided him with the best furniture available from the Parliamentary stocks, and that he was allowed to provide the finishing touches out of his own pocket.

It was within the very old part of

Parliamentary Estate with walls of stone, high ceilings and Victorian scroll cornicing. The huge windows overlooked Cloister Court, and they were framed by fine purple silk lined curtains that stretched the full length down, allowing them to caress the floor. The carpet was, of course, in the traditional green of the House of Commons, but Patrick had placed Persian rugs on top to ensure that the office reflected his own individuality.

Two handmade Chesterfield sofas sat proudly in the corner by the fireplace, the brown leather freshly cleaned and fed, whilst the main mahogany boardroom table had been pushed back to hold the plethora of drinks and snacks available to the guests. Josephine approached the table to see the plentiful buffet for herself and looked around. So many members of the political elite in one place. A normal Tuesday night.

This evening had one difference though, Josephine thought. This was the evening that she was going to start the fight back. She looked at her watch. Though he wasn't there yet, she knew that this was not an evening that Charlie would miss. Her eyes wandered over the assembled crowd and she wondered whom she could trust amongst the sharp suits and elegant dresses.

She spotted Jeremy slowly moving his way round the room, talking to everyone. He looked up from his conversation, noticing her watching him. His eyes crinkled, smiling at her, but in a flash, it was gone, and his attention was with the person he was talking to, her hand on his arm.

Josephine looked closely at the figure alongside him. She would recognise that hair cut anywhere. Freya. A new MP, she had seemed to have caught the mood of the Government. A slow burning and self-depreciating maiden speech had meant that she had been left alone by the Whips to find her own way, and she seemed to have used this to spend night after night scribing amendments to any bill that took her fancy - and the Energy Bill was no different.

She thought of envelope after envelope that arrived in the internal post, a missive from the Speakers Office regarding the inclusion of these amendments in the committee meetings. They all seemed to follow a similar line though, further clarifications surrounding the fiscal strategy. Further guidelines to ensure the money trickled into the industry. Nothing unusual about that. In fact, ahead of an election transparency had to be positively encouraged. However, it was unusual for quite this number to get approved without any real debate or opposition.

Suddenly Freya made him laugh at loud. A guttural reaction, and Josephine couldn't help but breath in sharply. How could he be having fun on a night like this. She suddenly doubted herself. Maybe she overstepped the mark with Charlie. Maybe she had got caught in someone else's fight.

Maybe she shouldn't have pushed him. Maybe it wasn't her place.

Dismissing the thought quickly, she saw the back of his head. He was there, playing the crowd. Charlie really did never change. Still smart and lithe, charm itself. He was dressed impeccably in a crisp black suit with an outlandish tie that could only be pulled off by someone that was classically handsome. His magnetic smile attracting the crowds, he was still able to flirt with the women, and the men at his whim if his mood took him.

Her eyes narrowed. There was no end to what he would do if it benefited his mission, she knew that now. Indeed, quickly enough, with reassurances of phone numbers and drinks promised, Charlie had managed to slip away from the crowd and take position at the side of the room. Patrick quickly joined him, and they soon looked to be locked in a very intent conversation. Girls lined up to pass him, flicking their hair to catch his attention, but they now went largely ignored, to be picked up at a later stage.

She watched the body language of the two men. God knows what they were discussing. He still came to the office but didn't engage with her anymore apart from the bare necessities. Their liaison had stopped almost as quickly as it had started, though no one would have known there had ever been anything other than a work relationship in the first place. He seemed to be able to mask it all, and she was certainly not going to highlight it. She felt embarrassed and stupid. It was obvious to her now that she had completely overplayed it in her own head and that it had meant nothing to him.

Bright eyes, he called her, burning like fire. She thought it was a compliment. Instead, he burned her like she meant nothing. Emotion, she had begun to understand, did not stand a chance with him. She knew she was getting stronger, but sometimes, like now, watching him, still made her feel quite angry with herself.

She saw Rebekah watching her with quiet contemplation and broke the silence. "Watching him now is so confusing," she started. "I really thought Charlie wanted to know how it was all going because he was interested in helping me out, making sure I was on the right path, but I really was just useful, wasn't I?"

Rebekah felt saddened for her friend. What seemed to be becoming more apparent was that Charlie always expected to have the upper hand, that she wouldn't ask any questions regarding what he was doing, even if there was any provocation. After all, she hadn't hunted down such a connection. Josephine had trusted where the relationship had been going, that she had a mentor, a lover and a friend. In reality, she questioned one thing and he turned. "I know. But think about it this way," she smirked. "You have the joy of knowing that Sharon really does have your sloppy seconds."

Josephine couldn't help but laugh, a spontaneous noise that she really hadn't felt capable of for quite a while now. She saw Jeremy approaching and they held their arms out to welcome him. Swooping in quickly he had brought over more drinks. Handing them over, they greeted him in unison.

"What are you, my favourite two girls up to?" he asked,

"Oh, just musing on the futility of life," replied Rebekah. Well it wasn't a lie and she knew instinctively knew that Josephine wouldn't want him to know she had ever found herself under Charlie's power. Josephine smiled, happy to have someone in her life that she could trust.

Seeing them move across to the other side of the room, and out of lip-reading distance, Charlie made an excuse to leave Patrick to approach the drinks table. He couldn't be too unsubtle, but it was fair enough that he wanted another drink. After all, everyone else was tucking in spectacularly to Patrick's supply of whiskey straight from the Speakers own selection, and the wine from the cellars under the estate so there was no reason why he shouldn't make use of the hospitality too.

He knew he had to trust Jeremy to do his job though. Josephine had already got under his skin too much, and he wondered briefly if his ability to keep his temper had just made her more inquisitive. He shrugged to himself. It didn't matter. He would find out exactly what she knew and make sure she was silenced if it was going to spoil his plans. Nothing was going to get in his way this time. Charlie watched the girls as the conversation progressed. The girls seemed so innocent, and he wondered why he had been worried. They were no match for him.

He thought back to his time with Josephine. He smiled to himself. She was full of energy, young and beautiful. But she didn't know when to stop. Yes, he confirmed to himself. None of this was his fault. He was right to let her go, so she could find someone else, move on and be happier with them than he could ever have made her. In breaking her down, he was setting her free and making the ultimate sacrifice.

Then there was Jeremy. Still the patsy. Still in hock to those better than him, even though he hated it. He just didn't understand his place. Of course, that's what made him so perfect for a job like this. No one would suspect him. After all, everyone knew that there was universal promotion of the meritocracy now. No one would suspect that him of all people could be bought, that he wouldn't stand up and be counted. Charlie watched closely. Nothing could possibly go wrong. Knowledge was power and he was setting himself up to have it all.

Just at the moment, the phone rang and

recognising the number, he knew he had to take it. He quickly moved out of the room, and quickly walked towards a door that lead to a meeting space set back from the main corridor. Setting himself up in one of the breakout pods, he knew he would now be able to take care of business in private, and soon he was listening intently to what was being said on the other end.

Though he was trying to be quiet, his natural arrogance was ever-present and the message was obvious: "It's all in place," he was saying: "A number of amendments have been put down by the ever-obliging Freya, amendments that will be easy to follow in practice, that's a given. Of course, she has been given the credit, that the Government is following her lead but we both know the truth. Anyway, it doesn't matter, no one will object to anything like this so it's pretty much a done deal."

He laughed heartily. The voice on the other end purred away: "I agree. Once this final piece is in the place, there will be no going back. Older technology will be obsolete with us at the forefront of the new world order in every sense of the word and those that doubted us behind the door desperate and on the edge." He stood up to his full height: "Well, it couldn't happen to a nicer set of people don't you think?"

His voice lowered, turning his head and slightly sneering he said, "No, I am the government. I will make sure that no one will forget that and try

271

and throw a spanner in the works. I have been locked out before, and I will not be locked out again."

With that he put the phone down, his eyes closed thinking about the legacy he was about to put in place. This was not just on making this a success for the Government. This was a much more personal campaign, with potentially unsuspecting individuals to be sacrificed in order to make good his own potential.

He walked back into the main room, and spotted Jeremy, who was just leaving the girls side. He went up behind him and cleared his throat. Jeremy's shoulders tightened. He knew he would be getting the Spanish Inquisition, but he didn't realise it would be so immediate. He turned around, and Charlie got straight to the point. "So, what did the girls say?"

Jeremy looked serious: "Well, I have set the scene nicely, but I need a little more time to get a complete picture of all their dealings. Don't worry though it's in hand."

Charlie looked at Jeremy, taking in his facial expression and body language. Jeremy stood still. He didn't know what else Charlie could possibly want. He had done everything that had been asked of him so far. Charlie cocked his head and put his arm around Jeremy's shoulders. "The girls won't know what's hit them. Not that it matters. That's what they are there for. To do what the

272

Government needs of them."

Jeremy was a good dog. He deserved a treat. "Right," he said, "Come with me, let's get out of here and go to dinner. I think we deserve a proper drink and I know a club with no signs, where you have to knock three times to get in. No one would even know it was there, so all inhibitions are left at the door." Charlie continued, obviously up for a hard night out. Jeremy nodded in agreement. Maybe a blow-out was just what they needed.

Heading out of the door, laughing to themselves, a forlorn figure, stood unnoticed behind the column, in silence. She took it all in. Josephine couldn't quite believe what she had heard. It really was true that in politics you could only trust yourself. She looked round. Rebekah was approaching her hurriedly, seeing the look on her face. "Are you ok? What's happened?" she asked.

"We've been betrayed, again," she started. She didn't know where to put herself, she didn't know what to do. She knew one thing though. Whatever she had said or discussed with Jeremy had gone straight back to Charlie. She had no quarter. She had no break. The nightmare just went on and on.

"What do you want to do?" asked Rebekah

"Can we go somewhere that I have never been with him. A loud bar perhaps, where there is dancing. He hates dancing." She laughed for a second, forgetting that everything she thought she

273

knew about him was falling apart, and that really, she might know nothing about him at all.

Chapter 22

Josephine sat at her desk with her head in her hands. "I don't know what to do," she said to Rebekah.

Rebekah put her hand on her friends back to comfort her: "No one was to know. Obviously the time he spent in Charlie's company had more of an impact than we could have ever realised."

Before she could respond, the postman hurtled through the door with a letter and handed it to Rebekah. They sat in silence as Rebekah finished reading through the contents, and then she smiled, a light bulb going off in her head: "So, lets' think what we do know. We know that Charlie is at least implicated, and that Sharon is playing her part in this sordid situation, so let's stir the pot."

She laid the card on the table. Josephine looked at the invite and smiled. "I see what you mean. Let's speak to Tarquin about the table plan. We can make sure it's just so at the Awards next week."

"Indeed," Rebekah whispered complicity: "Maybe play on some insecurities? After all, it's always a hot bed of gossip, when tempers are most likely to fray as people compete for the top prizes and recognition they deserve. It could be the perfect opportunity to stir up a few emotions."

Tarquin, mused Rebekah. A very old friend,

they had always hung around in the same bars as they were starting out in this odd and complicated world. Of course, busy schedules now meant that those endless sessions of champagne and vodka tended to be a thing of the past, but they still made every effort to go out every three months to their favourite restaurant for an afternoon of drinking, eating and politician spotting.

She brought out her diary and flipped through the pages. It was time for another catch up. The timing was perfect. "Yes," Rebekah nodded, "I can easily sort this." She quickly looked at her watch and wondered out loud. "Indeed, every man has to eat, let's see where he is now!" She texted him quickly, then put her phone down. It hadn't long been back on the table when she caught her breath and watched it ping with a message. She texted back quickly to confirm and leaning across the table, she gave Josephine a hug. She headed out the door, putting her coat on, a determined look on her face.

The route to the restaurant was simple. Just a few doors down from the office, she was soon opening the familiar red doors she knew so well. Even a change of ownership didn't charge the feel of the place. She nodded at the maitre d' who responded by immediately guiding her through the restaurant towards the furthest booth towards the very north of the dining room: "We reserved your usual spot as soon as we heard you were coming in.

Your friend is already here."

Tarquin was sitting at the table, but all she could see were his perfectly manicured nails. He sat, his body relaxed as he read his broadsheet, unlike most others in the restaurant who seemed to prefer an online edition. She approached and he brought the paper down before rising to welcome her to the table. He was dashing in a pinstripe suit, his dark brown hair immaculate, his eyes warm and welcoming. He moved towards her so that he could pull out her chair. "Hello gorgeous," he drawled, the slight tinge of an American accent overlaying the perfect received pronunciation accent that had been instilled into him from his highly expensive public-school education.

"It's so good to see you," he continued and pulled his napkin onto his lap. He continued: "I was just thinking we needed to catch up and here you are - a true sight for sore eyes." Rebekah looked him up and down, a perfect specimen of a man. He would be a perfect catch for any girl that managed to get him to open up, get him to commit. He was an unusual creature though, occasionally driven by a natural human lust but other than that a closed book, as if there was something he would just not give away. Someone who really didn't need other people.

The only one he ever seemed to really trust was Rebekah, but then they had always had a pure type of love. Like a sister for a brother, their relationship completely bypassed sexuality. He looked at her and smiled, reading her face with the skill of a psychiatrist. "So, apart from my dashing good looks and sparkling personality, I get the feeling you need something else from me?"

Rebekah knew there was no point messing around, and that getting business out of the way would mean they could then talk about more personal matters quicker. "I need to you to help me with the table plan at the Lloyd George Awards," she said.

He smiled, his bright white teeth bright in the light. "Well, you always did have a flair for party arrangements," he acknowledged, his way of saying that he was happy to give her what she needed. He brought out his lap-top "This is how it stands at the moment. What were you thinking?"

"Do you trust me?" she asked, and he immediately replied "absolutely." With that, she took the computer off him and made a couple of quick adjustments before passing it back. Looking at the screen, he saw what she had done, kissed his fingertips and blew them away. "Es bellisimo!" he exclaimed, and the deed was done.

Closing the laptop with a snap, he changed tone. "Now," he said, "Let's get on with lunch. I am afraid I have got myself into a little bit of trouble and I need your help regarding how I can possibly resolve it."

Rebekah smiled. It was going to be a fun

afternoon. "Course!" she said pouring herself a glass of wine. "I think we have a lot to discuss."

Chapter 23

The room was buzzing. The names of the shortlisted individuals and teams rolled out over the teleprompter, along with photos that had been taken in the offices the week earlier to increase the fizz surrounding the evening. Certainly, everyone was dressed in their best outfits, the sparkling jewellery drawn out for such an occasion a competition in itself.

Josephine herself had gone for a long black dress with a deep green trim and a slit to the hip to show off her long legs. It was one of a couple of favourite dresses that she had had for many years, and it always hit the mark. She matched it with a beautiful emerald necklace she had purchased many years before, a surprise piece she found in a quaint shop near Oxford Street that she had visited many times since.

She walked over at the table plan and smiled as she took in the layout of the room. Her pleasure soon faded though. She saw Jeremy at one of the tables slowly changing round some cards. She sighed as Sharon approached him and put her arm on his shoulder. Taking the cards out of his hands, she swiftly moved between two tables, and then with a wink her careful plan was in bits. Josephine frowned. They had wanted to keep Jeremy away from them all so he couldn't stick his nosy beak in.

Instead, he was now sitting with Sharon, in prime situ to just stir more trouble.

Rebekah soon came in with Sam, and Josephine approached them. Seeing the unease on her friend's face, Rebekah warmly reached out to her friend, and swiftly lifted two drinks from a passing waiter's tray. Handing one to her friend, they both took a quick sip and looked around at the throng. The room was almost at capacity already because everyone wanted to take advantage of the free bar. It wasn't long, however, until the bell was rung for dinner. Sam picked up Rebekah and swept her into the hall, leaving the girls to quickly clasp hands, their own private signal of good luck.

Josephine was going stag but it didn't bother her at the best of times, let alone when she had work to do. She approached her table and wandered round to find where she was sitting. Standing behind her chair a everyone looked to take their place, she looked round the room. It was obvious why the organisers always paid a lot of money to have the function here. The room itself stretched as far as the eye could see. It was outlined by huge red velvet curtains, that were draped over massive bell ropes that managed to maintain the weight of the material. Each of the tables were decorated with a crisp white tablecloth, whilst in the middle of the tables there was a magnificent floral centre pieces that contained the most beautiful black and white orchids. She looked up. Each one must have been a couple of feet tall on its own.

Completely distracted for a moment, she didn't notice Charlie appear next to her. Turning around, he cleared his throat and she saw a slight look of confusion on his face. The reality of them being together for the first time in so long hit them both. Looking him up and down, she was sure she saw a small amount of nerves, so she spoke first as they sat next to each other on chairs sumptuously covered in black velvet.

"Well this is a turn up for the books isn't it?" she said. Seeing him relax slightly, she proffered the wine that was sitting on the table and he gladly accepted. Pouring the wine, she looked him up and down. The old familiar body she had known so well, in her sphere once again.

Taking a sip from his newly poured drink, she saw Jeremy over on the other table, talking closely to Sharon. Watching them, her mind became clear, and she knew what she had to do. Charlie always wanted to be the centre of everyone's world whether he returned the favour or not, and he would find it deeply frustrating to play second fiddle to someone else. A small victory maybe, but with that she turned to the man on her left and started to make small talk.

A bustle from the kitchens began. Soon enough, the waitresses emerged from behind closed doors to bring the starters, and Charlie watched them for a moment distracted by their syncronised actions. Satisfied that they were making decent progress, he found himself looking at Josephine's long blonde hair curled down her back. He couldn't help but be frustrated. He was there, the man who had held her tightly in his arms, taught her what she knew, and she seemed to be more interested in the fop next to her. He looked at the young man. He had nothing about him, certainly nothing that could match Charlie, but there she was eating her bread roll, making small talk with him and laughing at his jokes and weak attempts to flirt. All the while, he sat there with her back firmly in his direction.

He started to break the bread on his side plate, desperate to keep control of his emotions. He moved his eyes down quickly and concentrated on spreading the butter on the bread one mouthful at a time. It was like his own personal hell. Suddenly he didn't care anymore. Shocked at his feelings, but unable to help himself, he had to get her attention. He had to make her understand his view. He moved slightly so their knees were ever so slightly closer, the thick material of his black suit briefly brushing her leg.

Prepared for most things, she didn't expect any physical contact from him, and she couldn't help but breathe in slightly, a slight sensitivity that just hadn't been quite snuffed out. She knew she had to say something but for a moment she didn't know what. She turned around, and Charlie felt that he was back on top. However, before he could

283

reconcile the triumphant feeling that he was expecting to follow, he just saw the girl he had known, and a slight sadness came over him. He had been used to getting his way with staff all over the estate and he had ended up treating her the same.

He reached out to her, his fingertips approaching hers. "Look at you," he started, "So sure of yourself now. It's so good to see." She moved towards him slightly as her equilibrium was knocked. In her mind she was transported back to their first date, when it was just the two of them again, and he had unnerved her so much that she had ended up talking to herself in the bathroom of the pub in order to try and work out what she wanted from this new flirtation. "Thank you," she managed. "Professionally I owe you a lot. You took the time to show me the ropes. You didn't need to do that." He looked at her, his blue eyes taking on the way he had looked at her all that time ago before other stuff got in the way.

"It was my pleasure," he continued, "Such a bright young thing. You never sold your soul and even now I admire that so much." She looked at him quizzically. He looked down, his brow slightly furrowing: "I was brought up in a household where it didn't matter how you got to the end point, the only thing that mattered was being successful. Having the biggest house, the biggest car, the biggest bank account. Of course, it was always made easier for future generations considering the family connections, the automatic education and the family name, but that was a double-edged sword".

He stopped for a second before continuing, "It made it even more of a kick in the teeth when I was not given a position in the family firm. Swept aside for Fat Bertie, my brother. It just seemed to make life a bit more difficult, that I had to prove myself more, and since then I have had a lot of conflicting emotions, as if I can't quit decide what - or who - is important to me."

He stopped. He was trying to hold back and looked Josephine straight in the eyes once more. She was truly puzzled. She thought back to the image Jeremy had given her about Charlie's background. The bullish cad that only ever did what he wanted that didn't care how anyone else might feel but just wanted to do his own thing. The man that nothing touched so he could concentrate on his work, because that was all that drove him. But then of course, he had turned out to not be so very different. Had she judged him too harshly? Had she just needed to wait until he was ready? Of course, typically his timing was appalling. He would choose now to make this appeal to her softer side, just as she was beginning to close the chapter and close the loop.

She knew she had to steel herself, but she sighed internally. It was very hard to continue feeling so angry with him: "So this meant that when I came to Parliament, I wanted to make my mark. I wanted to show that I was better than the others. I could work hard and play hard. I could bring down opposition bills for breakfast and then go out all night. There were few that really did touch me, but you were one. You seemed to just want to do good, and it made me feel good to be part of that for the time that I was." He picked up the bottle and looked at her, "You were so pure, so unwilling to be tainted by anything or anyone. Unlike others, with only an eye for the main chance."

She looked at his face as he poured the water. A face she had felt up close, seen in anger and seen in ecstasy: "Still?" he said, smiling, "I know my girl." Within two seconds of those words coming out of his mouth his mood suddenly changed, and she saw a sudden fear in his eyes. She then sensed a figure behind him and realised the change wasn't from something he had said, something he had admitted, but it was from the new arrival on the scene.

Taking in a breath, she realised who it was. He mouthed her name in silence as if, somehow, he had to be contrite for his behaviour just now. He turned around and saw the expression on her face. Sharon cocked her head to one side walking away without any words, her manner saying everything. Without a word of explanation, he followed her, leaving Josephine on her own, confused about what had been happening for the last few minutes. She put down her napkin onto the table. She knew one thing though. He hadn't changed. Not really. He still cared more for himself, for the alliances that he had undertaken, even if he knew they were somehow destructive and harmful, and that he would do anything to protect those. Even lie.

She then noticed another movement from the other table, and Jeremy quickly joined her, filing up the now vacant space. She eyed him in silence, unwilling to give anything away. "Hello," she acknowledged coldly, "Having fun with your new friend? I will say you have been busy with all your chatting and reporting general shenanigans," she couldn't help but snap. Jeremy looked down,

"Please trust me," he asked soulfully. Looking up, he got no response, and not knowing what to say, he left the table.

Walking down the corridor, in eerie silence, Charlie realised he was no longer in charge. He was unused to anyone else's mood or feelings telling him what to do, but he knew he had to keep her on track and make sure that the thunderous mood that was building up in her was brought back under control.

The two of them moved away and they found a corner in one of the many seating areas. He faced her, and with that her mood exploded. "How could you!" she started, "with that!" she continued, "When I am risking so much for you. So much for us. It wasn't easy explaining to an accountant why I was suddenly a shareholder in a business that's not only something I know nothing about, but one where the main activity is miles away."

He started to try and explain but was quickly cut off: "You know that for me, it's not about the money. I know that's what drives you, with your weird moral code, your obsession with destroying your family's business, and that the end always justifies the means. For me though, I am helping you out: your lover, your fighter, your rock. A rock you turn you have no problem with turning your back on though, a rock you lock out at the first opportunity. You know what - I hold all the cards. I am the shareholder, not you. Maybe I'll lock you out. See how you like it!"

Sharon's voice was getting louder, and Charlie flapped his hands to try and get her to quieten down. It only made her angrier. "Don't you try and shush me!" she continued, "I have hosted you, and him, that ludicrous man so that you can do your dirty deals in privacy. I have smiled at him and been your go-between to ensure that he had all the information he needed to ensure the patent matches exactly, and this is how you pay me back. Flirtation with that one, now, when you don't need to because you have me." She looked straight at him: "Oh yes, I knew. It all fell into place as you told me what you wanted to do. You made her feel good to make sure that she owed you, but I don't need reminding that you even looked at her, and yet here I am.."

Finally, she stopped and slumped down. Her outrage had left her with no more energy, and he sat down next to her. "You know that I am grateful. You know all my reasons. Legislation is there to make businesses money. It's there to make sure the strongest win, and I - we - are the strongest. Soon enough time will pass that we will be able to forget all about the means and it'll just be you and me, not bound by any rules, any stupid codes of vested interest. You know I only talk to that sanctimonious cow to make sure she is on side. To make sure she suspects nothing."

With that, Sharon smiled. She had him exactly where she wanted him. She knew that he was hers, and that he was just playing a game. She put her hands round his face. "That's all I needed to hear," she said, "We are in this together. So, let's go and solidify our alliance once more." He smiled and he drew her into his arms, kissing her deeply, and drawing her away.

Behind a pillar, a sigh of relief crossed Jeremy's face. He knew that Josephine would believe him now, that he hadn't betrayed her. The portable digital recorder would make sure of that.

Chapter 24

"All of it?" she stammered down the phone, "on its way now?" Her heart leapt into her mouth, not quite able to believe that Charlie and Sharon had been quite that stupid. She mumbled some thanks, sitting down, not quite believing that she was finally going to be able to see this through. That this package would seal her story.

At the same moment, she heard a motorbike whiz outside the house and stop outside. She quickly moved towards the door and before he had even managed to get his helmet off, she had whipped the packet from him and signed the chit. Leaving him slightly bemused on the step she ran back into the house and tore open the envelope, looking at the words on the paper in front of her.

She smiled. It was all there. She picked up the phone to Jeremy and her call was answered immediately: "I have it," she said "and I am going to see the powers-that-be now. Can I come to your office so we can head over together?"

"Yes," he replied, "I am so looking forward to see that bastard get his comeuppance."

She breathed a sigh of relief. This was the most difficult thing she had done. "Thank you so much, see you soon," and she put down the phone before heading outside the house on the hunt for a cab. A mere moment had passed when she saw the flashing yellow light. "1, Parliament Street, quickly!" she said, knowing she had to be specific or she would end up in the wrong part of the Parliamentary Estate.

Looking at the intense expression on her face, the cabbie knew she was serious, and he headed off with his foot on the right pedal. She looked at the package in her hands and put it carefully in her handbag, unaware that the cabbie was watching her through his mirror. He wondered what she was holding but knew he could never ask. All he knew was that there was obviously something serious going down, and he was a small but important part of it. He just hoped he was on the right side.

They raced through the streets whilst sirens wailed through the park towards Whitehall. Soon he pulled up outside the big building he had never been in, but his working life had always been surrounded by. She quickly got out before thanking him and using her pass to disappear behind the locked gates. He drove off. His job done.

Within five minutes she was at Jeremy's office and he was waiting at the door. He welcomed her with a smile. "You ready?" she smiled and tapped her handbag conspiratorially. Jeremy looked at her. It was the only place he wanted to be. He had been waiting for a moment like this for a long time. Charlie was finally going to be judged as anyone else would be.

Jeremy was nervous and he stepped back towards the door, keen to get the package delivered. She put her hand on his shoulder and stopped him. "Just before we go," she said slowly, "What happened? Why did I hear you talking to Charlie about me, about Rebekah, about what we were working on?"

Jeremy sighed slowly and knew what he had to say for their sake and his, he didn't care anymore. "Well it turns out," he started "that to achieve what he wants, Charlie is not below threats and a bit of grubby blackmail. I had to tell him what we have been discussing or he would have told my association about things I am not proud of."

Josephine gasped as he continued: "I have already told you that I had already known him a long time before we went up to university together. What I didn't tell you is that for a while his group of posh boys suddenly took a bit of a shine to having a piece of rough like me around. I can't say that the lunches and dinners weren't nice. Certainly nicer than being on the outside of Charlie's group like it was at school."

He stopped for a second, obviously slightly struggling with the memories that had now been forced into his mind. "It all came to a head one night though. They had got some gear in. Just pot, but they were obviously regularly using, they knew exactly where to go, and it arrived in the private dining room on a silver platter for crying out loud. The honour of going first was given to me and I didn't know how much to do so needless to say it went through my system quickly and I got absolutely stoned. I can't remember much more of the evening, but I do remember the sore hand I had the next day and the fact that the neighbours door was bashed in. Turns out I had got the wrong room but got into a rage thinking someone was playing a joke on me and had locked my dorm room so I would have to sleep in the corridor or something. So, I bashed it in."

Josephine said: "And Charlie bailed you out." Jeremy nodded: "Club rules were that no one told tales. No one wanted the drug use to go public, so they concocted a way of putting the blame elsewhere. Anyway, the janitor got blamed, and he got fired. I was weak but I knew that because I was the local MPs son, such a disgrace would get my father into trouble. So, I kept it to myself, but the feeling of guilt always stuck with me and I made didn't hang around with them anymore. They weren't impressed, they felt they had been kind to let me hang around with them, and my leaving of the group was a betrayal of that. They didn't see that all I saw was that I did the wrong thing, and that I didn't want to be part of a group that could feel it was above the law."

He stopped, spent from the years of pent up anxiety this had caused and glad to get a release.

"So anyway, it was at that moment I knew one day I would make it right. And that's what's happened now. I managed to play both sides and position Sharon in the best position to watch you and Charlie. She always thought you two might have history you know." He looked at her. Her face slightly fell. He quickly put his finger on her lips: "And so what if you do. Charlie is a mistake we all seem to make, don't we?"

Josephine couldn't help but smile. He looked at her intently: "You know I would never betray you. I just couldn't." His voiced quietened: "What I didn't factor in was how hurt you must have been when you thought I had, and I am sorry for that. That's my mistake."

She looked him up and down. She looked at his figure, the way he was standing, and knew he was telling the truth. That he had kept that in for too many years, and now he had got rid of the guilt. Jeremy approached her and put his arm protectively around her. They started walking through the building together. "So, something like this, needs two pairs of safe hands," she said, and she clasped his hand over hers, the envelope the bond that had brought them together. "I better phone ahead to warn them of our arrival."

Soon, they had arrived at Members Lobby, and they both flashed their badges giving their access to the main entrance of the Whip's Office. Her heels clicked across the tiles and she was momentarily back in time, thinking about the first time she had come into this building, and how nervous she had felt then. Now she was here again, hardened perhaps, but still with butterflies in her stomach. She couldn't believe what a way she had come in such a short period of time.

They knocked on the door of the Chief Whip, and the heavy door opened. Josephine's face fell. She realised there had been a recent reshuffle, but it had slipped her mind that now Bernard had been promoted from a pairing whip to the highest honour in that office.

Bernard looked them both up and down and clocked the paperwork in her hand. "Come in Josephine," he said "Jeremy, you should stay here. Clara can get you a coffee whilst you wait." Jeremy nodded. He knew there was no point in arguing with him. If anything, it would just distract away from the mission.

He saw Clara scurry towards the coffee machine silently, the look of someone who had been in a job for far too long on her face. He didn't have the heart to tell her that he disliked coffee and so accepted her offering with a quick nod. Clare moved back behind her desk, he looked at the big wooden door and wondered what they were saying to Josephine, and if she was holding her own in a tough, tough world.

Having closed the door and beckoned Josephine over, Bernard leant back in his chair, and put his hands together. She was certainly bold. Jeremy hadn't said much about why Josephine needed an immediate meeting with him, but the implication was certainly there, and it made him very uneasy. He assessed her body language. He couldn't help but wonder if she had just been tainted by the cynical side of the world in which they lived or if there really was something to her story. All he knew was that he had to be very careful. He had to get this right. The implications spoke for themselves. Someone he had personally trusted had potentially betrayed the office given to him at the highest level.

Josephine looked round the room. She understood that she was being assessed for any weakness and straightened her back, her jaw set. "I know this is all a little bit of a bombshell, especially just before an election," she started "But everything you need to know is here." She put the papers on the table, knowing that she could never unsay these words or undo these actions. He reached out and pulled the paperwork towards him, his eyes giving nothing away as he took the paperwork to read it.

Just at that moment the door opened. "I hope you don't mind," he started, his eyes briefly coming over the papers, "but we need to make sure there was no uncertainty and no inconsistency about exactly what you are saying. I don't want anything to fall between the gaps." He looked at Liam and smiled, beckoning him to the table, "and

the best way of doing that is a second pair of ears."
She caught his eye and sighed slightly. She had seen
Liam's picture on the new intake list of the last
election, and now there he was, to assess whether
or not what she said was true, and yet she couldn't
have her support by her side. He was cast adrift
outside waiting for the outcome.

Liam sat down earnestly, and Josephine
breathed slowly. This was beginning to feel more
and more like she was on trial. She would have to
be able to prove herself categorically. She was
letting the whips office know some serious
allegations and as there was a second pair of ears,
she knew that it would all be noted, with her name
intrinsically attached whether something was done
about it or not.

She leaned forward and moving her eyes
from man to man she repeated herself again: "It's
all there." Bernard looked up again from the
transcript, his mind racing but a cool expression on
his face. His eyes narrowed: "Yes, there is a lot of
information in here," he agreed "but of course, for
there to be a transcript there would have to be a
recorder. So, one has to ask - why was such an
article at such an event, and how do we know that
no one else has a copy of the recording? It was
almost as if you were waiting for him to trip up, are
you sure this isn't a honey trip in some way."

"Yes," piped up Liam "why would you
have such a device with you? Hardly spur of the

moment." Josephine's heckles began to rise. They hadn't even acknowledged what she was trying to say. "All I have wanted to do is my job. To make sure the right people benefit and that everyone that has something to add is able to. The flip side of this is that we need to ensure that there were no risks to the Government strategy through impropriety. Trust me, this is not what I wanted. I just wanted peace and quiet but there was little I could do when a press contact started linking a business primed to thrive in this new world with the man responsible for Government involvement." She looked down at the documents: "Instead I got that."

Bernard was taken aback. This was an unexpected addition to the piece. He knew the press were gearing up to the election, but he hadn't realised that they had any information that he hadn't willingly given or approved. He took his position as guardian of the party's reputation very seriously and he didn't want anyone to think he had missed anything. He looked at Liam, who was busy scribbling notes, and put his hand on the young boys arm: "Just a second, Liam, we know we are dealing with confidential information here, and even in the Whips Office there are two different levels of what needs to be officially recorded and reported back."

Liam stopped writing immediately. It was more than his job was worth, and he had spent three years sucking up to get to become the junior whip. Up to this point, his main job had been to organise the whips dinners. He didn't want to cook his own goose. Josephine knew she had now got his attention and stayed silent to see where the next move would come from. "Press?" Bernard said slowly, "I didn't realise there was any press involvement."

Josephine smiled. She knew he was trying to goad her for information, and that Bernard was wondering how far out of control he had actually been. He spoke slowly, watching her every move: "This is a very serious claim," he started "and I will need a full amount of time with the transcript in order to assess what it means and what the exact implications are. But I have to ask this, how do you know it was not just all fluff or nonsense that was said in anger? After all, it's not like you have been here for long, and could properly understand the context of what was being said."

Josephine's eyes thinned slightly. Did he genuinely not believe her? "You take your time," she replied. "I have another copy so I will read through it again to make sure every word stands up to scrutiny." She rolled her eyes "but I am pretty sure it's self-explanatory".

Bernard stood up. "Well thank you then, I think you can let us work out how this incident will further inform our party procedure and due diligence. We will get back to you in due course. Liam can you show the lady out?"

Standing up, she was shocked. Liam approached her but before he could usher her out, she turned and looked Bernard straight in the eye. "It has to be said Chief, I am rather disappointed in your reaction. Of course, I understand that Charlie is a well known and loved Member of this House. This is not something I would have brought up lightly and I think it has more implications all round than on party procedure or due diligence." "Perhaps," Bernard countered, his voice monotone, giving nothing away. "And now it's down to us." Pointing at the door, Liam scuttled over, and it was time for her to leave. The meeting terminated.

The solid door closed behind her, and Jeremy was waiting in the ante room. "What happened?" he asked, and Josephine just sat down,

"I don't think they believed me," she said quietly. "I think I might have put my reputation on the line for absolutely nothing."

He saw the girl sitting by him, her back hunched as if she had been given a physical beating. Her fair skin ashen and her hands slightly trembling. He couldn't help himself and he drew her close, his arm around her. He helped her stand and quietly put her head on his shoulder. He helped her to her feet, and out the door, leaving the ornate oak office behind.

Chapter 25

From inside the Chief's office, Bernard had enforced silence until the main door clicked shut and he knew they had both gone. The door was heavy, but he could not risk anyone overhearing him. He had spent the time checking the transcript and there was no doubt that what had been caught on tape was actually deeply embarrassing. With an election coming up, and such a close call for the centre ground in politics at the moment, the government did not need any scandals.

"It does seem that Charlie has been using his privilege to feather his own nest. The link between him and the company is unmistakable. In addition, it's obvious that he was willingly aided and abetted by Sharon. I knew she was in love with him which would mean she was willingly influenced but it doesn't make any difference to the result. They are both up to their necks."

"So, what are we going to do?" Liam asked. He had never seen anything like this unfold and suddenly felt very important. He had only just become a Minister and now he could tease his family and friends about what he was privy too, therefore further cementing his position, and his own feelings of self-worth.

Bernard knew what he needed to do, but he didn't like it. "We are going to have to call him in and get him to explain himself," he said sadly. "There is never any excuse for a member of the party, no matter how important to risk the party so much for one man's gain."

He opened the door and called to his secretary. "Get Charlie here now!" The door closed and Bernard started thinking about how on earth he was going to approach it. He had been trusted to resolve this, but it was an absolute minefield in every single way.

Soon enough, his time for thinking was over and Charlie had arrived. Walking in, Charlie had the air of someone who didn't know what was coming. Indeed, the way he looked round, greeting the staff, he was expecting some kind of a promotion or gong. The arrogance of the man really was nauseating. Bernard hesitated. though. He was obviously also a sly mover.

Charlie was used to being called at such short notice to dispatch some justice to another MP. He really hoped it was Jeremy. It was surely his time. Bernard motioned for him to sit down and seeing the look on his face, started quickly: "I'm afraid that this meeting is not about rooting out bad behaviour in one of your colleagues. It's about your own personal behaviour that's come under scrutiny."

Charlie leaned back, not quite knowing how to take this. How could he possibly be under investigation? He had done nothing but give his time, effort and commitment to the Party - at the detriment of his own personal position. Bernard put a copy of the transcript down and motioned for Charlie to start reading. Charlie looked down and back up again without acknowledgement of what was in front of him. He crossed his arms: "What's this nonsense?"

Bernard motioned again and Charlie sighed looking down. Suddenly his demeanour changed as he started to read the text. Charlie started: "And? Isn't it good to test the system and ensure that it actually benefits those it's supposed to? If there was anything done that was illegal," he snapped, "Wouldn't I be in front of a criminal investigation instead of you, here."

Bernard couldn't quite believe his ears, "It's only because of some sympathetic ears that we have been able to deal with this internally. Otherwise the press could have hounded you - and Sharon - exposing all sorts of sordid secrets over time. And then there is this Charlie! There is a difference between testing a system out in theoretical terms and using insider knowledge of the process to maximise personal gain. I am disappointed you can't tell the difference."

Charlie looked at his old friend, "So, what are you going to do with this disappointment?"

Bernard said, "I am sorry old friend, but the situation is pretty stark. The shareholder nomination scheme has to be terminated. It's up to you if the shares go to Sharon, like has been in the public domain, or Conor, but you need to make that call now, and you have to resign your seat. You can say it's for personal reasons, and it's not like you have a jilted wife used to the trappings of a lifestyle you are about to lose to reason with, but this needs to stop here. And now."

Charlie scowled "Sympathetic ears, huh? Dealing with this internally? Sounds like this is an insider job to me." He waited for Bernard's reaction. He couldn't put his finger on it on what had been said or how, but he had an inkling he knew who had been involved in at least part of this plot.

Bernard looked back and shook his head giving nothing away, "So, what's the decision?" Charlie looked at his old friend. "Fine, Conor should get the shares. It's him who's put in all the effort". Bernard nodded, slightly shocked. Sharon might have put herself on the line, but she was always last in line when it came down to the bit. "Sign here," he said, "and we will say nothing more about this for now. You will remain a member of the Party, but needless to say we will be keeping an eye on you until the polls close and we know this matter is over for good." Charlie snapped open his fountain pen, signed with a flourish and walked out, knocking some paperwork from a side table onto the floor as he left.

Chapter 26

Charlie sat in front of the TV. He couldn't believe he couldn't even be there, his political career stifled because of his own Whips Office - people he had classed as friends. He swirled the whisky round his glass. Conor had been understanding of his position, though they both knew that this project would have worked so much better with the two of them at the helm. Sharon had been less sympathetic, but he knew he would win her over eventually.

The clock chimed quietly. It was 3.30am and the results were now coming thick and fast. He couldn't believe how well the Government was doing - they were on for a resounding victory. He stood up and emptying the strong nectar coloured liquid in one mouthful, he refilled his whisky glass.

Sitting back down, the screen flicked to number 10 and he stopped and watched the camera's panning over all those standing around the Prime Minister. There she was, with him. Standing without a care in the world. He still didn't know how she fitted in but to think that she had not been part of this would be naive in the extreme.

His brain turned over and he heard a key in the door. Conor walked into the room, another bottle in hand. "In commiseration," he started, "and it looks like their majority has gone up." He walked into the sitting room and took a glass from the cabinet.

Charlie smiled sarcastically "Yes," he agreed, "it's amazing how people seem to rise at the most inopportune moments.."

He held up his glass and it clinked for the first time that night. Charlie looked his friend up and down: "It has to be said, the preparation for the big green revolution seems to be suiting you down to the ground. You'll be planting your own allotments next. You are obviously eating a lot of vegetables considering how much weight you have lost."

Conor tapped his belly "Oh it's the opposite of that" he said, "Not a healthy lifestyle but a restricted one."

Charlie looked at his friend, "Well good for you", he sighed, "but you won't find me restricting anything. It's time for us to plan for our future. No regrets." Conor smiled. His friend would always look to the future, and it was something he so admired.

Chapter 27

It was a few hours later, when the sun shone through the window, that Charlie woke up. His mind was slightly fuzzy but he had flashing memories of Conor setting himself up in the spare room and pulled himself up slowly so he could greet his old friend with a cup of tea. Walking slowly over to the kettle, he switched on the radio. "The victory for the Government was overwhelming," it blasted. "The flagship policies on environmental issues were a key reason that the younger floating voters decided to support the incoming Government, but with that, we are now going to Number 10 so we can hear from the Prime Minister make his victory speech."

Charlie sighed, the sanguine tones of a Prime Minister locked in place for another five years. "It has been a great honour to lead this great country up until now, and it's a privilege that you continue to have faith in me so that my team can bring our manifesto pledges to fruition. We are committed to not just economic development for this, our great country, but also ensure that we can leave a true and proper legacy for our children. One we can be proud of."

Charlie pulled the cups from the cabinet and the kettle whistled. The speech continued: "Of course to do this, we need to constantly look at ourselves, our own achievements and our own experience. We will therefore be undertaking a rank and file evaluation to make sure the best people are leading us in each department." Charlie slammed his fist on the kitchen service. All the effort he had put in, and nothing to show for it. It was going to be a depressing time ahead indeed, now he was cut off. Again.

Suddenly the door-bell rung. Charlie looked at the door and shrugged his shoulders. He didn't want to be disturbed. A couple of minutes later it rang again, and then a third time. He could ignore it no longer and opened it on the latch. In front of him stood two uniformed officers. He opened the door fully. He knew the man on the right. Jock had been his official police guard for a few years before he had had to turn his back on all he had known and gone on the beat.

He went to smile acknowledgment to a friendly face, but then saw their serious expressions. "Charlie, I have some bad news," he began: "there has been an accident."

Charlie went white. "Who?" he slowly asked. "Mr. Black," the police officer continued. "I saw that he left here at 5.40am this morning and started to follow him in the car as soon as I saw that he was driving under the influence so I could stop him before he did any damage. He stopped at a crossroads and I went to put on my lights but then suddenly he veered forward. There was a truck. It will have been instant"… His voice trailed off.

Charlie went as white as a sheet. "But I don't understand, he stayed here last night." Charlie rushed from the door towards the room in which Conor had stayed so many times, but like a bad dream he wasn't there. Charlie looked at the policeman, "I had no idea. I was sure he was staying here. Have you told his family?"

The police officer nodded slowly: "We have two people with his mother and father now, but I wanted to be the person to tell you."

"Yes, yes," Charlie replied absent mindedly, wondering what was going on. How the world had got so twisted. "I need to sit down. Can you give me some time please?"

"Of course," the two policemen replied. "We will need to question you soon, but we can give you some time to process what's happened."

Charlie nodded closed the door. He put his head against the wood, and he could hear his heart pumping in his chest. He walked slowly back to the spare room, his mind full of questions. Why hadn't Conor just stayed put? He went into the room and looked round. The bed was crumpled so Conor had obviously taken rest for at least a time, but he was not there now. He was gone.

Charlie felt his legs go just as he reached the side of the mattress. He pulled himself up and onto the last imprint of his friend and he put his face into the pillow. He pulled it towards him a piece of paper floated out. He picked it up, and saw his old friends writing:

"Dearest Charlie,

If you have this, I have left the house by now. Last night was so important to me, to reminisce and mull over old times, whilst preparing for new times.

I am sorry that you will doing it alone, but there was nothing I could do. My health was the one thing I had no influence on. It was failing me, but no one could think of my death as anything other than a terrible accident as I have ensured there is no record of the brain tumour that was growing in my mind, taking over cell by cell. And no one questions the actions of a dead man.

"So, I would urge you to speak to Adam Paul, my accountant. He will show you all the details, but we are all set once more. Sharon was very hurt when you chose to leave the shares to me, but I persuaded her you were just trying to protect her, and that it's her turn to protect you one more. No one will know. You will be able to be hidden in plain sight, but we will be able to ensure that those who delayed our work and sullied our names truly pay. I know you will do us all proud. Your friend, always CB"

Charlie looked at the note, read it for a second time and walked into the sitting room. Kneeling down by the fire, he lit a match. It quickly caught and putting the flame to the piece of paper, he watched as it started to burn. He bowed his head and threw the note into the fireplace. Turning to the TV, he cocked his head as he saw the news replaying the nights events. He knew what he needed to do.

Printed in Great Britain
by Amazon

40176309R00180